ETERNALLY YOURS

BRENDA JACKSON
ETERNALLY YOURS

ARABESQUE®

ETERNALLY YOURS

An Arabesque novel published by Kimani Press February 2008

First published by Kensington Publishing Corp. in 1997

ISBN-13: 978-1-61523-648-0

Copyright © 1997 by Brenda Streater Jackson

Printed in U.S.A.

Clayton Madaris's time has come, and this book is dedicated to all my avid readers who agree with me.

SPECIAL THANKS

To my family and friends for their continued support.

To Denise Coleman, Lynn Sims and Chimeka Hodge, who helped with my Christmas shopping so I could meet my deadline.

To Brenda Arnette Simmons for her feedback on the finished product.

To attorney Cecil Howard of Tallahassee, Florida, who took precious time from his busy schedule to talk to me and who helped me to understand the fundamentals of family law.

To a very special and dear friend, Syneda Walker. I appreciate the friendship and most of all, the laughs and good times.

And last but not least, to my Heavenly Father, who makes all things possible.

THE MADARIS FAMILY AND FRIENDS SERIES

Dear Readers,

I love writing family sagas, and I am so happy that Harlequin is reissuing my very first family series, the Madaris family. It's been twelve years and fifty books since I first introduced the Madaris family. During that time, this special family and their friends have won their way into readers' hearts. I am ecstatic about sharing these award-winning stories with readers all over again—especially those who have never met the Madaris clan up close and personal—in this special-edition reissue, with more to follow in the coming months.

I never dreamed when I penned my first novel, *Tonight and Forever,* and introduced the Madaris family, that what I was doing was taking readers on a journey where heartfelt romance, sizzling passion and true love awaited them at every turn. I had no idea that the Madaris family and their friends would become characters that readers would come to know and care so much about. I invite you to relax, unwind and see what all the hoopla is about. Let Justin, Dex, Clayton, Uncle Jake and their many friends indulge your fantasies with love stories that are so passionate and sizzling they will take your breath away. There is nothing better than falling in love with one of those Madaris men and their circle of friends and family.

For a complete list of all the books in this series, as well as the reissue publication dates for each novel, please visit my Web site at www.brendajackson.net.

If you would like to receive my monthly newsletter please visit and sign up at http://www.brendajackson.net/page/newsletter.htm.

I also invite you to drop me an e-mail at WriterBJackson@aol.com. I love hearing from my readers.

All the best,

Brenda Jackson

THE MADARIS FAMILY

Milton Madaris, Sr. and Felicia Laverne Lee Madaris

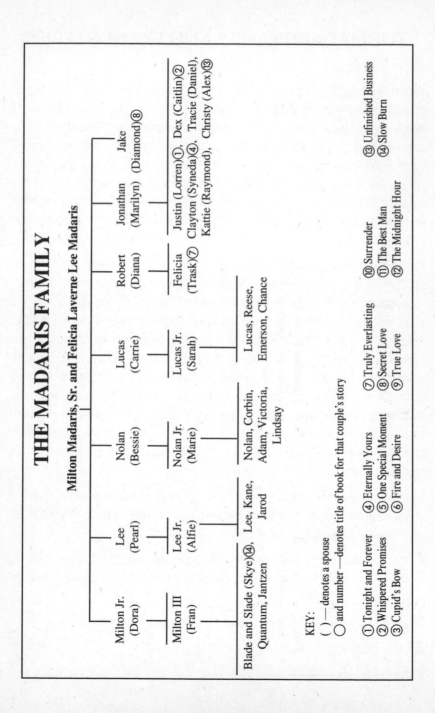

Milton Jr. (Dora)
- Milton III (Fran)
  - Blade and Slade (Skye)⑭, Lee, Kane, Jarod
  - Quantum, Jantzen

Lee (Pearl)
- Lee Jr. (Alfie)
  - Lee, Kane, Jarod

Nolan (Bessie)
- Nolan Jr. (Marie)
  - Nolan, Corbin, Adam, Victoria, Lindsay

Lucas (Carrie)
- Lucas Jr. (Sarah)
  - Lucas, Reese, Emerson, Chance

Robert (Diana)
- Felicia (Trask)⑦

Jonathan (Marilyn)
- Justin (Lorren)①, Dex (Caitlin)②
- Clayton (Syneda)④, Tracie (Daniel),
- Kattie (Raymond), Christy (Alex)⑬

Jake (Diamond)⑧

KEY:
( ) — denotes a spouse
◯ and number —denotes title of book for that couple's story

① Tonight and Forever
② Whispered Promises
③ Cupid's Bow
④ Eternally Yours
⑤ One Special Moment
⑥ Fire and Desire
⑦ Truly Everlasting
⑧ Secret Love
⑨ True Love
⑩ Surrender
⑪ The Best Man
⑫ The Midnight Hour
⑬ Unfinished Business
⑭ Slow Burn

THE MADARIS FRIENDS

Maurice and Stella Grant

Angelique Hamilton Chenault

Kyle Garwood (Kimara)③

Trevor (Corinthians)⑥,
Regina (Mitch)⑪

Sterling Hamilton (Colby)⑤,
Nicholas Chenault (Shayla)⑨

Ashton Sinclair
(Netherland)⑩

Drake Warren
(Tori)⑫

Trent Jordache
(Brenna)⑨

Nedwyn Lansing
(Diana)⑭

KEY:
( ) — denotes a spouse
◯ and number —denotes title of book for that couple's story

① Tonight and Forever
② Whispered Promises
③ Cupid's Bow

④ Eternally Yours
⑤ One Special Moment
⑥ Fire and Desire

⑦ Truly Everlasting
⑧ Secret Love
⑨ True Love

⑩ Surrender
⑪ The Best Man
⑫ The Midnight Hour

⑬ Unfinished Business
⑭ Slow Burn

To every thing there is a season, and a time to every purpose under the heaven:

—*Ecclesiastes* 3:1

There is a right time for everything.

—*Ecclesiastes* 3:1

Chapter 1

"Your bed or mine?"

Clayton Madaris glanced up from his meal and gazed into the eyes of the woman who'd asked the question. She was beautiful, and her sensuous proposition was something any man would jump at. No hot-blooded male in his right mind would ever think of turning it down.

So why was he contemplating doing just that?

An impassive expression masked his handsome features. His hesitation had nothing to do with the fact that he'd just met her that morning. Like him, she was an attorney attending a convention in D.C. He had come to enough of these conferences to be prepared for the expected. One would be surprised just how many unmarried, as well as married people took advantage of the three-day convention to engage in short, no-strings-attached affairs. In all his thirty-five years, there had never been a time when he'd been hesitant about making love to a willing woman, granted the situation wasn't a risky one.

So what was wrong with him tonight?

His dinner companion undoubtedly was wondering the same thing and had no plans to stick around and find out. He sensed her agitation with his silence. Her eyes narrowed. "I won't make the same offer twice," she said quietly. There was a feverish edge to her voice.

Clayton nodded slowly, his eyes never leaving her face. He knew her type. She was a woman hungry for physical intimacy. Her eyes had sent him silent, intimate messages all day. There was no doubt in his mind that although he'd just disappointed her by not jumping at her offer, she wouldn't give up on him. She *would* make the offer again.

His smile was slow. "Sorry. Not tonight..."

Evidently not happy with his response, she pushed her plate aside and stood, giving him a measured look. "Perhaps another time, then?"

Clayton stared up at her before answering. "Perhaps."

After she left he simply sat, quietly eating the rest of his meal and drinking his coffee.

A short while later, after taking care of the dinner bill, he rode up the elevator alone to the fifth floor. During the ride he tried coming to terms with his sudden lack of interest in an affair. It wasn't like him to turn down any woman's advances or not make a score or two of his own. It definitely wasn't his style. Enjoying the opposite sex was something he had been overly fond of doing since his first time with Paula Stone when he'd been sixteen.

So what was his problem now?

The huge metal elevator doors swooshed open. Taking a deep breath he stepped out and began walking down the long hallway leading to his room. Opening the door to his suite, he walked into the sitting area, then through open double doors to the large bedroom.

He leaned his shoulder against the doorjamb, looking at the king-size bed. No one, especially those who considered him a player of the third degree, would believe he'd actually slept in the huge bed alone. And definitely not by choice.

He smiled as he pushed himself away from the door. There's a first time for everything, he thought, removing his tie and jacket and going into the bathroom. Peeling off the rest of his clothes, he stepped into the shower, dismissing the fact he'd taken a shower just before dinner.

Since becoming an attorney over ten years ago, he'd discovered his most soothing moments were in the shower while warm water caressed his skin. It was during that time he possessed the ability to blank out any thoughts other than those needing his undivided attention. In the end, whatever plagued his mind was usually put in perspective. At the moment, he needed to think about why he'd just refused an offer of no-strings-attached sex.

Adjusting the water, he picked up the scented soap and lazily lathered himself as he mentally analyzed the situation.

For some reason, he was becoming bored with the way his life was going. Somehow he was getting tired of his routine of chasing and bedding women. He twisted his lips in a wry grin. Now that was a laugh, especially since the main reason he had constantly shunned any sort of commitment with a woman was the fear of that very thing—boredom. He was the type of person who found any kind of routine deadly. He'd always been afraid of committing himself to someone only to lose interest with that person and end up feeling trapped.

His thoughts fell on his two older brothers, Justin, the physician, and Dex, the geologist in oil exploration. Both were happily married and neither appeared bored. If anything they seemed to be having the time of their lives with their wives, Lorren and Caitlin. Was it possible he'd been wrong? Was there a woman out there somewhere who could forever excite, stimulate and amuse him?

He shuddered at the way his thoughts were going; shocked that he could even consider such a thing. His credo in life for the longest time had been "The only men who aren't fools are bachelors." But he couldn't help wondering why lately he had been subconsciously longing for more than a little black book filled with the names of available women.

As the water from the shower pounded his body, he tossed the problem around in his mind, pulling it apart, analyzing and dissecting it. But he still couldn't come up with any answers.

With a groan he turned off the water and grabbed a towel. Stepping out of the shower, he began drying himself off. There were a lot of questions to which he needed answers. And he knew those answers wouldn't come from taking just one shower. The main problem might be that he had been working too hard lately. Too many court cases and too many late nights spent poring over them. A tired body occasionally filled the mind with foolish thoughts. And what could be more foolish than the notion that he was longing for a steady relationship with a woman?

Clayton shook his head to clear his muddled mind. What he needed was to get away for a while. He had some vacation time coming up. And it was time he took it.

Syneda Walters looked across her desk at the elegantly groomed woman sitting in front of it. She schooled her expression not to show her irritation and annoyance—or her pity. Bracing her elbows on the arm of the chair, she leaned forward. "Ms. Armstrong, I hope you'll reconsider your decision."

"But he has told me he's sorry about everything and really didn't mean to hurt me. He's been under a lot of stress lately. He loves me."

Syneda sighed, letting her well-manicured fingers run agitatedly over the desk surface. She could barely restrain herself from calling the woman all kinds of fool for letting a man abuse her. Yet the woman sat defending a man who evidently got his kicks using her as a punching bag.

Rubbing the ache at the back of her neck, Syneda stared beyond the woman and out the window. It was a beautiful day in early May. The midday sun slanted across the sky and reflected off another building. Its golden rays gleamed brilliantly in the blue sky. She watched as a flock of birds flew by and wished she could somehow fly away with them.

"Ms. Walters?"

Syneda's eyes again rested on the woman's tear-stained face. The bruises hadn't quite faded and were not adequately concealed with the use of makeup. "Yes?"

"You just don't understand."

Syneda allowed her eyes to close for a moment. Then pushing her chair back she rose and sat on the edge of her desk facing the woman. "You're right, Mrs. Armstrong, I don't understand," she replied quietly. "I don't understand several things. First, how can a man who claims he loves a woman physically hurt her the way your husband has repeatedly hurt you? Second, how can a woman who cares anything about herself let him do it and get away with it?"

Mary Armstrong blew her nose in a well-used napkin. "But he's my husband," the woman implored, pleading understanding.

Syneda didn't give her any. "He's also your abuser. Look, Mrs. Armstrong, you've only been in the marriage for three years and he's doing this to you now. What do you think he'll be doing to you three more years from now?"

"He'll change."

"That's what you said a few months ago." Syneda gave a disgusted shake of her head. "It's time for you to make changes. Don't live under a false conception you're worth less than you really are. Don't ever believe you deserve to be beaten. No one deserves that. And please stop thinking you're nothing without him."

There was a moment of silence in the room. Then the woman spoke. Her voice quavered with indecisiveness. "What do you suggest I do?"

"As your attorney I suggest the first thing you should do is get some counseling. And I highly recommend that you bring charges against your husband."

"Will he be arrested?"

"That's a good possibility."

The woman's face paled. "What will happen to his practice? He's an outstanding member of the community."

Syneda let out a huff of breath that was more disgust than anger. "He's also an abuser. As far as his medical practice is concerned, if I were you I'd let him worry about that."

"He loves me, and he's sorry that he's hurt me. I can't let him lose everything. I can't do that to him."

Syneda stood. "Then there's nothing I can do. We'll be more than happy to help you, Mrs. Armstrong, when you're ready to first help yourself. Good day."

Syneda continued to gaze at the closed door after Mrs. Armstrong had left. She let out a deep sigh of frustration. She was not having a good day. To be more specific, it had not been a good week. It had started with the case she'd lost on Monday, and the week had gone downhill from there.

She rubbed her forehead, trying to relieve the throbbing at her temples. Even after five years she often wondered about her decision to practice family law. But then, she silently admitted, the profession she had chosen was important to her because she'd always managed to feel she had somehow made a difference in someone's life; whether it was getting them out of a hellish marriage, taking on their fight for custody rights, or in a case like Mary Armstrong's, helping them to realize options in life other than one filled with physical abuse.

A quick knock sounded at the door. "Come in."

The door opened and her secretary stuck her head inside. "I'm leaving for lunch now. Do you have anything you want me to take care of before I go?"

Syneda shook her head. "No, Joanna. There's nothing that can't wait until you return."

Joanna nodded. "All right. And Lorren Madaris called while you were with Mrs. Armstrong."

"Thanks, and enjoy your lunch."

"I will," Joanna replied, closing the door behind her.

Syneda picked up the phone and began dialing. Lorren Madaris was her best friend. Both of them had grown up as the foster children of Nora and Paul Phillips. "Lorren? How was Hawaii?"

"It was great. Justin and I had a wonderful time."

"I'm glad."

"What about you? What was the outcome of that case you were working on?"

Syneda studied her manicured nail for a long moment before answering. "We lost." She shook her head and tried shrugging off her disappointment. "As far as I'm concerned the judge's decision was wrong. No one can convince me that Kasey Jamison should have been returned to her biological mother. Where was the woman when Kasey really needed her? If you ask me she showed up five years too late. You of all people know how I feel about parents who desert their kids."

There was a slight pause before Lorren replied. "Yes, I know. And you're thinking about your father, aren't you?"

Syneda's body tensed. "I don't have a father, Lorren."

Lorren said nothing for a while, then broke the silence. "So what're your plans now about the case?"

"For one thing, I won't give up. I feel like I've let Kasey down, not to mention her adoptive parents. I plan to appeal the judge's decision."

"Don't let things get you down. You did your best."

"But in this case, my best wasn't good enough." Syneda stood. She let out a deep sigh of frustration, not wanting to talk about the Jamison case any longer, not even to her best friend. "Lorren, I'll get back with you later. I need to prepare for my next client."

"Okay. You take care."

"I will."

As Syneda hung up the phone, a part of her mind slipped into a past she had done everything in her power to forget. Eighteen years ago this week, at the age of ten, she had received her mother's deathbed promise that the father Syneda never knew would be coming for her.

Syneda sighed deeply, remembering how her mother had died

of an acute case of pneumonia. Even after the juvenile authorities had come and taken Syneda away because she'd had no other relatives, her mother's words, "Your father will come," had been her comfort and hope. Weeks later, after she'd been placed in the foster home with Mamma Nora and Poppa Paul, she still believed her father would come for her. She would never forget how she would stand in front of her bedroom window, watching and waiting patiently each day for him.

For an entire year she had waited before accepting he was not coming. She began pitying her mother for dying believing in the love and devotion of a man. If his actions were proof of the love two people were supposed to share, then Syneda wanted no part of love. As far as she was concerned, love was like a circle. There was no point in it. She swore to never blindly love a man and put her complete trust and faith in one like her mother had done.

Syneda's thoughts drifted back to the present when she heard a group of fellow attorneys conversing outside of her door. She quickly wiped away the tears that had filled her eyes and released a quivering breath. Just as she had told Lorren a few minutes ago, she didn't have a father.

"Hello."

"Clayton?"

"Lorren? Is anything wrong?"

"No. I'm glad I was able to reach you before you left the hotel for the airport. Will your flight make a layover in New York?"

"Yes, why?"

"I need to ask a favor of you."

Clayton Madaris smiled. "Sure. What is it?"

"Will you check on Syneda when you get to New York?"

"Why? Is something wrong?"

"I talked to her a few minutes ago, and she's down in the dumps. She lost an important case."

Clayton frowned. "I'm sorry to hear that. No attorney likes to lose."

"It wasn't about just winning the case, Clayton. This case was very important to Syneda."

He glanced at his watch. "All right, Lorren. I'll check on her when I get to New York."

"Thanks, Clayton. You're the greatest. Next to Justin, of course."

Clayton laughed. "Of course."

"By the way, how was the convention?"

"Not bad. I had a nice time."

Lorren laughed. "Knowing you, I'm sure you did."

Clayton chuckled. "I'll call you after I've seen Syneda."

"Thanks."

"Hold your horses, I'm coming!"

Syneda's nylon-clad toes luxuriated in the deep smoke-gray carpeting as she made her way to the door. A smile touched her lips when she glanced through the peephole. She quickly opened the door.

"Clayton! What on earth are you doing here?"

Clayton stepped into the room and turned to face the attractive light-brown-skinned woman standing before him. Thick, golden-bronze hair fell to the shoulders of her tall and slender figure. She looked cute in a short-sleeved blue blouse and a flowing flowered skirt. Her full lips formed a wide smile that shone in her sea-green eyes.

He returned her smile. "I'm here at the request of Lorren. You know what a worrywart she is."

Syneda laughed as she took Clayton's hand and led him over to the sofa. She always enjoyed seeing him. He was Lorren's brother-in-law, and since their first meeting a couple of years ago, they had become good friends. The two of them were attorneys and somehow could never agree on various issues, legal or otherwise. They were both extremely opinionated and at times their different viewpoints led to numerous debates and sparring matches at the Madaris family celebrations and holiday gatherings. She had gone head-to-head with him on just about every topic imaginable, from the government's policy on illegal immigrants to whether or not there were actual UFOs.

"Can I get you something to drink, Clayton?"

"No, I'm fine."

Syneda sat across from him in a chair, tucking her legs beneath her. "Lorren was always the mothering type. Now you would think the kids would be enough. Don't tell me she sent you all the way from Houston to check on me?"

Clayton's attention had been drawn to three framed photographs that sat on a nearby table. One was of Justin and Lorren, their son, Vincent, and daughter, Justina. Another photo showed Dex and Caitlin, with their daughter, Jordan. The last photo was of her foster mother, Mama Nora. He smiled at the photographs before turning his attention back to Syneda to answer her question.

"No, I've been in D.C. for the past three days attending the National Bar Association convention. She knew my flight had a layover here and suggested I look you up."

"How was the convention?"

"Pretty good. I'm sorry you missed it. Senator Lansing was the keynote speaker, and as usual he kept the audience spellbound."

Syneda nodded. She knew the one thing she and Clayton did agree on was Senator Nedwyn Lansing of Texas. He was admired by both of them and had a reputation for taking a stand on more unpopular issues than anyone in Congress. "What was this year's convention theme?"

"Law and order."

"Not very original was it?"

Clayton laughed. "No, not very."

Syneda smiled. "I know Justin, Lorren and the kids are all doing fine. How's the rest of the Madaris clan?"

Clayton smiled. "My parents are doing great. They're off again. This time the ever-traveling retirees are headed for the mountains in Tennessee."

He leaned forward in his seat. "Since Christy's home from college for the summer, she went with them," he said of his youngest sister. "Traci and Kattie and their families are doing all right. With me being their only single brother, they've been playing the roles of ardent matchmakers lately."

Syneda grinned. "How're Dex and Caitlin?"

"They're fine. The baby isn't due for another six months but Dex is coming unglued already. Since he and Caitlin weren't together when she was pregnant with Jordan, he's really into this pregnancy big-time." Clayton laughed. "Sometimes I wonder who's really having this baby, him or Caitlin. He swears he's been having morning sickness." Clayton shook his head. "By the way, you missed Jordan's birthday party."

"Yeah, and I hated that. Unfortunately I was deeply involved in a case and couldn't get away." A cloud covered Syneda's features. "We went to court on Monday and lost."

Clayton noticed the shadow of disappointment in her eyes. "Do you want to talk about it?"

She nodded. She did want to discuss it. Maybe doing so would unleash all the frustration, anger and resentment that had plagued her since the judge's decision. Although she and Clayton usually took opposing sides on most issues, she knew that like her, he was a dedicated attorney, and hopefully on this one he would understand how she felt, even if he didn't agree with the position she had taken.

Syneda took a deep breath. "It was a custody fight. The natural mother gave the child up at birth six years ago. She fought the adoptive parents for custody...and won. That has happened a lot lately, and I don't like the message being sent to adoptive parents. They don't have any protection against this sort of thing under our present legal system."

Clayton frowned. "In the last two cases that received national attention, I thought the only reason the child was returned to its natural parents was because the natural fathers had not given their consent."

"True, but in our case the consent was given. However, the biological mother claims that at the age of fifteen, she'd been too young to know her own mind and had been coerced by her parents to give up her child. She contends the contract was between her parents and the Jamisons, and that she wasn't a part of it. How's that for a new angle?"

Clayton shuddered at the thought of a fifteen-year-old giving birth. "You're right. That is a new angle."

Syneda leaned back in her seat. "As far as I'm concerned, the real issue is not why she gave up the child. No one seems concerned with what's best for Kasey. She's being snatched from the only parents she's ever known and is being given to a stranger. That's cruel punishment for any child, especially a five-year-old."

Clayton nodded. "Hopefully things will work out. But you can't allow what's happened to get you depressed."

"I know I shouldn't but at times I can't help wondering if what I do really makes a difference."

"Of course it does."

Syneda smiled. "Do you know this is the first time we've been able to talk about a case and not take opposing sides?"

Clayton chuckled as he rested back comfortably in his seat. "Just because I didn't oppose anything you said doesn't mean I fully agree. Tonight you needed someone to just listen to your thoughts and feelings, and not force theirs on you. I gave you what I thought you needed. But what I really think you need is a vacation."

"I took a vacation earlier this year."

"I mean a real vacation. You usually use your vacation time to mess around here and not go anywhere. You need a real vacation to get away, relax and do nothing. I'm sure you can take time off from your job if you need it, so what's the problem?"

Syneda shrugged. "There isn't a problem. I just never thought about it."

"Well, I'm giving you something to think about. What about going someplace with that guy you're seeing?"

"Marcus and I are no longer seeing each other," she said slowly. "We decided it was for the best."

"Mmm. Could it be you're also suffering from a broken heart?"

Syneda frowned. "Not hardly."

Suddenly Clayton sat up straight. His eyes gleamed bright with an idea. Before checking out of the hotel, he had phoned his parents and asked their permission to spend a week at their time-share condo in Florida. They had given him the okay. "I have a wonderful idea," he said.

"What?"

"My parents have a condo in Saint Augustine, Florida. It's right on the ocean. I'm leaving next Sunday and will be there for a week. Come with me."

Syneda's brows arched in surprise. "Excuse me? Did I hear you correctly? You want me to go on vacation with you?"

A wide grin broke across Clayton's face "Sure. Why not? You need a rest and I think it's a wonderful idea."

She shook her head. "Clayton, get real. You know I can't go on vacation with you."

"Why not?"

"For a number of reasons."

"Name one."

"My work. I've appealed the Jamison case."

"So. It'll be a while before the courts review it. If you ask me, you need a vacation to deal with what you'll be up against when they do."

"True, but I still can't go anywhere with you."

"Why?"

Syneda refused to believe the man was so overlooking the obvious. It was rumored that no woman spent too many hours alone with Clayton Madaris and managed to keep her reputation clean. She considered herself a modern woman—and in some people's opinion she carried her fight for sexual equality too far—but she was cautious by nature in some things, although impetuous and aggressive in others. In this case, she needed to carefully weigh Clayton's invitation.

"What will people think, Madaris? Specifically, what will your family think?"

Clayton inwardly smiled. She always resorted to calling him by his last name whenever she was getting all fired up to stand her ground against him about something.

"If I remember correctly, my family has extended itself to become your family. They won't think anything of it. For Pete's sake, Syneda, they know we don't think of each other as sexual beings, and they know we aren't romantically involved." He chuckled. "If anything, they'll wonder how we'll spend a week together without doing each other in. We're usually completely at odds over just about everything."

Syneda laughed. "That's an understatement."

He grinned. "We aren't compatible. You know that as well as I do. There's nothing sexual between us. We're good friends, nothing more."

Syneda nodded in agreement. "But I wouldn't be any fun. What if you meet someone while we're there and want to get it on with them? I'll just be in the way."

"Women will be off-limits to me that week. I'll be on vacation for rest and relaxation, nothing more."

"Maybe you should get away by yourself."

Last night he would have agreed with her, but now he didn't think so. He liked Syneda. She was intelligent, witty, highly spirited and fun to be around, even when she was giving him hell about something. Besides, he could tell by the tone of her voice when she had talked about the case she'd lost that she needed a vacation as much as he did.

"The beach isn't any fun when you're by yourself," he said. "I plan to unwind and relax and have a good time. I want to just chill and do whatever I want to do, whenever I want to do it."

"And you think you can do that with me?"

"Yep, just as long as we agree not to talk shop. For one week I don't want to be an attorney, a player or anyone's lover. I don't want any worries or problems. We both need that. I think the two of us going away together is a wonderful idea."

Syneda still wasn't easily convinced. She gazed at the man

sitting across from her, who was impeccably dressed in an expensive printed tie, Brooks Brothers' shirt, and a costly dark blue suit.

Like his two older brothers, Clayton Madaris was a good-looking man who possessed sharply defined features. She had noticed those things the first time they had met. She'd immediately taken in his dimpled smile and dark brown eyes. A short beard—something he'd grown since she had last seen him—covered his nut-brown complexion, and his neatly trimmed mustache enhanced his full lips. His broad shoulders and towering height—almost six feet two inches—made him totally masculine. And his charismatic nature was like a magnet that attracted women to him in droves. But what he had said earlier was true. He wasn't her type, and neither was she his.

In Texas, Clayton had a reputation for being a ladies' man. And according to his sisters, Traci and Kattie, he kept a huge case of condoms in his closet and used them with as much zeal and vigor as a shoemaker used leather. However, in spite of his more than active love life, she had to admit he did have a few redeeming qualities. He generously spent his free time helping others. He was an active member of Big Brothers of America, and he spent a lot of time doing such noble community services as aiding senior citizens, the homeless and underprivileged kids. He was also a wonderful and adoring uncle to his nieces and nephews.

Clayton's sigh echoed loudly in the room. "I really don't understand the problem. You and I both know that all the two of us can and ever will be is friends. I think by getting away, we'll be doing us both a favor."

Syneda launched one objection after another, and Clayton had a reason to shoot down every one of them. "Are you sure about this, Clayton? I'd hate to be a bother."

"You won't be. The condo has two bedrooms and two bathrooms. It'll be plenty big enough for the two of us. You can fly to Houston and from there we can take a direct flight to Florida. Just think about the fun we'll have spending an entire week on the beach of the nation's oldest city, not to mention all the historical sites we can check out while we're there. Come on, let's go for it."

A smile touched Syneda's lips. Clayton was right, she really did need to get away for a while. And a trip to Florida sounded mighty tempting. "All right, I'll go."

Clayton came over and pulled her into his arms and gave her a big hug. "Great! We'll have a good time together. We won't argue at all about anything. You'll see."

Chapter 2

Clayton and Syneda argued as they boarded the plane for Florida. Clayton had fronted the expenses and flatly refused to let Syneda reimburse him.

"I can afford to pay my own way, Madaris," Syneda said, glaring at him.

"I didn't say you couldn't. Just consider it my treat."

"But, I'd rather—"

"Let's drop it, Syneda," Clayton snapped.

Angry frustration swept over Syneda's features. "Fine with me. It's your money," she replied curtly after they had taken their designated seats.

"I'm glad you finally realized that," he said, getting in the last word.

Syneda decided not to respond. She didn't want to appear ungrateful, but she had a hang-up about a man doing anything for her. She had learned early in life not to depend on one.

After fastening her seat belt, she turned to Clayton. "What did your family say about us going away together?"

Clayton settled back in his seat. "They didn't have a thing to say." Syneda raised a brow. "Not anything?"

"Not anything." He smiled. "Except for Dex."

She lifted her head. "Dex? What did he have to say?"

Clayton chuckled. "Dex didn't say anything. He just made the sign of the cross. I guess he thinks we're going to do each other in on this trip."

Syneda couldn't help but laugh. "Are we really that bad?"

"I guess, but we'll get along okay this trip. We did agree to be on our best behavior and not discuss any controversial topics. Remember?"

Syneda met his gaze then smiled slowly. "Well..." She dodged an answer, turning to look out of the window as the plane lifted off.

"Syneda..." Clayton said her name in a warning tone.

She turned back to him with her smile still in place. "Oh, all right. I remember, and I plan on keeping my end of our agreement. We'll get along just fine."

Dallas, Texas

The sun was setting in the afternoon sky when the man alighted from the parked car. Instead of being dressed in a business suit, which over the years had become his usual mode of dress while out in public, he had worn only a lightweight jacket and dress slacks. With the person he was going to visit, he could always be himself.

He crossed the dusty road and climbed the grassy hill before entering the meticulously cared-for grounds. In his hand he carried two bouquets of mixed flowers.

The walk seemed to take forever as he weaved his way toward the hillside and the marked stone. He was fully aware of the tears that misted his eyes as he knelt to place the flowers next to the grave. The headstone, although worn with time, still clearly showed the name and inscription written on it.

JAN WALTERS—REST IN PEACE

A knot of pain and sorrow formed in his throat. He closed his eyes as poignant memories resurfaced. It had been exactly thirty years ago today that they had met. It had been a day that changed his life forever. It was a day that brought him here every year, after finding out about her death fifteen years ago. By that time she had been dead three years already.

His heart grew heavy when he thought about all the wasted years they could have had together. They had begun dating during their senior year of college. Then a few days after graduation, after he had left for the Air Force Academy, she had left town without telling him or anyone where she had gone.

He stood, straightening his tall frame. The woman in the marked grave would have his heart until the day he died. He also knew that he would continue to come here each year and share this special day with her. It was their day.

Tears gathered in his eyes and slowly spilled down his cheeks as he turned toward the direction where his car was parked.

Until next year.

"This view of the ocean is breathtaking, Clayton," Syneda said, leaning against the railing. From the balcony she watched the blue waters of the Atlantic Ocean ripple gently toward the shoreline of St. Augustine Beach.

"It sure is," Clayton replied, coming to join her. He handed her a glass of wine. "Compliments of the management. They also left some entertainment brochures, as well as a visitors' guidebook to all the places to check out while we're here."

Syneda accepted the glass.

"Thanks." She looked out toward the ocean again. "I just can't believe all of this."

"All of what?" Clayton asked, sitting down in a patio chair.

"All of this! The ocean view, the size of this condo, the list of activities lined up for us, this city's history. Everything! And don't you dare sit there and pretend not to be moved by all of it. This place is wonderful, and I plan on enjoying myself immensely the next seven days. Thanks again for inviting me."

"You're welcome." He took a sip of his wine. "I told you what Dex's reaction was to us vacationing together. What did Lorren have to say about it?"

Syneda set her glass on a small table and reclined in a nearby lounger. "At first she didn't believe it. She couldn't imagine the two of us being anywhere together for too long without arguing about something. But after I explained we agreed to stay away from controversial issues, she thought it was a great idea. According to her, no one will think twice about us going away together. She said everyone knows the differences in our personalities and philosophies make the two of us ever getting it on impossible."

"See there. What did I tell you? You were worrying for nothing."

"Maybe, but a girl has to know when to safeguard her reputation." She grinned.

Clayton frowned. "You don't think your reputation is safe with me?"

Syneda smiled. "Let's put it this way, Clayton. Everyone knows about your womanizing lifestyle."

"Really? And what exactly do *you* know?"

Syneda gave him a rueful smile. "For starters, thanks to your sisters, I know all about that case of condoms in your closet. Do you deny it?"

He chuckled, thinking he needed to have a talk with his sisters for getting into his business. "No. I don't deny it. It's better to be safe than sorry."

"Have you ever given any thought to just doing without?"

He gave her a slow grin. "I've been doing without for a couple of months, and I don't like it too much."

She laughed. "Poor baby. What's the matter? The women are finally resisting that Clayton Madaris charm?"

Clayton laughed. "No, that's not it. Would you believe for the past couple of months, I've had a totally insane idea running through my head."

"What sort of insane idea?"

"I've been thinking that maybe it's time for me to stop playing around and get serious about someone."

Syneda almost choked on her wine. "You gotta be kiddin'. I can't imagine you ever getting serious about any woman."

Clayton grinned at the startled expression on her face. "Neither can I, and that's the reason I desperately needed a vacation. I needed to get away to rid my mind of such foolish thoughts. I must be going crazy to even consider such a thing."

"I totally agree."

He smiled. "I'm glad someone does. However, my family would disagree with you. They think it's past time for me to settle down."

Syneda shook her head. "The reason I agree with you is because I understand completely. Falling in love isn't for everyone. I know it's definitely not for me."

Clayton raised a brow. "Really? I thought most women dreamed of their wedding day."

"Well, I'm not like most women. I have no intention of ever falling in love," Syneda said matter-of-factly. She stared at him, eyes bright with curiosity. "What has held you back from ever getting serious with a woman?"

"Fear."

"Fear? Fear of what?"

"Fear of becoming bored with the relationship. Because of my parents' rather close relationship, marriage to me means 'forever after' and 'till death do us part.' The thought of spending the rest of my life with the same woman is enough to give me nightmares. I'd be afraid of eventually becoming bored with her and feeling trapped. For Pete's sake, Syneda, forever after is a hell of a long time. Any kind of routine would drive me nuts."

He then smiled. "I enjoy spontaneity, creativity and excitement. I don't want to be tied to a woman who would eventually have me settled into a dull life."

He lifted his dark brow. "What about you? What's your hang-up about falling in love?"

Syneda took a long, deep breath before answering. She met his inquiring gaze. "As far as I'm concerned, falling in love means becoming dependent on that person for your happiness. I did that once and will never do it again."

She stood. "I think I'll go unpack and turn in early. Our flight wore me out. What would you like to do tomorrow?"

Clayton set his glass on the table next to hers and also stood. "How about if we go on one of those sightseeing tours around town."

"That sounds like fun. Well, good night, Clayton. I'll see you in the morning."

"Good night, Syneda."

Clayton watched as she walked off through the living room and toward the bedroom she had chosen to use. He couldn't help wondering about the man who had evidently hurt Syneda to make her feel the way she felt about falling in love.

Leaning against the balcony Clayton took his first sip of morning coffee and then released a satisfied sigh. "Ahh, good stuff," he commented as he looked out at the ocean to enjoy the early-morning sunrise. He had gotten up before dawn to make coffee, and had tried to be quiet while moving around in the kitchen. He hadn't wanted to awaken Syneda.

Rest, unwind a bit, have some fun and clear his overworked mind were the only things on his agenda this week. He turned and was about to go back inside when his gaze caught sight of a lone figure walking along the beach. The first thing he thought was that the woman, dressed in running shorts and a halter top, probably had the best body he'd ever seen. He couldn't make out her face because she was wearing a big straw hat and sunglasses, but he suspected any woman with a body like that had to have a terrific face to go along with it.

He stood transfixed, mesmerized, as she strolled along the beach apparently looking for seashells. A fragment of something teased at his consciousness. Had he met her before somewhere? There was something about her walk that was familiar to him for some reason.

He momentarily closed his eyes thinking his mind was playing tricks on him. There was no way he could ever have met this woman and not remember it. He reopened his eyes in time to watch her lean down to pick up a seashell and put it in the basket she was carrying. From his position high on the balcony, he could see the shorts she was wearing, which were already cut close to her hip bone, had ridden higher and showed a very good-looking backside.

Clayton drummed his fingers against the railing. Perspiration began forming on his forehead. For crying out loud, he was on vacation to unwind and just looking at the woman had him all wound up. He wiped his forehead thinking this wasn't good. Women were supposed to be off limits to him this week.

He was just about to leave when the woman turned and looked up in his direction and waved. He frowned, not understanding the friendly gesture. He had not known she had seen him watching her and had definitely not expected her to acknowledge it. Not knowing what else to do, he waved back.

Only after she'd taken off her sunglasses and removed the big straw hat from her head did he recognize her.

The woman was Syneda.

Clayton turned and whispered in Syneda's ear. "Our tour guide has the hots for you. He's been checking you out ever since we boarded this train."

Syneda ungraciously shoved a handful of popcorn into her mouth, followed by a big gulp of cola before responding. "You're imagining things."

"No, I'm not. I know when a man is interested in a woman."

Syneda giggled. "I guess you would, being an expert in womanizing and all."

Clayton frowned. "It's not funny, Syneda."

"Yes, it is. Men have been girl watching for ages. Will you stop being so uptight? What's wrong with you?"

Clayton took a deep breath. He was asking himself that same question. It had all begun that morning when he had seen her on the beach. Then later, things had gotten worse when they had decided to take an early-morning swim before breakfast. She had joined him by the pool wearing the sexiest bikini he had ever seen. He had always thought she had a great pair of legs, and the bathing suit only made how great they were more obvious. His mouth, along with every male's around poolside, had watered as they gazed at the sight of her delectable breasts swelling out of her bikini top and her well-rounded hips filling the bikini bottom. For one brief moment he'd experienced the oddest sensation— a heat flowing through his body and settling down toward his midsection. He had also felt something else, too: possessiveness. He hadn't liked the idea of the other men looking at her. Then he'd shaken off the feeling, but now it was coming back. And he knew at that moment, without a doubt, he was in serious trouble.

"Clayton?"

Unwilling to consider just what was happening to him, he took a deep breath and met Syneda's bemused gaze. "What?"

"I asked what's wrong with you?"

"Nothing is wrong with me," he replied, placing a hand in the small of her back and leading her toward the nation's oldest jail. "By the way. Where's the rest of your outfit?"

Syneda took a quick look at herself. She was wearing a printed backless skort set. The sides were held together in a few places by snaps. A wide-brimmed straw hat whose band matched her outfit covered her head. "What's wrong with my outfit?"

Clayton raised his eyes heavenward. It was obvious she wasn't wearing a bra, and from the cut of the garment one would question if she was wearing underwear, as well. He was tempted to ask her but thought better of doing so. "There's not much to it."

Syneda laughed as she eyed Clayton from under her hat. "That's the idea, Clayton. This is Florida. It gets too hot for a lot of clothes. The fewer the better."

"I'm sorry you feel that way," Clayton replied drily.

Syneda raised a brow. "Why?"

"I'm going to be spending all of my time keeping the men around here in line."

The guide led them back to the sightseeing train and then on to the next stop. After touring the Fountain of Youth, Zorayda's Castle and the Lightner Museum, they caught another bus to have lunch in a popular restaurant in the Lincolnville Historical District.

Lincolnville constituted the heart of the city's black community. It was a large residential neighborhood whose occupants could trace their ancestors' origins to the city's sixteenth-century founding.

After lunch they took a carriage ride through the Colonial Historical District before doing some extensive walking while touring the old homes along George Street.

It was midafternoon when they decided to call it a day. Clayton draped his arm across Syneda's shoulder as they walked from the bus stop in front of the condos.

At the door Syneda turned to face him. "I can't believe all the sights we took in today. There is so much to do and see here. And I can't believe how architecturally grand the buildings are. They were simply amazing."

"Yeah, amazing," Clayton replied, feigning interest as he unlocked the door and ushered her inside. The only thing that had held his attention all day was her and that outfit she had on. He had been ever mindful of more than a few male stares sent her way. She hadn't noticed but he sure had.

Syneda dropped her purse onto the entry table. "Where do you want to go for dinner, Clayton?"

"I'll let you decide. The only thing I want to do right now is rest my poor aching feet."

Syneda laughed. "Aren't you used to walking?"

"No."

"How do you stay in such good shape?" she asked as she eyed his masculine body outlined in the shorts and top he wore. He was in great physical shape. "Surely all those nights spent in bed with women didn't do it," she teased.

Clayton gave her a wan smile. "I keep in shape in a lot of ways. I work out at least twice a week at the gym, and I play basketball with the guys every chance I get."

"Oh, I see." She looked down at her watch. "It's four now. How about if we go out for dinner around seven. That will give you a couple hours to rest up."

"That sounds good to me. What will you be doing while I'm resting up?"

"I think I'll go to the beach and build a sandcastle. The beaches around here have the whitest and silkiest sand I've ever seen."

Clayton frowned. "What will you wear?"

"Where?"

"To the beach."

"Clayton, that's a silly question. I'll be wearing a bathing suit."

"The one you had on this morning?"

"No, not that one," Syneda replied, turning toward the direction of her bedroom. "But it's one similar to it. Why?"

"Wait up. I think I'll build that sandcastle with you."

Syneda turned around and gave him a surprised look. "I thought you were tired."

"I've suddenly found myself with a new burst of energy."

Later that evening Clayton and Syneda entered a restaurant that the condo's management had recommended. It was a place on Anastasia Island known for fresh seafood and tropical drinks. After enjoying a feast of assorted seafoods, they left the restaurant section of the establishment to enter its lounge. They were led by a waiter to an empty table in the back that had a wonderful view of the ocean.

After the waiter departed with their drink orders, Clayton rested back in his chair. "I'm curious as to where you buy your clothes."

Syneda raised a brow. "Why?"

"Just curious." In fact, he was more than curious. He was having a difficult time keeping his eyes off her long, smooth legs that were showing from the outfit she had on, a minilength sundress with three tiers of ruffles on the hem. The outfit was blatantly sexy. Too sexy.

"I buy my things from a number of places. I don't shop at any one particular store. That reminds me. I need to go shopping while I'm here. I want to get something for the kids."

Clayton knew what kids she was referring to: his nieces and nephews who called her Aunt Neda. "Are you enjoying yourself, Syneda?"

"Yes. I'm feeling more relaxed than I have in days," she replied with a smile. "I want to thank you again for inviting me."

"My pleasure."

Syneda smiled. "When the waiter returns with our drinks I want to propose a toast."

"To what?"

"Our friendship."

Clayton swallowed hard. Friendship was the last thing on his mind and he felt guilty as sin. His mouth was watering over the sight of her, and she wanted to toast their friendship. And if her outfit wasn't bad enough, the perfume she had on was drifting around and through him. If only she knew how enticing the fragrance was. Her light makeup was immaculate and her hair appeared soft to the touch. He had taken this trip to clear his mind, but being around Syneda was beginning to turn his brains to mush.

"Do you want to dance?" he asked abruptly.

"The waiter hasn't returned with our drinks yet."

"He'll hold them," Clayton answered tersely, reaching across the small table and taking her hand. A slow-moving song was playing as he led her to the dance floor, which was crowded with other couples.

He knew it had been a mistake to ask her to dance the minute he took her into his arms and pulled her close. Her hands automatically folded loosely behind his neck, which caused her breasts to press against his chest.

Syneda tilted her head back and looked up at him. "What about you, Clayton? Are you enjoying yourself?"

Clayton looked down at her. She looked absolutely stunning. "Yes."

"Are you sure?"

"I'm positive," he replied, pulling her closer.

They continued the dance in silence. He was so engrossed in the feel of having her in his arms that at first he didn't notice the tap on his shoulder. When he did, he turned and looked into the face of a man he'd noticed eyeing Syneda when they had first entered the lounge.

"May I cut in?" the man asked with a deep southern accent.

"No, you can't."

"Why not?" the man asked gruffly, obviously put off by Clayton's rudeness.

Clayton faced the man squarely. "Because I said so, that's why. Now back off."

"Clayton!"

"Excuse us," Clayton said to the man he'd been tempted to bring down a notch moments earlier. Taking Syneda's hand he led her back to their table.

"Clayton, what in the world is wrong with you? That was downright rude."

"I was protecting your sweet behind since you don't seem to notice it needs protecting. That guy's been drooling over you ever since we entered this place. He's just one of many men who are undressing you with their eyes."

"They're not!"

"They are, too! Just look at that outfit you're wearing. It invites stares."

Syneda stared at him with anger reflecting in her eyes and her mouth open. "I don't believe you, Clayton. There's nothing wrong with my outfit."

"Not if you're a woman looking for a pickup."

"How dare you—"

"You didn't want to come on vacation with me for fear of cramping my style. Maybe I should have made sure I wouldn't be cramping yours," he said curtly.

Syneda stood. "I'm leaving."

Throwing more than enough money on the table to cover the drinks they had ordered but not yet gotten, Clayton followed a fuming Syneda out of the door. Leaving the lounge, they rode in silence along the shoreline road that led back to the condos. As soon as he opened the door to the condo, Syneda entered and went straight to her bedroom, slamming the door behind her.

Clayton let out a disgusted sigh as he poured a drink and stepped out on the terrace. He stood transfixed for an hour or so looking at the ocean that was lit only by the moon's glow. He turned around when he heard a movement behind him. Syneda stood before him. She had changed into a nightshirt.

"Clayton, I'm sorry. I can't believe we had an argument after agreeing not to."

Clayton held open his arms and she walked into them. He pulled her close to him. "I'm the one who should be apologizing, Syneda. I behaved like a jerk tonight and I apologize. There was nothing wrong with the way you were dressed. You looked sensational. I guess I'm so used to eyeing women myself that I know what goes through other men's minds when I see them doing it. And I don't want them thinking about you that way. I guess I've taken it upon myself to be your protector while we're here."

"Yeah, so I've noticed. But Clayton, you don't have to protect me. I'm twenty-eight and old enough to take care of myself. Have you forgotten that I live alone in New York?"

Clayton smiled down at her. "Deep down I know you can take care of yourself, but that doesn't keep me from wanting to do it for you."

Syneda grinned. "I guess with three younger sisters you're used to it."

"Maybe so," Clayton replied, although deep down he had a feeling the root of his problem was jealousy, plain and simple.

Syneda stepped back out of his arms. "I'm really enjoying myself, but I don't think you are. Maybe I should leave tomorrow and return to New York. You're so busy looking out for me that you're not relaxing at all."

Clayton brushed a stray curl from her face. "No. I'm fine, and I don't want you to leave. I enjoy your company. Like today, for instance. I had a great time building that sandcastle with you on the beach. And tomorrow is our day to spend shopping at the malls, remember."

Syneda smiled. "How could I possibly forget something as important as that?"

Encircling her with a protective arm, Clayton drew her closer to him. For a long moment there was no conversation between them. They just held each other. Clayton was going through pure torture. Everything about Syneda was sexy, and he felt a quickening in the lower part of his body. If he didn't separate himself from her, he couldn't be held accountable for his actions. "Syneda?"

"Umm?"

"I think we should call it a night, don't you?"

Syneda stepped out of his arms and peered up at him through a sweep of long lashes. A smile covered her lips. "Friends again?"

Clayton returned her smile as a surge of warmth passed through him. "Yes, friends again."

"Good. As much as we argue at times, I like having you for my friend."

"And I feel likewise."

Syneda leaned up on tiptoe and kissed his cheek. "Good night, Clayton."

"Good night, Syneda."

He watched as she turned to leave. He couldn't help but notice how the sleeper she wore clung to her body, accentuating her shapely hips and tiny waist. He had a feeling he was in for a long, sleepless night.

Chapter 3

"Don't tell me we've finally done something that's tired you out," Clayton said, grinning. He handed Syneda a cold can of soda. "I was beginning to think you were blessed with never-ending energy."

Syneda took the soda and flopped down in the nearest chair. "Shopping always tires me out," she replied after taking a sip of the drink. She set the can on a nearby table and began removing her sandals. "The stores at that mall were wonderful. Just look at all this stuff."

"I'm looking," Clayton replied, glancing around at the bags and boxes littering the floor. "Have you forgotten that I helped you carry most of it?"

Syneda smiled. "I really appreciate you being with me. I couldn't have purchased nearly as much stuff had you not been there."

Clayton glanced around the room shaking his head. "Yeah, your Master Card company should thank me profusely. I wonder if they'll be willing to give me some kind of a kickback since you spent a fortune today."

Syneda laughed. "I doubt it." She stood to collect her boxes. "Do you mind if we order out tonight? I don't think I have the energy to get dressed to go anyplace."

"That's no problem. What do you have a taste for?"

"How about lobster?"

"That sounds good to me. I'll order delivery from a restuarant nearby."

"Thanks, Clayton, you're such a sweetheart."

Less than an hour later, a just-showered Syneda stood leaning against the railing on the terrace enjoying the view of the ocean. Clayton had left her a note saying he was going downstairs to the pool for a swim.

From her position on the terrace she could see him below, and for some reason her eyes kept straying toward him. She became entranced by the movement of his muscular legs as he dived into the pool, by the firmness of his stomach beneath his swim trunks and by the mass of dark hair covering his chest. He looked tough, lean and sinewy. His powerful well-muscled toast-brown body moved through the water with easy grace.

"For heaven's sake, what am I staring at?" she exclaimed in dazed exasperation. "You would think I've never seen a good-looking male body before." And what really bothered her was the fact the body she was ogling belonged to Clayton.

She forced her gaze to move from the pool area back to the view of the ocean. But as if they had a will of their own, her eyes strayed back to Clayton time and time again, and each time she felt a flutter deep in the pit of her stomach. He might be downstairs swimming in the pool, but she was upstairs swimming through a haze of feelings and desires that were almost drowning her.

Knowing the only way she would be able to stay above water and stop looking at him was to move from her present spot, she walked over to stretch out on the lounger to take a nap.

Syneda had nearly dozed off to sleep when she heard Clayton return. She opened her eyes to find him standing next to the lounger. She couldn't help but let her gaze settle on the line of body hair that tapered from his navel into the waistband of his swim trunks.

"Did I wake you?" he asked, stretching down in the lounger opposite hers.

She pulled herself into a sitting position. "Not really. How was your swim?"

"Super. It relaxed me tremendously," he replied.

And it unsettled me, Syneda thought.

"What's on the agenda for tomorrow?" he asked.

Biting her lower lip, she looked away. "I thought I would give you a break and make it a do-your-own-thing day. That way you can be free of me for a while." *And I can be free of you to sort through all these strange feelings I'm beginning to have,* she thought.

"I like having you around."

"Oh," she replied. Her eyes were again drawn to the thick mat of hair on his chest. Awkwardly, she cleared her throat. Her eyes met his. "Well, then, let's not make any plans. We'll let it be a whatever-happens sort of day."

"All right."

They spent the rest of the afternoon relaxing on the terrace enjoying the ocean view and trying not to let it be obvious that they were also enjoying the view of each other.

Later that evening after enjoying a superb lobster dinner, they sat around on the floor drinking the remainder of the wine.

"You have butter on your nose."

Syneda twitched her nose. "I do?"

Clayton laughed. "Yes, you do."

When Clayton reached over to wipe it off, their gazes locked and held for several seconds. A mite too long to be at ease.

"Thanks, Clayton," Syneda said awkwardly, taking another sip of wine. Her mind was clouded with uneasiness. *For crying out loud, Syneda Tremain Walters, pull yourself together. You're acting like a bimbo. The man is Clayton, for Pete's sake. You know, Lorren's brother-in-law, the one who changes women as often as he changes socks, the one who has a case of condoms in his closet, and the one who is definitely not your type.*

"Here's something we can do tomorrow night."

Syneda glanced up to find Clayton looking in the entertainment brochure. "What?"

"Take a cruise around Anastasia Island aboard the *Rivership Romance.*"

Syneda almost choked on her drink. "A romance ship?"

"Yes."

"Why would you want to do something like that?" she asked. A shadow of caution touched her.

Clayton shrugged. "Because it sounds like fun, and we are here to have fun, aren't we?" he asked, his voice carefully colored in neutral shades.

"Yes, but we'll be out of place aboard that ship."

"Why?"

"Because most of the people there will either be married or lovers."

"And you'll feel out of place because we're not either of those things?" he asked, regarding her quizzically for a moment.

"Won't you?"

"Nope. It wouldn't bother me at all. But since it evidently will bother you, forget I suggested it."

Although her misgivings were increasing by the minute, Syneda felt like a complete heel. The last thing she wanted was to be a bore, especially after he had been nice enough to invite her on this trip with him. "We'll go."

Clayton shook his head. "We can do something else."

"No, I'm fine with going."

"Are you sure?"

"I'm positive."

"All right. I'll make reservations."

Syneda stood quickly, collecting her empty wineglass. She

smiled down at him, although inwardly she struggled with uncertainty. "Well, I guess I'll retire early. It was a tiring day."

Clayton couldn't help but look up at her. His eyes scanned her,
beginning with the polished toes of her bare feet to the golden-
bronze hair atop her head. He met her eyes. He could almost drown
in them and wondered why he had never felt like doing so before.
Then there was that cute little dimple that appeared in her cheek
each time she smiled. Why did he suddenly find it totally alluring?
His senses began spinning. The scent of her perfume seemed to
float around him. It was as sensuous as he found her to be. He
inhaled deeply as a need as primitive as mankind touched him. "All
right, Syneda. I'll see you in the morning," he replied huskily.

Syneda took a deep breath and feigned a yawn. "Not too early
though. I can barely keep my eyes open so I may sleep in late
tomorrow. If I'm not up by the time you want breakfast just go
on without me. I'll grab something later. Good night." She
hurried off to her bedroom.

As soon as she was in the privacy of her bedroom, Syneda
rushed into the connecting bathroom. The reflection staring back
almost startled her. Her features were basically the same, except
she had gotten a little browner from the time she had spent in the
sun. But that wasn't the only noticeable difference. Her eyes were
glazed with a look that definitely spelled trouble. What bothered
her was the fact Clayton Madaris was the one responsible for that
look being there. And to make matters worse, she would be
spending tomorrow night with him on board a romance cruise ship.

*Good grief! What am I going to do? I'm becoming attracted
to Clayton Madaris!*

"Wake up, sleepyhead."

Syneda heard the deep masculine sound in her ear at the same
moment she felt the warm breath on her neck. She opened one
eye slowly, then the other. Her eyes met the sparkling brown ones
that held a flicker of mischief in their dark depth. She became
instantly wide-awake.

"Clayton! What are you doing in here?"

Clayton was lying down beside her, facing her. "I came to make sure you were still alive."

Syneda became aware of her state of dress and tugged her nightshirt down. "Of course I'm alive. I told you last night that I'd probably sleep through breakfast. Did you forget?"

He gave her a lopsided grin. "No, I didn't forget. I just didn't think you meant you would also sleep through lunch."

"Lunch! What time is it?"

"Around one-thirty."

"One-thirty! I didn't mean to sleep so late," she said, pulling herself up in a sitting position. She forced her gaze from his lips, full and inviting. Somehow they had never intrigued her before as they were doing now.

"You must have really been tired."

"Yes, I was." She didn't bother to add that she had lain awake most of the night thinking about him. She suddenly felt uncomfortable at his closeness, and a confusing rush of desire whirled inside her. He was dressed in a blue pullover shirt and a pair of white shorts. The masculine fragrance of his cologne was beginning to dull her senses.

She suddenly realized while she had been staring at him, he'd been doing likewise with her. "I need to get dressed."

"Don't let me stop you. Just pretend that I'm not here."

"Fat chance, Clayton Madaris!"

Clayton laughed throatily, and a disarmingly generous smile extended to his eyes. "I was afraid you'd say that."

Syneda watched him stretch his body before standing. "Okay, Miss Walters, I'll leave you to dress in peace. But if you're not ready to go in twenty minutes, I'm coming back for you."

Syneda watched as he left the room, closing the door behind him. She tried going back into her mind, into central control, to reset her emotions. She was not ready for the thoughts and feelings she'd begun having around Clayton.

* * *

"Senator, I'm glad you're back, sir. How was your trip?"

"The trip was nice, Braxter. It's always good to get away and spend some time with an old friend." Senator Nedwyn Lansing studied the young man in front of him. As a senator's top aide, Braxter Montgomery at the age of thirty was the best there was. A graduate of Georgetown University, he had begun working for him over six years ago, serving him through almost two full terms. During that time he had gotten to know Braxter as well as the other members of his immediate staff. They were people he could depend on. But only a few he felt he could trust completely. Braxter was one of them.

"Is something bothering you, Braxter?"

"There's nothing bothering me, sir. But there is something I'm concerned about."

"You worry too much."

"I'm supposed to. That's part of my job."

The senator nodded. "All right. Let's sit and talk."

The two men took seats that were facing each other. "Okay, let's have it, Braxter. What's so concerning that you've missed lunch?"

Braxter eyed the forty-nine-year-old, light-complexioned black man with hazel eyes sitting across from him. He was a man he highly respected. Most people did. Where most senators did good things for their image, Senator Lansing did good things for the people he represented. He was often referred to by the media as the "people's servant." His life was an open book.

It was a known fact he'd been a sharecropper's son from a small town in Texas not far from the border. His mother had died when he was five. With hard work and dedication, he had completed high school and because of his academic achievements, he had obtained a four-year scholarship to attend the University of Texas in Houston.

It was also well-known that he had never been married, although he'd been steadily dating a law professor at Howard University for the past couple of years. The only thing that had always puzzled

Braxter was the senator's annual trip to Texas this time every year; the one he had just returned from. It was a trip he never talked about, other than to say he had gone to visit a friend.

"What I'm concerned about, sir, is your blockage of the Harris Bill."

Senator Lansing raised a brow. "What about it? That bill needed to be blocked. I flatly refuse to support any legislation that proposes cuts in education."

"Yes, Senator, and I agree with you. But blocking that bill won't be a popular move on your part. Especially with certain people."

The senator nodded, knowing Braxter was referring to the creator of the bill, John Harris, and a few other senators who were considered Harris's cronies. "I can't waste my time worrying about some people, Braxter. I want to do what's right for the majority of the people in this country, not just a limited, socially acceptable few. Every child regardless of race, creed, color or social standing is entitled to a good education."

Braxter smiled. He enjoyed seeing the senator fired up over an important issue. But his job as a senator's aide was to make him aware of what he could possibly be up against. Especially since the kickoff for his reelection campaign was less than two months away.

"I totally agree with everything you're saying. And according to recent polls, the American people are behind you all the way."

"Then I guess those people whose noses are out of joint will just have to get over it."

"I really don't know if they will, sir. By blocking that bill, you've stepped on a few toes. I have a feeling they'll step back."

Senator Lansing smiled. "Let them. I have nothing to hide."

"Do you remember the first time we met, Syneda?"

Syneda almost blushed under Clayton's warm stare. They were lying side by side on loungers at the pool. "Yes, it was almost two years ago, the night of Justin's cookout to celebrate his purchase of the ranch." A smile touched her lips. "He was very much interested in Lorren that night."

Clayton chuckled. "Yes, he was, wasn't he." Clayton thought about the night he and Syneda had met. When he'd first met her he had thought she was about as explosive as a stick of dynamite next to a blazing torch. Just about any controversial subject could set her off. She had disagreed with him on just about everything. It had been a first for him. Most women agreed with practically everything he said.

There was a brief moment of silence before Syneda spoke. "Clayton?"

"Umm?"

"Why did you ask me if I remembered when we first met?"

"I was just wondering."

Syneda gazed over at him but couldn't see his eyes behind the aviator-style sunglasses he wore. She wondered what his thoughts were and tried ignoring the funny, shivering sensation in her midsection just being near him was causing. Despite her best intentions, her eyes kept straying to him.

"Syneda?"

"Yes?"

"Did you bring a different bathing suit for every day?" he asked, lifting his sunglasses and squinting at her inquiringly.

She swallowed. Had he been checking her out the way she'd been doing him? "No, why?"

"Because I haven't seen you wear the same suit twice."

"Are you complaining?" she asked. The smile on his lips sent her pulse spinning.

He gave her body a thorough once-over, which made Syneda's breath lodge in her throat. His gaze moved over her, traveling from her bare feet, up her thighs, past her waist. His gaze paused momentarily on her breasts, before moving to her face where it held hers.

"No. You won't get any complaints out of me. I think you look great. I don't know what happened between you and that guy you were seeing, but it was definitely his loss," Clayton replied huskily.

The dark brown eyes that held hers appeared to have darkened. What Syneda saw reflected in them made her lose all conscious thought. She read appreciation, attraction, awareness and something she hadn't counted on: desire. Were those the things she saw in his eyes or the things she was afraid he saw in hers?

Stifling a low groan, she quickly came to her feet when she felt an odd rush of heat flare in her belly before moving lower. "Thanks for the compliment, Clayton. I think I'll go back to the condo for a while. There's a book I bought yesterday that I want to start reading before we leave for the cruise tonight," she said hastily, pulling on her cover-up and grabbing her beach bag. "What time will we be leaving for the cruise?"

"Around seven," he answered, the huskiness lingering in his tone.

"Okay. I'll be ready. See you later."

Clayton watched Syneda walk back toward the condo. He took a deep breath with every step she took and with each sway of her hips. How in blazes was he going to get through the evening pretending their relationship hadn't changed? How was he going to spend the rest of the week with her and pretend not to want her when he wanted her like he'd wanted no other woman before?

Going into her bedroom to wake her had been a *big* mistake. He had found her sprawled atop the covers wearing a loose cotton nightshirt. Evidently sometime during her sleep, the sexy garment had risen to her hips revealing a pair of luscious thighs. And if that hadn't been bad enough, the first few buttons had been undone and had shown a hefty view of the slopes of her breasts.

Lunch with her had been even worse. He had sat across from her in a booth at a sandwich shop eating a submarine sandwich when he happened to notice the peaks of those same breasts poking through the front of her thin blouse. He had almost choked on the bite he'd just taken out of his sandwich. Desire, hot and rampant, had consumed him, had hardened him, and had made him fully aware of how much he wanted her.

Clayton sighed deeply. He would no longer fight the inevitable. He wondered how Syneda would handle the fact that he had every intention of getting close to her. Very close. He was a man who believed in going after what he wanted.

And he wanted her.

Chapter 4

"**I**'m ready, Clayton."

Clayton turned his attention away from the television to cast his gaze upon Syneda as she entered the room. He was utterly spellbound as he stood to his feet. She looked absolutely radiant.

While waiting for her he had begun watching a sitcom that he had found rather enjoyable. However, all thoughts of the television program left his mind when he saw her. He could only stare at the stunning woman standing across the room.

She was dressed in a fuchsia-colored dress that fit like a glove.

A knot formed deep in Clayton's throat. He was totally captivated, and before he could stop his mouth from saying aloud his innermost thoughts, the words flowed from his lips in a voice rich with masculine magnetism and sensual appeal. "You look great, Syneda."

The dark intensity in Clayton's eyes touched Syneda to the core. The dress she had chosen to wear was one she had bought earlier that year to attend the law firm's annual get-together. The style of the dress showed off her figure to alluring advantage. She had made quite a hit in it at the party.

"Thanks, and you look pretty good yourself." She thought he looked particularly handsome dressed in a charcoal-gray suit, white shirt and printed tie.

Anxious to get away from Clayton, if only for a minute to get her bearings and to stop her senses from spinning, she said, "I think I lied earlier."

"About what?"

"About being ready. I left my purse in the bedroom. I'll be right back."

Clayton drew in a deep breath when Syneda turned to leave the room. His gaze traveled over her from behind. Her dress had a daring deep V-back that seemed to end at her waist. His skin felt flushed, his tongue felt thick in his mouth and his eyes felt swollen from expanding. He stared at her bare back, small waist, soft curves and long shapely legs. He could feel the hammering of his heartbeat in his chest and was no longer stunned at the rush of pleasure that surged through him.

Syneda hurried off into her bedroom. Pausing just inside the door, she took a long, deep breath. What was happening to her? Clayton wasn't a man she had just met. Why was being around him affecting her this way? Why was every sensory nerve in her body sharpened with maddening awareness of him? With no answers but a determination to enjoy herself during the evening, she took another deep breath before snatching her purse off the bed. Moments later she returned to the living room where Clayton was waiting.

"I'm really ready this time."

"No more than I am," Clayton replied softly. Taking her hand he led her out of the condo.

"What a beautiful ship," Syneda said to Clayton as they boarded the *Rivership Romance*. It was a 110-foot triple-deck catamaran that was positively elegant. On board was an interior of Tiffany lamps and plushly carpeted dining salons and a lounge.

The exterior contained promenade decks with seating that provided a stunning view of the ocean.

"Welcome aboard. I'm Captain Johnstone," a tall man dressed in a starched white captain's uniform greeted. "Tonight we're featuring live entertainment and a full cocktail service. Dinner will be served promptly at eight and will include a selection of several mouthwatering dishes. Our crabmeat-stuffed whitefish baked in parchment is usually a favorite."

"That sounds delectable," Syneda replied, flashing the captain a warm smile.

"It is and we're here to please. We want you to enjoy yourselves."

"Thank you and I'm sure *we* will," Clayton replied, ushering Syneda on board. He hadn't liked the smile the good captain had given Syneda.

"Just as I thought," Syneda said moments later after grabbing a treat off the table of tantalizing hors d'oeuvres.

"What?" Clayton asked, also grabbing a plump chilled shrimp off the table.

"All the people here are paired off. And from the looks of things they're just as I predicted, either married or lovers. Just look at them."

Clayton did look. Most of the people were hugging and kissing, walking along the deck holding hands, or on the dance floor moving to slow music.

"Don't let it bother you, Syneda," Clayton said quietly, his eyes holding hers as he casually leaned against the ship's railing. "If you feel uncomfortable, you should consider the old cliché, when in Rome do as the Romans do."

"Meaning what?"

"Meaning this."

Syneda didn't know what she expected, but it wasn't Clayton suddenly taking her into his arms, cupping her chin in one firm hand, tilting her head back and lowering his mouth to hers. Her heart began pounding wildly as Clayton's tongue began an erotic exploration of her mouth. His hands massaged the center of her back, touching her bare skin.

Her body began to vibrate with liquid fire. She surrendered completely to his masterful seduction. A deep ache that began in her abdomen radiated downward, to the very core of her. The kiss was like nothing she had ever experienced, and she was shocked to discover she wanted more.

Clayton lifted his mouth from hers and looked into wide, amazed eyes. What he saw in them almost took his breath away. He was too experienced not to recognize total desire in a woman. And he was inwardly elated to discover Syneda wanted him just as much as he wanted her. The burning question of the hour was where to go from here?

"Clayton, I—I…"

He silenced her by placing his finger against her slightly swollen and undeniably moist lips. "Don't say anything, Syneda. Not yet. We'll talk later. I think we have a lot to discuss." His body ached with the sweetness of taut sexual awareness. *Then maybe we shouldn't talk at all,* he thought, seeing signs of apprehension in her eyes.

After dinner the live band continued to provide the music. Clayton and Syneda walked along the promenade deck holding hands, not saying anything but very much aware of each other.

"Would you like to dance, Syneda?"

"Not if it's going to end like it did the last time we danced together a few nights ago," she replied teasingly.

"It won't. I promise." With deft fingers he led her onto the dance floor where couples were already moving slowly to the instrumental version of Billy Ocean's classic, "Suddenly." The music wrapped them and every other couple on the dance floor in a romantic web where everything else, except the person you were with, faded into oblivion.

It was quite obvious most of the people there were in love, Syneda thought. She and Clayton began to slow dance. She felt his hand tighten around her, gathering her closer to him. A gust of desire shook her. She never dreamed his hands would feel so warm, so gentle, so hypnotic. In response, she moved her hips against his rock-hard thighs and heard his sharp intake of breath.

"You feel good," Clayton whispered, his warm breath hot against her neck. She felt so right in his arms, so perfect. It was as if she had been made just for him. "I can't believe we've never—" He cut off his words and began chuckling to himself. "The music they're playing is very appropriate for our situation."

Syneda lifted her gaze to his. "How so?"

"We felt pretty comfortable about coming on vacation together because there was nothing romantic or sexual between us. Then whammo, *suddenly,* after two years, I discover you're the sexiest woman alive. What do you think of that?"

Syneda gave her head a wry shake, feeling totally off balance. Passion was flowing through her entire body. "I really don't want to think anything about it, Clayton," she replied in a husky voice. To think about it would make her see reason and remind her that nothing had changed. She and Clayton were still not compatible. At the moment she didn't want to dwell on that. All she wanted was to share this special moment with him. But then again, maybe she should think about it. Their not being compatible just might be a plus. Clayton could very well be the type of man she needed to become involved with. Especially after Marcus.

She had explained to Marcus Capers when they'd first begun dating that she wasn't in the market for a serious relationship. But as far as he'd been concerned, she was the perfect woman to settle down and begin a family with. He just couldn't get it through his head that she wanted no part of love and marriage.

After dating each other for a little over six months, he had proposed to her. She had turned him down. Syneda doubted she would have that kind of trouble with Clayton. Like her, he wanted no part of a commitment with anyone. He was a man who knew the rules and would play by them.

The band began playing another slow number, and Clayton pulled her back into his arms and held her close. He rubbed his hand, slowly, sensually over her bare back, tracing erotic patterns with his fingertips. Again she felt passion rising in her like the hottest fire, clouding her brain.

Syneda was so close to him she could hardly move without her body moving both seductively and suggestively against his. She couldn't help but feel his virile response to her movements. For the first time in her life, she felt an aching emptiness in her that demanded fulfillment. Clayton's face was so very near that all she needed to do was turn her head just a little to touch her lips to his.

Her pulse raced. The urge to do more than kiss Clayton was a physical ache deep within her, and her fervor mounted. "Clayton," she whispered. Her sea-green eyes held his dark ones.

"Yes? What do you want, Syneda?" he asked quietly, hoping it was the same thing he did.

They had stopped dancing and were standing in a secluded area of the dance floor. Syneda reached up and boldly traced his lips with her fingers. For a long while their eyes held. She drew a deep breath. She didn't understand what was happening to her, but she did know what was happening between them. Blame it on the magnificent sunrise she saw each morning upon wakening, or the plush condo and its gorgeous ocean view, or the cruise that was taking them around the island setting the mood for romance. No matter where the blame was placed, the result was the same.

She wanted him.

"What do you want, Syneda?" Clayton asked again.

The sexy huskiness of his voice made blood race through her body. She attempted to calm herself down, discovered she couldn't and decided the devil with it. Why fight it anymore? Known to be upfront, candid and straight to the point in her dealings with anyone, Syneda slowly moved closer and whispered in Clayton's ear. "I want you, Madaris. Bad."

Clayton crushed her to him. Sharp needles of sexual excitement were pricking his every nerve with the five words she had spoken. It was impossible to maintain any semblance of control, physically or emotionally. He drew in a tremulous breath. "And

I want you, too, baby." He then leaned down and kissed her deeply, tasting her fully.

The hours didn't pass fast enough for either of them before the ship finally returned to dock. Clayton drove the rental car back to the condo. Neither said anything. However, Syneda couldn't help but study his profile, exalting at the male strength and beauty of him. She couldn't stop her gaze from lingering on his lips. Lips that had masterfully kissed her for the first time that night and had her own still quivering in desire. They were lips that had awakened a craving within her so strong it had literally transformed her into another person; definitely not the cool, calm, levelheaded person she usually was.

She fidgeted restlessly in her seat, thinking about what would happen once they returned to the condo. She wanted the feel of Clayton's mouth on hers again. She wanted him to touch her all over. And more than anything, she wanted him to make love to her.

Sensing her anxiousness, a copy of his own, Clayton relieved one of his hands from the steering wheel and reached for her hand. Tenderly turning it over, he began tracing erotic circles in her palm. "This means I want you very much."

Syneda's breath caught in her throat. She was stunned by the wild and dangerous feelings coursing through her from his words.

"Here at last," Clayton said a few minutes later. At a brisk walk he came around to open the car door for her.

"Did you enjoy yourself tonight, Syneda?" he asked as they walked at a fast pace away from the car holding hands. Sexual tension between them was at its maximum. Small talk was the last thing either of them wanted to engage in.

"Yes, very much. What about you?"

His dimpled smile almost made her knees weaken. "I had a great time," he replied, increasing his pace. The door to the condo was now only a few feet away.

"I'm glad," Syneda said, almost having to run to keep up with him. Her heart was pounding with anticipation. When they finally made it to the door, he had the key in his hand. As they stood in front of the door facing each other, calming their deep, erratic breathing, Syneda gave Clayton a breathtaking smile.

He was surprised at his lightning-quick reaction to that smile. Drawing her closer, he enfolded her in his arms. Leaning down, he touched his lips to hers, kissing her deeply and simultaneously reaching for the door. Before he could use his key, the door was flung wide-open.

"It's about time the two of you got back!"

Clayton and Syneda broke apart and stared in surprised shock at the couple standing in the doorway.

"Justin! Lorren!" Syneda exclaimed in astonishment. She quickly recovered and threw her arms around them.

"Did we surprise you two?" Lorren Madaris asked speculatively, eyeing Clayton and Syneda with a sort of stunned expression on her face. "We arrived a few hours ago. When we discovered the two of you weren't here, Justin used the spare key to get in."

Clayton hugged Lorren and shook hands with his oldest brother. Although he and Syneda had been well hidden in the shadows, it was apparent they had been doing a lot more than chitchatting outside the door.

"Surprise is putting it mildly," Clayton muttered to them. His voice was as unwelcoming as his expression. "Your timing is lousy, big brother," he whispered for Justin's ears only.

Justin Madaris gave Clayton a hard look. "Apparently it was right on time," he whispered back.

"So what brings the two of you here?" Clayton asked, entering the condo, still holding Syneda's hand. "Whatever the reason, I hope it's a short visit." He wasn't kidding. And to make sure Justin and Lorren knew it, the tone of his voice was deadly serious.

Evidently it wasn't serious enough. Both Justin and Lorren were smiling with a look that said, "Now that we see what you're up to, not on your life, buddy."

After a moment of tense silence, Justin finally spoke. "Lorren has some news she just couldn't wait to share with Syneda. And your lack of phones in this condo made calling impossible."

"Our lack of phones was to ensure complete privacy and avoid untimely and uninvited interruptions," Clayton replied, placing emphasis on the last part of his sentence. "So what's your news, Lorren, that was so pressing you had to deliver it in person?" His eyes fell on the sister-in-law he had come to love and adore but at the moment wanted to strangle.

He couldn't help noticing her love-mussed clothes, tousled hair and slightly swollen lips. Despite not wanting to do so, he couldn't help smiling. Evidently Justin and Lorren had found a rather interesting way to pass the time while they had waited for him and Syneda to return.

Lorren's eyes sparkled with total happiness. "We're having another baby!"

"Lorren, that's wonderful! I'm so happy for the two of you." Syneda threw her arms around Lorren, sharing her excitement.

Clayton couldn't help but roar in laughter. Now he had two pregnant sisters-in-law. Evidently his brothers had taken the good book's directive to be fruitful and replenish the earth rather seriously. "Somehow Lorren being pregnant again doesn't surprise me," he said. "It really doesn't surprise me at all."

Senator John Harris sat across the table from the other three men in the large conference room. They were all staring at him as if he'd lost his mind. He hated it whenever they stared at him like that.

Finally one of the men, Senator Carl Booker, spoke. "I think you're taking all of this too personal, John."

"Because it *is* personal, Carl. Nedwyn Lansing and I have been at odds with each other since the first day we both arrived on Capitol Hill. The passage of that bill was important to me."

Matthew Williams, the oldest senator in the group, spoke. "But it didn't pass, so I suggest you get over it. What you're proposing to do is crazy. I'm not all that fond of Lansing, none of us are, but I wouldn't deliberately do anything to destroy his political career."

"That's why you and I are different, Mat. I would destroy his

career in a minute if I had the right ammunition. All I'm proposing is to get someone to dig into his past, just in case something
is there. No one can be that squeaky clean. Even George Washington had skeletons in his closet."

"Forget it, John," Senator Paul Dunlap said. "If the media hasn't
uncovered any dirt on Lansing, then there isn't any to be found."

The other men in the room nodded in full agreement.

Senator Harris fumed. "That's not necessarily true." One by
one he looked in the eyes of everyone at the table. "No one has
found out about that twenty-two-year-old woman you've been
two-timing your wife with for the past two years, Mat. Nor have
they found out about your lovely teenage daughter's recent
abortion, Paul. And last but not least, Carl, I really don't think
anyone knows a thing about your son's drug addiction."

Senator Harris's eyes crinkled at the corners at the surprised
look on each of the men's faces. He had just stated information
they all thought no one knew. "And don't insult my intelligence
by denying any of it. I have everything I need to prove otherwise."

"What do you want from us, Harris?" Dunlap asked in a voice
with an edge to it. "It's getting late and I would like to make it
home before midnight."

"I want all three of you to back me on this. Ruining Lansing has
to be a group effort. And another thing, he has too many close
friends who happen to be Fortune 500 CEOs. I find it hard to believe
he's never accepted any type of kickback from any of them."

"I assume you're referring to Garwood Industries, Remington Oil, and Turner Broadcasting Corporation?" Carl said. "Everyone knows those three are loyal financial contributors to
Lansing's campaign coffers."

"Yes."

"That can be explained," Paul replied. "Lansing and old man
Garwood were friends since Garwood Industries opened their
first Texas branch office. And since his grandfather's death, Kyle
Garwood has maintained a close relationship with Lansing."

After taking a drink of water he continued, "As far as his association with S. T. Remington is concerned, it's my understanding they were roommates in college. And as for Ted Turner, they became good friends during the time Lansing was the mayor's assistant in Beaumont, Texas. He encouraged the school board to do an experiment using cable television as a teaching tool for elementary and secondary students. It was a project that proved to be very successful and got Turner Broadcasting much recognition."

"Besides," Mat contributed, "none of us can deny the fact that Lansing has done more for the interest of the oil and cattle industries than anyone in Congress. That's why he's always gotten such strong support from the oil companies and the cattlemen."

Senator Harris slammed his hand down on the table. "There has to be something in his past that will drop his popularity with the voters," he thundered. "And I plan on finding out what it is and destroying him the same way he destroyed my bill."

Chapter 5

"Clayton and Syneda. I don't believe it."

Justin Madaris shook his head as he whispered the words to his wife as she lay in his arms.

"They're the last two people likely to end up together. Who would have thought they would have stopped opposing each other long enough to get interested in each other," he added.

Clayton and Syneda had retired to their separate bedrooms, and Justin and Lorren had made the sofa into an extra bed.

"I can't believe Clayton," Lorren said tersely. A thundercloud of indignant frowns bunched her brows together. "The nerve of him hitting on Syneda."

Justin rolled his eyes heavenward. "Aren't you getting a bit carried away?"

Lorren lifted her head to glare down at her husband. "If I am, I have every right to. I don't want Clayton and Syneda involved with each other."

"Why?"

"He'll hurt her."

"Have you ever considered letting Syneda handle her own love life, Lorren? She's a grown woman, you know. Besides, don't you think you're being a little too hard on Clayton?"

"No. I love Clayton dearly, but he's a man who loves women. Lots of them. And I don't want him adding my best friend to his flock. Having a constant supply of willing women has spoiled Clayton. I know just how he operates, and I don't want him operating on Syneda."

Justin smiled. "Is that why you ignored his hints that we check into a hotel tonight?"

A satisfied glint appeared in Lorren's eyes. "You got that right. He was trying to get rid of us. As far as I'm concerned, we arrived right on time."

Justin laughed, pulling Lorren closer into his arms. His eyes glowed with amusement. "Clayton didn't think so."

"I'm sure he didn't. Especially when Syneda retired to her own bedroom."

"What happens when we leave the day after tomorrow?"

"Hopefully by then you'll have talked Clayton out of this foolishness."

"Me?"

"Yes, you." Lorren looked at her husband with appealing eyes. "You have to do something. You're his older brother. He might listen to you."

Justin laughed shortly and shrugged. "Lorren, I respect Clayton's privacy. Besides, it's none of my business and neither is it yours."

"But Syneda is my best—"

Justin didn't let her finish. "It isn't our business, Lorren," he repeated. "We should have enough faith in Clayton to believe he won't deliberately hurt Syneda."

He cupped his wife's chin with his hand and lifted her eyes to meet his. "Clayton loves you. He knows how close you and Syneda are. He won't ever do anything to ruin that."

Lorren took a deep breath. "I hope you're right Justin," she said softly in a voice that seemed to come from a long way off.

"I believe I am. Besides, I think you've overlooked one very important fact here."

"What?"

"One of the reasons Clayton and Syneda were never interested in each other was because neither was the other's type. Syneda is nothing like those women Clayton normally dates, flashy with no substance. She's an attractive, intelligent woman who has a lot going for her. I feel confident she'll be able to handle him."

Justin grinned. "In fact, you may be worried about the wrong person. I don't know if he realizes it yet, but I think Clayton has finally met his match. You just might want to take out the prayer book for Clayton."

"Where is everyone?"

Justin raised his head from reading the newspaper and met his brother's eyes. It didn't take much from Clayton's brooding expression to figure out he hadn't enjoyed sleeping in his bed alone.

"Lorren and Syneda aren't here."

"Where are they?"

"They went shopping."

"Shopping? That's crazy. Syneda and I went shopping a few days ago."

Justin chuckled. "Evidently like most women she enjoys it. Lorren said not to expect them back until dinnertime. I guess we're stuck with each other until then."

Clayton gave his head a wry shake. "I could wring your wife's neck, Justin. She knew I was trying to get rid of the two of you last night, and she deliberately ignored my ploy. And now I have a feeling she's trying to keep Syneda from me today."

Justin smiled and shrugged his shoulders in mock resignation. "She feels Syneda needs protecting."

"Protecting?"

"Yes, protecting. Face it, Clayton, your reputation precedes you."

The two brothers stared at each other for a long time before Clayton finally looked away. He didn't need this, he told himself righteously. Why should he defend his actions to anyone, especially his family? He and Syneda were not teenagers, they were adults. They didn't need keepers, nor did they have to answer to anyone.

He let out a disgusted sigh before turning hard eyes to his brother. "I would never deliberately hurt Syneda, Justin."

"I know you wouldn't, Clayton."

A faint light appeared in the depths of Clayton's brown eyes. "Thanks," he said quietly. "I wish there was some way I could assure Lorren of that, but there isn't. Being attracted to each other was the last thing that Syneda and I planned on happening. It just did. The attraction became more than the two of us could handle last night."

"I gathered as much when I opened the door last night on you guys."

Clayton grinned. "Yeah, that was bad timing on your part. You and Lorren are welcome to stay here for another day but then I want the two of you out of here. The last thing Syneda and I need is outside interference. We're going to enjoy the rest of our vacation in peace and quiet without you and Lorren acting as chaperones. Now with that out of the way, let's go grab some breakfast."

Justin chuckled. "I don't know if there's a need. You've just said a mouthful."

A spectacular view of the yacht harbor and intercoastal water-way was the setting for the Clam Shell Restaurant, a popular favorite with locals, yachtsmen and tourists. The restaurant was renowned for its luncheon specials, which were best enjoyed while sipping a cooling tropical drink.

Syneda and Lorren had chosen a table on the wooden deck that provided a breathtaking view of the Comachee Cove Yacht Harbor.

"Isn't the food terrific, Lorren? Clayton and I had lunch here a few days ago and—"

"Just what's going on with you and Clayton?" Lorren asked pointedly.

"What do you mean?" Syneda replied innocently.

"Don't act crazy, girlfriend. You know exactly what I mean. When Justin opened the door on the two of you last night, it was obvious we had interrupted something."

Syneda's lips broke into a wide grin. "Clayton and I could have made the same assessment about you and Justin."

"We are not discussing me and Justin. We're discussing you and Clayton."

Syneda sighed. "Clayton and I discovered that we're sexually attracted to each other, and both feel we should explore our attraction. There's nothing wrong with enjoying a sexual encounter for no reason beyond the physical pleasures it would bring."

Lorren didn't say anything for a few minutes. Her expression was one of total shock and disbelief. Lately, Syneda's mood swings were extreme and unpredictable. "I don't believe what I'm hearing. You've never been a woman to let a man use her casually for a little quick, easy sex."

"And you think that's what he'll be doing?" Without giving Lorren a chance to reply, Syneda continued as her mouth curved into a smile, "Then there's no reason for me to feel guilty about using him, as well."

For the first time since the conversation she'd had with Justin the night before, Lorren gave serious thought to the possibility that Justin could be right. Her concern just might be directed at the wrong person. "What do you mean by that?"

Syneda leaned forward in her chair and met Lorren's level stare. "I've figured out what's been happening to me for the past few months."

"What?"

"I'm going through an emotional meltdown. Maybe it stems from the type of cases I've been handling lately or the fact that I'm approaching thirty in a couple of years. I don't know. All I know is that I'm sick and tired of being self-reliant, practical and levelheaded. This sister," she said, pointing at herself, "wants a new attitude."

"And you think messing around with Clayton is the answer?"

Syneda smiled. "No, but it's better than thinking seriously about getting my nose pierced, putting a tattoo somewhere on my body or shaving my head."

Lorren couldn't help grinning. "Why not get married? You could have with Marcus. That's what he wanted."

"But that's not what I wanted. I don't love him. I'm not in love with any man, and I'm certainly not interested in getting married. I think of a wedding ring as a neon sign flashing the words, 'You no longer have a life of your own.'"

"That's not true. Look at me and Justin, and Dex and Caitlin. No marriage is perfect, Syneda, and it sure doesn't make everything else in your life automatically fall into place. Nor is it a protection against career crises, economic disaster or loneliness. But I wouldn't trade it for anything."

"Yeah, you say that now, but I can remember a time when you wouldn't have. Your marriage to Scott was the pits."

"True, but it's the opposite with Justin. That just goes to show miracles can happen."

"But I don't want a miracle in my life, Lorren, nor do I need one. All I want out of life is happiness, namely mine. I don't want to be responsible for anyone else's. Nor do I want a man to become my other half. I just want to become my entire whole self, and I think I'll start with an affair."

Lorren sighed. "But why with Clayton?"

"Why not with Clayton? I like him, I trust him and I've recently discovered I'm attracted to him. Isn't that enough?"

"What do you think, Syneda? Will affairs be all you'll ever want?"

"Possibly."

"I don't believe this! You sound just like Clayton. His attitude on life seems to have rubbed off on you. I ought to say that the two of you deserve each other, but I can't. I want you to want more."

"But I can't allow myself to want more. Every time I feel myself wanting more, I remember Mama and how she died believing in a man who didn't come through for her or for me," Syneda replied quietly.

Lorren sighed deeply. She was among the few people who knew the situation regarding Syneda and her father. "All men aren't the same. For example, there's no comparison between Justin and Scott. One day you'll meet someone who's your soul mate, Syneda. Just like Adam was to Eve, like Ruby Dee was to Ozzie Davis, like—"

"Beauty was to the Beast?" Syneda cut in.

Lorren laughed. "Yes, just like Beauty was to the Beast. And like Prince Charming was to Cinderella, like—"

"I get the picture, Lorren."

"I hope you do, Syneda. I honestly hope you do."

Clayton glanced at his watch for perhaps the one hundredth time since he had awakened that morning to find Syneda gone. It was now four o'clock. Where were they? What he had told Justin earlier that day had been the truth. He could wring Lorren's neck.

He stood on the terrace drinking a glass of wine and staring moodily at the ocean. What would Syneda's attitude be toward him when she saw him again? Would she regret what had happened between them last night? Had Lorren convinced her she was making a mistake getting involved with him?

The sound of the doorbell interrupted his thoughts. Evidently Justin had returned. He had left a few hours ago to play a game of tennis with another physician he had met at lunch.

Leaving the terrace, he went to open the door.

"Telegram for Syneda Walters."

Clayton stared at the young man. "She's not here but I'll make sure she receives it," he said, taking the telegram and signing for it. He went into his pocket and handed the guy a bill that brought a bright smile to his face.

"Thank you, sir!"

Clayton was staring blankly at the sealed telegram when the

door opened again a few moments later. Lorren and Syneda walked in carrying a number of packages.

Clayton's eyes immediately met Syneda's. He was stunned by the rush of pleasure surging through him at the sight of her. His eyes wandered over her face for a long moment, and the slender hands holding the packages she placed on the sofa. She was wearing a printed romper and looked absolutely fantastic. The rare beauty of her sea-green eyes touched him. Her beauty was exquisite and overwhelming.

There was a noticeable pause in the room before Lorren cleared her throat. She couldn't help but pick up on the sexual magnetism radiating between Clayton and Syneda. At the moment, she wasn't quite sure which of the two individuals most needed her sympathy. "Hi, Clayton. Where's Justin?"

Clayton swallowed and forced his gaze from Syneda to his sister-in-law. All thoughts of wringing her neck were temporarily forgotten. "He's playing tennis with another doctor he met at lunch."

He then turned his sharp and assessing gaze back to Syneda. "How did shopping go?"

"It was okay," Syneda answered, almost unable to breathe. Clayton looked wonderful dressed in a pair of cutoff jeans and a tank top. He definitely had a monopoly on virility, she thought. His arresting good looks totally captivated her.

"I almost forgot. This came for you a few minutes ago," Clayton said.

Syneda forced her eyes from his to the item he was handing her. "A telegram?"

She tore into it and read it quickly. Regretful eyes met Clayton's. "It's from my firm. Something has come up and I have to get back to New York immediately."

"Why?" Clayton and Lorren exclaimed simultaneously.

"What's wrong?" Lorren asked as she threw her packages down next to Syneda's and gave her friend her absolute attention.

"A few weeks ago I was handling a case involving an abused wife. However, she wouldn't file for a divorce from her husband."

"Yes, I remember you mentioning it," Clayton replied, taking a step closer.

"She's been arrested."

"Why?"

"For shooting her husband. He's in critical condition."

"I don't understand," Lorren stated bemusedly. "Why would she be arrested? It was probably a case of self-defense."

"That has to be proven in a court of law," Clayton replied to Lorren's statement, taking the position of the attorney that he was.

"What does any of this have to do with you, Syneda?" he asked, his mouth set in a taut frown. "You're not a defense attorney."

"I know, but the woman asked for me and refuses to talk with anyone else. The firm has requested that I come back to New York as soon as possible," Syneda replied.

"But you're on vacation. Surely there's someone else who can help the woman until you return next week."

"Unfortunately there isn't. She feels comfortable with me. I have to go back." Syneda turned to Lorren. "Could you call the airlines for me and book me on the next available flight back to New York? There's a phone in the main office, which is located next to the tennis courts. I need to pack."

"Sure," Lorren replied and left immediately.

"I'll go back with you."

"That's not necessary, Clayton. You shouldn't ruin the rest of your vacation just because of me. Now, if you'll excuse me, I really need to begin packing."

Syneda went into her bedroom, leaving a disgusted Clayton standing in the middle of the floor.

A few minutes later Clayton entered her bedroom. "Things aren't over between us, Syneda."

She looked up at him. "What do you mean?"

"I think you know the answer to that," he replied huskily. "Things can never go back to being the way they were between us—"

"Until we've satisfied this lust for each other that's racking our bodies?"

Clayton took a step closer. "You think that's all it is?"

"Of course that's all it is. What else could it be? And I feel the best thing to do is to go ahead and get it out of our systems."

Clayton's pulse raced. "What exactly are you suggesting?"

"Exactly what it sounds like."

Clayton raised a brow. "An affair?"

"Yes, an affair. A short, fulfilling and mutually satisfying affair."

Clayton could not believe what he was hearing. Although he never had reason to inquire how serious they had been, he was well aware that since knowing her, she had been involved in a number of affairs. So why did her eagerness to engage in another surprise him? "Starting when?" he asked, studying her intently.

Syneda looked down at the bed. "Much to my regret, it has to be later. I have to return to New York."

Clayton couldn't shield the flints of desire and passion that shone in his eyes. "Can I visit you in New York?"

Syneda met his eyes. They touched her deeply. "Yes. You're welcome to come visit me anytime. You've always known that. Nothing has changed."

Clayton took a step closer. He took her hand in his. "Yes, things have. My next visit will be in a whole new light, won't it?"

Syneda glanced down at the floor, deliberately avoiding his eyes. "Yes."

Clayton lifted her chin so their eyes could connect. "What about your concern regarding what the family thinks?"

Syneda hunched her shoulders. Deep down she knew that an involvement with Clayton was a bad idea. They were all wrong for each other but her mind was made up. What she had told Lorren at lunch was the truth. As far as she was concerned, she was going through changes in her life and needed something or someone to shake things up a bit, and Clayton would certainly do that.

Then she spoke softly. "Justin and Lorren already know what's going on, and they'll keep it to themselves. No one else has to know."

"Are you suggesting that we keep things a secret?"

Syneda nodded. "There's no reason for anyone else to know. It won't last that long anyway."

Clayton looked at her for a long while. "You sound so sure of that."

"I'm not entering into this relationship with any misconceptions, Clayton."

"Meaning?"

"I only want to finish what was started here. A serious relationship is the last thing you or I want."

Clayton pulled Syneda into his arms. "You think you know me rather well, don't you?" he asked. Cupping her chin in his hand, he tilted her head back and lowered his head to hers. When his mouth opened over hers, she welcomed it. She felt the probing of his tongue as it delved deep into the warmth of her mouth.

Her eyes fluttered shut as his tongue rubbed against hers, as their mouths sealed in a searing kiss.

Syneda's arms crept slowly around Clayton's neck as she strained toward him. A hot, heady rise of pleasure exploded deep within her, filling her with profound heat. And at the same time, a multitude of sensations coursed down her middle and her belly.

They were panting and breathless when Clayton slowly lifted his head. Syneda's lips were slightly swollen, and her pupils were glazed with desire. She had the sexiest expression he'd ever seen, Clayton thought, gazing down at her. He then began wondering if a serious relationship was really, as she thought, the last thing he wanted.

Chapter 6

"I never did get a chance to thank you for coming back as soon as you did, Syneda. I hope I didn't ruin your vacation."

Syneda looked into the handsome face of the man sitting on the other side of her desk. Thomas Rackley, a widower in his early forties, was a well-liked defense attorney who had begun working with the firm two years ago. She had often accompanied him to dinner and the theater until he began dropping hints of wanting a more serious relationship. To avoid the risk of hurting him by their becoming too involved, she had suggested that they begin seeing other people. Not too soon thereafter, she had begun dating Marcus.

"You didn't totally ruin my vacation." Syneda grinned. "But had it been anyone other than you, I would have given them hell."

Thomas let out a deep chuckle, fully believing she would have. Moments later his smile faded. "I ran into Marcus Capers at a baseball game while you were away. So I hope the friend you were with didn't mind the interruption."

Syneda met his gaze. She knew the question that was on his

mind. If he'd seen Marcus, it meant he knew they hadn't gone away together. He was curious to know if she had gone on vacation with a male or a female, but was too much of a gentleman to ask. She took a deep breath. It was time to bring to an end that part of her relationship with Thomas forever. She didn't want him fostering any false hope; especially now that she was no longer dating Marcus.

They looked at each other for a long moment before Syneda answered. "He understood."

There was a pause in the room before Thomas replied. "I see."

Syneda decided to change subjects. "So how are things going with Mrs. Armstrong?" she asked quickly.

"Thanks to you, she has agreed to reveal the depth of her husband's cruelty. I believe once the prosecuting attorney reviews her case, the charges will be dropped. It was clearly a case of self-defense."

"And Dr. Armstrong?"

"His condition has changed from critical to stable. He'll live. However, he'll be getting quite a bit of bad publicity once the media gets ahold of what he's put his wife through."

"I'm just glad Mrs. Armstrong has finally realized she has other recourses than remaining in a situation that has caused her to be painfully abused. No one should have to suffer the physical and emotional batterings she's gone through."

Thomas nodded in agreement. He continued to stare at her. "I hope he's what you want, Syneda. You deserve to be happy," he said, switching back to their earlier conversation.

Syneda's thoughts immediately fell on Clayton. She had no doubt he would certainly rock her world a bit. "I believe he is, and thanks, you've been a good friend."

Thomas looked at her, his eyes compelling. "I wanted to be more."

"I know, but it wouldn't have worked out between us."

"Because of our ages?"

Syneda shook her head. Although he was forty-three to her

twenty-eight, their ages had never been an issue with her. "No, it wasn't that. I'm just not ready for what you want. I doubt if I ever will be. The love and marriage scene aren't for me."

He stood and held out his hand to her. "If you ever need a friend, I'm here for you."

Syneda accepted his hand and the offer of friendship that came with it. "Thanks, Thomas. I'll remember that."

When Syneda returned to her office from lunch, Joanna looked up from her desk. Her blue eyes were dazzling with merriment. "There was a delivery for you while you were out."

"Oh?" Syneda asked, pushing open the door to her office. The sight awaiting her was breathtaking. Four huge vases filled with roses sat in the middle of her desk. Speechless, she entered her office. The rose fragrance permeated the room.

"They're beautiful, aren't they?" Joanna asked, gazing at the four dozen peach-colored roses. "I wonder who sent them."

Quickly recovering from her initial shock, Syneda took in a deep breath. She hoped they weren't from Marcus.

"I placed the card on your desk next to your calendar."

"Thanks, Joanna. Please let Mr. Dickerson know I've returned, and I'm free to go over the Franklin case now."

Recognizing a dismissal, Joanna nodded and closed the door behind her.

Syneda walked over to her desk, picked up the envelope and pulled out the card. Her hand shook when she read the message inside. She couldn't help the smile that touched her lips nor could she prevent her heartbeat from quickening.

The card read: "A dozen roses for each day we spent together. Saint Augustine wasn't the same without you." It was signed "Clayton."

"Clayton." Syneda whispered the name as she leaned against the corner of her desk to slow down her breathing. Marcus hadn't sent the flowers as she had assumed. They had come from Clayton.

Nervously thumbing through the personal directory on her desk she located the numbers of her search. She picked up the phone and began dialing.

"Clayton Madaris's office."

"Yes, may I speak with Mr. Madaris, please?"

The woman's response was pleasant and businesslike. "I'm sorry but Mr. Madaris is unavailable. Would you like to leave a message?"

"Yes, please tell him Syneda Walters called."

"Oh, Ms. Walters. Mr. Madaris left instructions to put you through should you call. Please hold for a minute."

The secretary clicked off the line and Syneda nervously toyed with the telephone cord while waiting for Clayton to come to the phone.

"Syneda?" Clayton asked coming on the line.

Tremors raced through Syneda at the deep masculine sound of her name from Clayton's lips. Her hands on the telephone tightened as blood coursed hotly through her veins. Even over the telephone, he was reaching out to her and the sensations were like a soft caress. She tried to sound natural when she replied. "Yes, Clayton. The flowers are beautiful. You shouldn't have."

"I couldn't help myself," he said huskily. "I meant what I said on the card. I want to see you, Syneda. Soon. This weekend. Is that possible?"

Syneda took a deep breath. "Yes."

"How about if I fly in on Friday afternoon?"

A lump formed in Syneda's throat. The silkiness of his suggestion touched her everywhere. "I'd like that."

There was a slight pause before he asked, "Are you sure?"

"Yes, I'm sure."

Another pause. "Do you want to go out to dinner when I get there?" he asked.

"If you'd like. Or we can have something delivered. Let's decide when you get here."

"Okay. I'll see you on Friday."

"Until then, Clayton."

"Yes, until then."

Clayton hung up the phone and glanced down at the legal brief he'd been working on before Syneda's call. He pushed it aside as he sat back in his chair.

He hadn't realized he'd been holding his breath until the plans had been finalized for his visit to see her. He had been in knots all week at the thought that after returning to New York, she would have had second thoughts about continuing what they had started in Saint Augustine.

He shifted uneasily in his chair, wondering what had actually happened to bring him to such a state over a woman. There had never been a time when a woman had consumed his every thought. There were too many females out there to get hung up on just one. Women had a way of making the most sensible man act foolish. So what in the world was happening to him?

After Justin and Lorren had left to return to Texas, he had tried resting, relaxing and enjoying his time alone. But he hadn't been able to do any of those things. Instead he had thought of Syneda. He had spent an uncomfortable amount of time thinking about her and had begun feeling resentful. Resentful that any woman's overpowering allure could bring forth such a need in him.

So he had tried not to think about needing her and wanting her. He had even made up his mind not to contact her when he returned to Texas from Florida. But something had happened to him that he hadn't counted on, something that had gone beyond any rational thought. It was something that—after taking more showers than he could count—still had him mystified until he had finally faced the truth. Syneda had been able to do something no other woman had done. She had somehow exposed deep feelings within him.

Before the trip to Florida, his relationships with women had been uncomplicated. Over the years he had dated a number of incredibly attractive women, but never did one have him thinking more about passion than winning court cases. Why was this thing with Syneda, of all people, different?

Why had kissing and touching her caused tremors deep within his body days after they'd parted? He shook his head, thinking how in the last couple of days he'd lain in bed thinking about her and wanting her. It didn't take much for him to close his eyes and visualize her in every outfit she'd worn while they were in Florida. Right at this very moment, he would do just about anything to have her in his arms, with her soft, warm body pressed close to his.

He took a deep breath. It was an effort to breathe. A first for him. His features tightened at the thought that he was losing control. Again.

Clayton stood and moved to one of the windows facing downtown Houston. The only excuse he could come up with for his reactions was that it had been some time, sixty-four days to be exact, since he'd slept with a woman. Why was he putting himself through unnecessary misery? All he had to do was pick up the phone. He knew a number of women who'd be more than willing to take care of his needs. But for some strange reason not just any woman would do.

He wanted Syneda.

He again shook his head. He hoped Syneda was right when she said the two of them were dealing strictly with a case of lust. Pure and simple. A deep sigh escaped him. He had a feeling anything involving Syneda wouldn't be pure and simple. And he had a sinking feeling that no matter what happened between them this weekend, his life would never be the same.

He frowned. That thought bothered him more than anything.

Later that day Syneda sat at her desk going over her notes from her last appointment. Margie Sessions wanted a divorce from her husband of thirty-four years, a husband she claimed had been unfaithful.

Although the woman had tried not to show it, it was obvious

she was deeply hurt. The pain was evident in her eyes, her speech and in the way she had paced the room for nearly an hour while providing an account of how she had discovered her husband's infidelity.

Listening attentively while observing the woman, Syneda also found it blatantly obvious that even after discovering his unfaithfulness, the woman was still very much in love with the man.

Syneda had convinced the woman to think things through before making any hasty decisions. "If you decide to go through with this," she'd told her, "I hope you're prepared for the emotional pain you'll have to endure. That pain may be far worse than what you're going through now—although you may feel nothing is worse than finding out your husband has been unfaithful to you. The two of you share three children and six grandchildren, not to mention a wealth of cherished good memories."

"Are you saying I should just forget what he did? That I should let him get away with it and do nothing?"

"No, Mrs. Sessions, that's not what I'm saying. I just want you to be sure that you're ready to deal with the emotional turmoil this divorce may cause you. I have no qualms about representing you. I'm tough, and I fight hard for my clients. But there are some things you need to think about. During the years of your marriage, the two of you have accumulated a lot of possessions, so there's also the physical settlement to deal with. However, as your attorney I have a moral obligation to advise you to try and salvage your marriage before thinking of ending it."

"There's nothing to think about. I can't remain married to him. I can't stop loving him, but I'll never trust him again. A marriage can't survive without trust, Ms. Walters."

Margie Sessions's story wasn't a new one. Syneda had heard similar ones during the years since she had begun practicing family law. The anger, the hurt, the sense of betrayal, and the need for revenge were emotions most of her clients wanting divorces encountered.

Syneda had just reached for a small recorder to dictate her

office notes when the buzzer sounded on her desk. "Yes, Joanna, what is it?"

"You have a call from Lorren Madaris."

"Please put her through."

A few seconds later she heard Lorren's voice. "Syneda?"

Syneda smiled. "Lorren. How are you?"

"I'm fine. I went to the doctor today and he said everything is okay."

"You mean Justin isn't going to deliver this baby? I thought he did a great job with Justina."

Lorren giggled. "Be sure to tell him that when you see him again. He said delivering Justina aged him about twenty years."

Syneda grinned. "So what do you want this time, a girl or a boy?"

"It doesn't matter. We have both already, so whatever we're having this time is fine with us."

Syneda sighed. She was completely elated with her friend's happiness.

"Syneda, have you talked to Clayton lately?"

Syneda tried detecting censure in Lorren's voice and didn't note any. "Yes, I spoke with him earlier today. He's flying in this weekend."

"So you haven't changed your mind about what we talked about in Saint Augustine?"

"No, I haven't."

There was a slight pause. "Promise me you'll take care of yourself."

"Lorren, lighten up. Clayton and I are two adults who can handle things. We're having a weekend fling. Nothing more. I'll be fine."

Braxter Montgomery saw the woman across the parking lot as she raised the hood of her car. Being the only son of a single mother and the brother of two younger sisters, he believed in assisting women in distress and began walking toward her.

Only after he had gotten a few feet away from her did Braxton discover he'd suddenly forgotten how to breathe. The woman, whose age appeared to be around twenty-five or twenty-six, was gorgeous.

"Do you need any assistance?" He finally found his voice to ask. His eyes scanned her slender figure before glancing under the raised hood of her car. She glanced up from her close study of her car's engine and smiled beautiful dark eyes at him.

"I think so. My car won't start. Do you know anything about cars, Mr....?" She glanced at the identification badge he wore on his suit. "Mr. Montgomery?"

He smiled. "A little. Let me take a look." Handing her his jacket and briefcase, he began rolling up his sleeves. "That is, if you don't mind, Ms....?"

"Rogers," she supplied, shaking his hand. "Celeste Rogers."

"And Ms. Rogers, do you work around here?" Braxter asked. His tone was polite as he began fiddling with some of the equipment under her car's hood. He couldn't help noticing she wasn't wearing a wedding ring.

"No, I don't work around here, but a majority of my clientele do," she said, glancing at the Capitol Building in the background. "I own a travel agency, and today is my day for deliveries." She looked down at her car and frowned. "At least it was until my car decided to give out on me."

Braxter nodded. "Now, Ms. Rogers, you can try the ignition."

She smiled. "Please call me Celeste."

"Celeste," he said, liking the way the name sounded on his lips. "And I'm Braxter."

"All right." She walked around and slid into the car's seat. She smiled broadly when the car's engine roared to life. Getting out of the car she went back to where he stood, she smiled at him. "It's working again. What did you do?"

"It was just your distributor cap. It wasn't on tight enough." The expression on her face told him that, like most women, she knew nothing about what went on under the hood of a car.

"Well, whatever it was, I really appreciate your taking the time to help. How much do I owe you, Braxter?"

He checked his watch. "Nothing, but how about lunch? There's a great Chinese restaurant a few blocks from here. That is, if you like Chinese."

She hesitated a moment before answering. "I love Chinese, and lunch sounds wonderful."

"Great, we can drive over in my car."

She shook her head. "I prefer if you lead in your car. I'll follow in mine."

"Okay." Braxter said smiling. He wasn't the least offended that she'd graciously refused his offer to ride to the restaurant with him. Evidently, she was a cautious woman by nature. He liked that.

Celeste watched the handsome man walk off, heading back toward his parked car. She then got into hers. As she followed him out of the parking lot, she picked up her cellular phone and punched in a few numbers. She waited patiently for the voice on the other end before saying, "Yes, this is Celeste." Her lips formed in a faint, victorious grin. "I've made my connection."

Chapter 7

Syneda glanced around her living room, nervously gnawing at her bottom lip. Clayton was to arrive any minute.

For the first time since her decision to have this weekend interlude with him, she was beginning to feel uncertain and apprehensive. Unnerved by those feelings, and unsettled by the novelty of the actions she was about to take, she uncomfortably ran a hand through her hair.

At the sound of the doorbell, she hesitated briefly before turning toward the door. Drawing in a deep breath, she made an effort to maintain her composure. Sharp needles of sexual excitement and anticipation pricked every nerve in her body. "Yes?"

"It's Clayton."

She slowly opened the door and smiled. "Hello."

Clayton smiled back at her. "Hello, yourself. May I come in?"

"Sure." Syneda couldn't help noticing how his dark form was silhouetted by the dim lighting flowing through the entrance foyer. Although she couldn't see his features clearly, she could tell he was dressed in a dark suit and white dress shirt. He must have left the office and gone directly to the airport, she thought, moving aside.

Clayton stepped inside the apartment. After placing his traveling bag down, he closed the door behind him. He stared at Syneda, suddenly realizing just how much he had missed her since she'd left him in Florida. He felt an overwhelming joy at seeing her again.

He was having a difficult time assimilating what he was feeling as he continued to stare at her. Air became trapped in his lungs, and his heart pounded in his chest. His mind tried reminding him, uncomfortably, that no woman had ever had this sort of effect on him. No woman had ever made him feel such joy, such desperation…and such panic.

A part of him—that part that had always been in full control where women were concerned—was wavering under the sea-green gaze that held him captive.

And that thought was frightening.

He suddenly felt a strong urge to protect himself by turning and walking back out of the door and doing an easy escape before he got himself into something too deep, something he wasn't prepared for. But for the life of him he couldn't make the move to retreat.

"Clayton? Are you okay?"

The sound of Syneda's voice was soft, smooth, sexy and concerned. Reaching out, he gently pulled her into his arms. "Yes, I'm fine," he said, lowering his mouth to hers.

Their contact was electric as Clayton ground his lips against hers with a hunger that could not be denied. Syneda opened her mouth to his immediately. Heat rose in her body and a tightening started in the pit of her stomach. She trembled all over, unable to believe what was happening between them. It had not just been Florida after all, because even here in smog-filled New York, the sexual chemistry between them was even greater than before. Breath rushed in and out of her lungs and she couldn't help wondering why no man before Clayton had ever made this kind of passion rise so quickly within her. It made her become urgent, wanting to hold back nothing and lose control.

Clayton slowly raised his head and met dazed sea-green eyes. "You taste good," he whispered hoarsely against her lips. "I enjoy kissing you."

Syneda stared up into the dark eyes gazing down at her. The electric brown eyes were glowing like black fire. "You taste pretty good yourself. And I like kissing you, too."

Clayton grinned and kissed her again, long, deep and hard. His hand lightly cupped her bottom. Syneda could feel the muscles in her body come alive with his intimate touch and she pressed herself closer to him. The powerful muscular build of his shoulders felt heavenly beneath her hands as he pulled her even closer.

He reluctantly broke off the kiss, his breathing unsteady. "What's planned for this weekend?" he asked huskily, planting butterfly kisses against the corners of her mouth.

He felt her grin underneath his lips. "If you don't know, I'm not telling."

Clayton's chuckle echoed deep in his chest where Syneda placed her head. He tightened his arms around her. "So, what's first?" he asked.

Syneda lifted her head and looked up at him. "First, we talk."

Clayton bent down and brushed his lips against hers. "Talk about what?"

"Rules."

He raised his head and looked down at her. "Rules? What rules?"

She smiled at him. "Rules I'm sure you've followed countless times and won't have any problems not breaking. In fact, I bet they're similar to the ones you've probably used in your relationships."

"What are they?"

Her eyes, he noticed, suddenly became set beneath a high, serious brow. However, she still managed to contain her smile. "The first and most important one being that we won't expect anything beyond what we'll share this weekend. And second, we must never, ever let ourselves think that what we're sharing is in any way, shape, form or fashion associated with love." She gave him a fierce hug. "See, there, I told you they were probably similar to yours."

Clayton flinched. She was right, they were like some of his own rules. They were rules that had always governed his relationships with women, and for the first time the thought of those rules bothered him.

"That's why," she continued, "I'm so excited about this weekend. For once I can let myself go without worrying."

He frowned. "Worrying about what?"

"About someone wanting more than I could possibly give, and trying to keep him at arm's length. I know how you feel about love and commitment. You don't want them any more than I do."

A tender smile danced across Syneda's lips. "And there's something else I guess I should tell you…about me."

"And just what could that be?" he asked. Taking her hand he led her toward the sofa. She only presented him with a surprisingly relaxed smile when he sat down and pulled her into his lap.

"It's nothing that's a big deal, but it's something I think you should know."

He lifted his brow. Despite her smile, he had a feeling there was something mysterious lurking deep in the sea-green eyes staring back at him. "What is it?"

"I've never made love with a man before."

"What!"

If Syneda hadn't caught hold of the sofa, she would have fallen on the floor when Clayton unexpectedly jumped out of his seat.

"What do you mean you've never slept with a man before? That's stupid!"

Syneda stood then. The smile on her face was replaced with an angry frown. "What's stupid?"

"The notion that you're a virgin. That's impossible."

"And just why is it impossible?"

Clayton's eyes swept over Syneda as he tried coming to grips with what she was telling him. She stood before him as he'd seen her many times, with her hands on her hips, facing him squarely, ready to do battle. He met her glare head-on. He could believe a lot of things, but the thought that she had never slept with a man before wasn't one of them.

"I'm waiting for an answer, Madaris. Are you implying that all the time you've known me, you just assumed I've lived the life of some kind of slut?"

Clayton rolled his eyes heavenward. "I wasn't insinuating anything. All I'm saying is that you of all people would be the least likely candidate for a virgin." Clayton frowned, wondering if the words he'd just spoken to clear himself had done more damage than good.

"What I mean," he said quickly, "is that you're twenty-eight— for heaven's sake, you live by yourself, you're a career woman, a professional. You went to college, and I'm sure you dated while you were there. You date men now, and you're a very sexy woman. Besides that, you have modern ideals."

Syneda shook her head at the lack of logic in Clayton's way of thinking. "Let's get one thing straight. Having modern ideals doesn't mean you automatically toss aside old values. I control my own destiny, and I've never depended on the smooth talk of some man to guide me. I make my own decisions when it concerns my body. I never felt compelled to give myself to a man to prove anything. And why do women have to prove anything anyway? Why can't a man do the proving for a change?"

Clayton folded his arms across his chest and leaned against a wall. He knew Syneda was on a roll. He glanced around the room for signs of her soap box.

"And another thing," she continued. "Most women have the good sense to know most lines men are feeding them are usually a bunch of bull. But unfortunately, others are too flattered or too naive to figure it out, and that mistake is many of their downfalls. I could provide you with statistics on the number of women having babies out of wedlock. And those smooth-talking, irresponsible men, who refuse to claim their role as fathers, have moved on to hit some other unsuspecting female with the same line."

"Syneda—"

"No, Madaris, you started this so let me wrap it up." She came to stand in front of him. "And age has nothing to do with it. Neither does occupation or status in life. So what if I'm a single, twenty-eight-year-old attorney living on my own. That doesn't necessarily mean I have loose morals. What law says I have to sleep with any man I date? People shouldn't get intimately involved with each other until they're ready, both physically and mentally."

Clayton grabbed Syneda's hand. "I apologize if I offended you, I didn't mean to. It's just hard to believe."

When her frown darkened he added, "However, I do believe you. But what about that guy you recently broke up with? The one you had been dating for the past six or seven months."

Syneda yanked away from his grasp. "What about him?"

"Wasn't he special to you? Didn't the two of you ever want to…you know?"

"My relationship with Marcus is not open for discussion. All you need to know is that there has never been a special man in my life. And as far as me sleeping with him, I didn't want to and he respected my decision."

"The man was a fool. There's no way in hell you would have been my woman and not shared my bed."

"Then it's a good thing I'm not your woman, Madaris. So you can take your sexist way of thinking right back to Texas."

When she made a move to walk away, Clayton reached out and gently brought her against him. "Let me go, Clayton."

"Not on your life." He calmed her struggling and pulled her against him, holding her tight.

When he bent down and kissed her, she reluctantly returned it. "I want you to leave, Clayton," she said unconvincingly between their kisses.

"I'm staying, Syneda."

He picked her up in his arms and carried her back to the sofa. Sitting down, he again placed her in his lap and continued kissing her.

"Stay then," she muttered against his moist lips. "Just as long as you know I'm mad."

"Stay mad," he responded, against the angry quiver he felt while tasting her bottom lip. He lifted his head and looked down at her. "Nothing brings out passion quicker than anger."

"Then this weekend should be rather interesting since we argue most of the time, Madaris."

He traced the line of her lips with his finger. "Not this weekend," he replied easily. "For the next two days, we're going to spend time doing something else. We'll argue the next weekend we spend together."

Syneda gazed up at him, wanting to remind him that this would be their only weekend together. Instead, she pulled his face down and kissed him long and deeply.

Clayton stood with her in his arms and carried her to the bedroom. Once there he gently placed her on the bed. The colorful bedcover was pulled back invitingly. He stood back to look down at her.

"I'm not a very good hostess. I didn't even offer you a drink," Syneda said silkily.

"You offered me something a whole lot better and definitely more precious."

"What?"

"Yourself."

His words made what little control Syneda had slip even further. It was evident that he wanted her. His body was growing hard with desire. He reached down and drew her up slowly toward him. His lips touched hers lightly at first, nibbling at her mouth softly.

Syneda moaned as she opened her mouth fully to him and tightened her arms around his neck. Her tongue slipped into his mouth and met his, returning his kiss with an intensity and hunger that he absorbed.

Syneda, Clayton discovered, had an intensely passionate nature and it set him on fire. A tremor inside him heated his thighs and groin. Pulling her into his arms, he ran his hands over the slender curves of her body through her clothes, bestowing kisses on her that were more hot and demanding than any of his others had been.

Still holding her, he swept back the bedcovers with a one-handed motion, and placed her on the mauve-colored sheet, gently coming down on top of her. They kissed again. No words needed to be spoken.

Syneda clung to Clayton, kissing him with as much hunger as he was kissing her. Everything was swept from her mind except him and how he was making her feel.

Clayton was driven by a need to become a part of her. He undressed her quickly, removing every stitch of her clothing. When she lay unclothed before him, he let his hands glide over to the slender curves of her body.

Syneda's breath caught. She closed her eyes. A flash of blazing heat roared within her. "Clayton." She whispered his name in a yearning urgency.

"I'm here, baby. The only place I'm going is inside of you."

His words made her sizzle. She reached up and pulled his head down to her, capturing his mouth with hers. She conveyed to him in her kiss just how much she wanted him.

Clayton's breath grew ragged. He felt possessive, protective and vulnerable. Those feelings were strange to him, but for some reason, quickly acceptable. With their mouths still joined, he somehow managed to unbutton his shirt. However, he had to break their kiss to completely remove it.

"Clayton, please," Syneda pleaded. She wanted him. She wanted his hands on her, she wanted his kisses.

"Just a second, sweetheart," he breathed against her neck as he tugged on the belt to his pants with shaking hands. He removed the foil packet from his pocket. He intended to take every precaution to keep her safe.

Moments later Syneda gazed at the magnificent nude male body before her. "You're beautiful, Clayton."

He grinned broadly, rejoining her in bed. "Thank you. You're beautiful, too."

Syneda smiled. She felt neither shy nor ashamed with Clayton, just a sense of wanting and readiness. What she was about to share with him somehow felt right. It felt like this was how it was supposed to be.

She caught her breath when she felt his lips open against her skin as he placed kisses over her body.

"Sweet. You taste very sweet," he whispered. His hand began moving slowly up her hips, tenderly stroking her bare skin. She thought she would go up in flames when his hands moved upward, his touch lingering just below her breasts.

Syneda arched her back, welcoming the feel of his hands on her, feeling her body's response to him. She searched for words to describe how she felt but couldn't come up with any. Nothing had ever felt like this before. When he began stroking her breasts, a moan of pleasure escaped her followed by the words, "I want you, Clayton."

Her words inflamed him. Instinctively he ground his hips against her, feeling himself grow harder, heavier, less in control. He willed himself to hang on. He wanted their first time together to be special.

Desire, deeper than he'd ever known before tore through him. He couldn't last much longer. He lowered his head and let his lips take hers with an all-consuming hunger. Her taste filled him completely. He wanted this woman and it wasn't just due to a physical need. He felt an even stronger need, one he had never felt before in his life. It was the need a man had to bind a woman to him forever.

He raised his head slightly and looked deeply into her eyes, wondering why he felt this way, and why with this woman. Some emotion he had never felt before coursed through his entire body. Shivers passed through him when he leaned down and kissed her again. It was a surprisingly gentle kiss as his lips brushed lightly over hers. Then he lifted his head and their eyes met once more.

"Syneda, are you sure?"

Syneda looked up at him in a passion-filled state. She heard his words. His voice was a mere whisper but his features were as serious as the question he was asking her again.

"Are you sure about this, Syneda?"

She met his gaze, fully understanding what he was asking her. If she had any apprehensions about what they were about to do, he was giving her the opportunity to stop things from going any further. For them to go beyond the bounds of friends to become lovers would be a mutual decision.

She had no apprehensions. Maybe it was because of the tenderness she saw in the dark brown eyes looking down at her, or the feel of the light strokes his fingers were tracing from her throat to her breast, and the feel of the heat of him pressed against her. And when she felt his hand dip low to touch her stomach, she thought her breathing had stopped.

She was lost.

A part of her, a part she had never shared with any man was taking over. It was that part she seldom allowed to surface. It was a part of her that up until now, had kept her from losing all concept of reason and logic. But now she felt vulnerable to the man who held her in his arms. She was steadily losing control of her senses and was rapidly spiraling beyond what she had the ability to contain.

She couldn't stop herself from cupping his face in her hands and saying. "I'm sure, Clayton. Very sure."

As if he'd been waiting to hear her say those words, Clayton crushed her to him in a torrid kiss at the same time he joined their bodies as one, making Syneda totally aware of the heat of him deep within her. He stopped moving, giving her body time to adjust to his.

Moments later, Clayton moved again and Syneda gave a sharp intake of breath. She reveled in the fullness of him inside her, filling an emptiness she'd just discovered existed. She couldn't help giving herself up to the enthralling sensuality flowing between them.

The ultimate pleasure of their lovemaking exploded, wrapping them in a delicious convulsion of ecstasy. The long, shattering release carried them to the heights of sensual splendor where they were somehow united in body, soul and spirit.

It was a long time before either of them could move. They lay together completely depleted of strength.

"Clayton," Syneda whispered drowsily. Her body was totally satiated. She wanted to do nothing but sleep. However, it appeared Clayton had other ideas. She felt his strong hands pull her closer to him. She felt his fingers as they began to trace lightly over her body. She felt the hardness of him pressing against her.

He was ready again.

She wondered how on earth such a degree of sensuality and passion could exist between two people. He had already taken her to the peak of sexual pleasure. Surely, something that strong, potent and powerful could not be repeated. At least not this soon.

Syneda tuned out her thoughts when she felt his hand touch her intimately. She automatically began responding, giving herself up to the luscious waves of pleasure rippling through her all over again.

Clayton only paused briefly in his ministrations to protect her again before sheathing himself deep inside her.

Syneda sighed heavily as her body matched the primitive sensual rhythm of his. Soon after, once again, they flowed together in a sensual haze of passioned fulfillment.

Hours later Syneda's last thought before sleep overtook her was that it could be repeated. Several times.

Clayton's chest expanded as he drew in a deep breath. Never before had he experienced anything liked he'd done tonight with Syneda. He tilted his head back to watch her sleep. Her hair fell like a silky curtain on either side of her face, and she wore such a peaceful and serene look.

He gathered her closer to him. From the time he had begun high school, women had always been readily available to him. And like most men, he appreciated them, desired them and enjoyed them. But never until tonight had he actually loved one.

Oh, God, he loved her!

That sudden realization settled on him with the weight of a ton of bricks, and it scared the hell out of him. He probably would have bolted out of bed right then and there if Syneda had not been sound asleep in his arms. Instead he looked down at Syneda, really looked at her before pressing his head back against the pillow and closing his eyes. *What in the world had he gotten himself into?*

Clayton released a deep sigh as he held Syneda even closer, lightly caressing her back and shoulders. He suddenly understood as he had never understood before. There could be no other explanation for what he had been feeling since he had seen her that morning walking on the beach, and the jealousy, possessiveness, wanting and need he'd been experiencing ever since. And it had nothing to do with lust. He'd been there, he'd done that. What he was feeling now was totally different. What he felt for Syneda went a lot deeper than just the physical relationship they had just shared. He loved her. There could be no other explanation for what he was feeling at this very minute. He slowly opened his eyes.

A part of him still wanted to run for cover and deny the strong emotions he felt. That was the part of him that had been a bachelor all of his life and had been quite proud of that status. But another part of him, the part that had recently had him subconsciously longing for something more, acknowledged the fact that for the first time in his life he had actually made love with a woman. There was an astounding difference in having sex with a woman and making love to one.

Tonight he had made love to Syneda. Every movement of his body, every touch he had bestowed upon her, and every kiss he had given her had conveyed the words his lips had not spoken. There was no way he could deny that he loved her.

He didn't fully understand how it had happened and why it had happened. All he knew was that it had happened. Somehow, once they had gotten to Florida, he had begun to stop thinking of her as just a good friend and an antagonist. He'd begun regarding her as a very desirable woman. He had appreciated her fun-loving nature, her intelligence and sensitivity.

He shook his head and grinned ruefully, wondering how on earth he would survive a relationship with Syneda. She was definitely a handful. She could be outright stubborn at times, temperamental and too outspoken. He would even conclude that she was somewhat of a female chauvinist. But one thing was for certain, a life with her would never, ever be boring.

A smile touched Clayton's lips at the thought that Syneda was now his. He knew he would have to give her plenty of time to adjust to the notion that she belonged to anyone but herself. But he was willing to give her all the time she needed, because he had no intention of ever letting her go.

Chapter 8

A slow, lazy smile spread across Syneda's face when she felt the warmth of Clayton's lips near her ear. "It's morning," he whispered.

She opened one eye and peered up at him. He was standing next to the bed leaning over her. And from the casual way he was dressed, she could only assume he'd been up for some time. "I hate morning people, Clayton. Don't you believe in sleeping late?"

"I'm usually up before the crack of dawn every day, including Saturdays," he said, sitting on the bed beside her. "But I would not have had any problem staying in bed late this morning," he added, his meaning clear. "None whatsoever." He leaned down and kissed her. "Are you ready to get up now?"

Syneda closed her eyes and snuggled deeper under the covers. "No! And I forgot to mention rule number three."

"Which is?"

"Don't ever wake me up on Saturdays before nine o'clock."

"It's nine-fifteen."

"Then don't ever wake me on Saturdays before ten."

Clayton laughed. "I admire a woman who's flexible only when it suits her."

Syneda began to turn away from him but Clayton touched his lips to her shoulder. "I'm serving breakfast at ten."

She opened her eyes. A frown lowered her dark eyebrows. "Breakfast? There's nothing here to eat for breakfast."

Clayton stood. "So I noticed. I walked down to that deli on the corner and grabbed us something. See you at ten." He turned and walked out of the bedroom.

Clayton had no trouble finding his way around Syneda's kitchen. There wasn't much to it; at least in the way of supplies. It was one his father would refer to as an unstocked kitchen. During his search, he'd been unable to find any dishes, glasses or silverware. He wondered if that meant she dined out every day.

"What are you looking for?"

Clayton looked up. Syneda was leaning against the door frame wearing nothing but his dress shirt. The shirt hit her midthigh and she looked very sexy in it.

They stared at each other for a long, silent moment, and he knew her thoughts were probably similar to his. He couldn't help but remember them together, wrapped in each other's arms last night.

"You're late. It's almost ten-thirty," Clayton finally said, breaking the silence. Didn't she know what seeing her dressed in his shirt was doing to him? The only reason he had gotten up and left her alone in bed was to give her and her body a break. They had made love through most of the night. The more he was around her, the more he wanted her. He couldn't seem to keep his hands off her.

Syneda laughed softly. "Better late than never. Now what were you looking for?"

"Place settings."

"Oh. Everything's in the dishwasher."

Clayton moved to the dishwasher and opened it. He then turned and raised a brow at her. "Saving space?"

"What do you mean?" Syneda came into the kitchen and sat down at the table.

Clayton couldn't help noticing how the shirt had ridden higher when she'd sat down, exposing one luscious-looking bare thigh. He tore his gaze away from her thigh and back up to her face. "A month's supply of place settings are in your dishwasher."

Syneda shrugged. "They're clean, aren't they?"

Clayton nodded. "Yes, they're clean. But don't you put your dishes away in the cabinets after they're washed?"

"No. But I suppose you do."

"Yes."

Syneda's lips tightened and she glared at him. "Well, I don't. I see no sense in going to all that trouble when I'll be using them again. So don't start in on me, Madaris."

Clayton grinned. "Are we about to get into an argument?"

"If you start it, I'll sure enough finish it for you," she said, giving him a look that said she meant business.

"Does that go for anything else I start?" he asked in a challenging voice, walking toward her.

Syneda stood and met his gaze. "Just try me."

Clayton looked at her, his dark eyes thoughtful. He had one hell of a woman on his hands. She was full of fire, and he was determined to make sure her fire burned just for him. He swept her into his arms. "You're on."

She glowered up at him. "You have a one-track mind, Madaris. I wasn't talking about this and you know it. And what about breakfast?"

He smiled down at her. "We'll have it in bed."

So much for wanting to do the right thing and leave her alone for a while, Clayton thought, snuggling closer to the woman in his arms. He and Syneda were two strong, stubborn, argumentative people who were accustomed to having their own way. It seemed it was only while in the throes of heated passion they were totally and completely of one accord.

He gathered her closer to him. Even while she slept, his hands continued to caress her. He would never get tired of touching her.

He glanced at the clock. It was past noon. They hadn't eaten breakfast yet, but during the past couple of hours neither of them had cared. They'd been too busy satisfying another type of hunger.

He frowned. Syneda was turning into a sort of a mystery. She was definitely full of surprises. There were some things about her that he didn't understand; things that didn't make sense. Like the spiel she'd given him about why she'd remained a virgin. Had she been talking for Syneda or was she the spokesperson for someone else? Had some man once fed her or someone she'd cared for a line they had believed? And then there was the question that he had pondered since their trip to Florida. Who was the man responsible for her never wanting to love again?

He wrapped his arms around Syneda. She belonged to him now. She was his. And he would always see to her happiness.

His thoughts quieted and, like the woman he held in his arms, he drifted off to sleep.

Syneda's eyes slowly opened and they flickered over the sleeping man holding her in his arms. He was as solid as a rock. His muscular thighs were entwined with hers in an unnervingly sexual way, almost holding her to him in bondage. If she'd wanted to get out of bed, she'd have to wake him to do so.

She snuggled closer to him, satisfied for the moment to remain just where she was as memories washed over her. Last night when he had stood before her completely undressed, she couldn't help appreciating his powerful masculine frame. No wonder women were drawn to him. His physique absolutely radiated virility. She shivered when she remembered the sheer male size of him and the arousing effect seeing him had had on her. At first she had felt wary wondering how on earth she would handle it all.

A satisfying smile touched her lips. Somehow she *had* handled all of him, and had enjoyed every tantalizing moment doing so. He had entered her easily, filling her with all his masculine power and strength. She had felt very little pain.

"I hope that smile is for me."

Clayton's words startled her. She thought he was still asleep.

"No, sorry. It's for someone else." She could tell by the gleam in his eyes that he didn't believe her.

"Then maybe I better try this all over again," he said, leaning over her on one elbow.

"If we try this anymore today, I won't be able to walk for a week."

"Did the bath help any?"

Syneda noticed the concern in his voice. Last night after they'd made love a number of times, he had gotten up and gone into the bathroom. A few minutes later, she had heard the sound of running water. He'd come back and gathered her up in his arms. Carrying her into the bathroom, he had eased her body into the warm sudsy water. Dropping to his knees beside the tub, he had taken her bath sponge and gently lathered the soreness from her aching muscles. It had felt heavenly.

She gazed up into his eyes. "Yes, the bath last night helped tremendously. Thanks for taking such good care of me. But then, somehow I knew that you would. Under that rough and tough exterior is a very caring man. You're a gentleman in every sense of the word."

"A gentleman?" At her nod, he shrugged. "I don't know about that. A part of me feels a real gentleman would have walked out the door last night and left you alone after discovering you were a virgin."

"But I wanted you as much as you wanted me. It was just that simple."

"There's nothing simple about being the first with a woman, Syneda. Some men may take it lightly. I don't."

Their gazes held and Syneda felt the seriousness in his words.

"No, you wouldn't. Even with your womanizing ways, I knew deep down that you wouldn't. And that was one of the reasons for my decision to let it be you, Clayton."

"And the other reason?"

When moments passed and she said nothing, Clayton reached out and caressed her cheek with his finger. "Talk to me, Syneda. We're friends, remember. And after last night, I'd say we're very close friends." A smile touched his lips. "As close as any two friends could possibly be."

Syneda nodded. "The other reason is because you play by the rules."

"A man playing by the rules is very important to you, isn't it?"

"Yes."

"Why? Why are you so against falling in love?"

She frowned. "I've told you all this before, when we were in Florida. You and I are a lot alike. Love isn't for everybody. Take you for instance—"

"We're not talking about me, we're talking about you. You never told me what happened to make you so against falling in love."

Syneda quickly turned away from him. "I'm hungry. I think I'll go find something to eat," she said, attempting to get up from the bed and clearly sidestepping his question. But Clayton's huge muscular thigh across hers wouldn't budge.

She turned back to him. "Clayton," she said warningly. "Kindly move your leg off me."

"Not until you answer my question. Who was he, Syneda? Who was the man that hurt you so?"

She held her head down for a moment and when she lifted it again, Clayton couldn't help noticing the tears misting her eyes. "Please don't ask me about him, Clayton," she said softly.

"Syneda." He gathered her close in his arms. The last thing he wanted to do was to make her cry. In the two and a half years that he had known her, he had never seen her cry, except for the tears she'd shed at Justin and Lorren's rushed wedding. But those had been tears of joy. What he saw in her eyes now were clearly tears of pain. His entire body shook. He was used to seeing fire and anger in her eyes, not hurt and pain.

"Talk to me baby. Please talk to me. Who was he?"

Twisting agony in her midsection made Syneda not want to talk about it. But another part of her, the part Clayton could so effortlessly bring out, wanted to share that period of her life with him.

"My father."

"Your father?" He frowned. "I don't understand."

Syneda drew a shuddering breath. The subject of the man who had fathered her was one she didn't like to discuss with anyone. But for some reason, she wanted to talk about it with Clayton.

"I never knew my father. From the information I was able to gather while growing up, my mother got pregnant while attending college. It must have been in her senior year because she did manage to graduate with a degree in nursing. She was an only child, and she, too, had been born out of wedlock."

Syneda's expression saddened. "There were two generations of Walters women who allowed men to feed them lines. I was determined not to follow in their footsteps and become a third."

She took a deep breath before continuing. "When I was ten, my mother caught a rare form of pneumonia and had to be hospitalized."

"Did you stay with your grandmother while your mother was in the hospital?" Clayton asked, pulling her closer into his arms.

"No, by that time, my grandmother had died. There was a lady my mother knew, another nurse name Clara Boyd who kept me. They weren't exactly close friends but she was a coworker who agreed to take me in while my mom got better. The only thing was my mom never got better. She died in the hospital."

A tender, pained smile came into Syneda's features. "The really sad thing is that she died still very much in love with my father. And for some reason, she died believing that he still loved her, too, and that he was deserving of both her love and trust. I don't understand how and why she could believe such a thing because he never came to see us."

Syneda quivered slightly. "For as long as I live, I'll never forget the day Clara took me to see Mom in the hospital. She had lost a lot of weight and I kept thinking how different she looked. She could barely talk but I remember her telling me that my father would be coming for me. She said Clara had already called him and he had agreed to come for me. She said he would love me and take good care of me."

Clayton stroked her shoulder gently. "What happened?"

Syneda lifted her head slightly to look at Clayton. The hurt, pain and tears in her eyes made his insides ache. "He never came. After my mom's funeral, I waited and waited but he never came. Even after the authorities turned me over to Mama Nora because I didn't have any other family, and Clara didn't want the responsibility of taking care of me, I still believed he would come. I believed it because my mom believed. She died believing it, so I figured she couldn't be wrong. I remember waking up each day at Mama Nora's thinking that this would be the day. Sometimes for hours, I would stand by my bedroom window watching and waiting. But he never came."

Clayton's hands tightened around her and he pulled her closer into his arms, silently cursing the man who had caused her so much pain. "Why did he tell Clara he would come if he had no intention of doing so?"

"I found out the truth later. Mama Nora and Poppa Paul told me the entire story years later when they thought I was old enough to handle it. Evidently the authorities questioned Clara, and she admitted to lying to my mom. She had called the man as my mother had asked her to do, but according to Clara, he had denied being my father. Clara said she didn't have the heart to tell my mother what he'd said, so she let her die believing I would be taken care of."

"What about the authorities? Couldn't they pursue it before making you a ward of the state? Evidently, Clara had this man's name and phone number, surely there was something they could do."

"Possibly, but they didn't get the chance to question Clara any further. I understand not long after my mom died, she quit her job at the hospital and moved to another city without leaving a forwarding address."

"So you still don't know who your father is?"

"No, and as far as I'm concerned, Clayton, I never had a father."

Her eyes closed momentarily, and when her lashes lifted again, her eyes revealed deep inner pain. "That period in my life was very difficult. It was during that time that Lorren and I became the very best of friends. She would stand by the window and wait with me every day, and then later when I found out the truth, that my father wasn't coming, her being there made a very painful time easy for me. And then I had Mama Nora and her husband Papa Paul. They were also there for me. One day Papa Paul explained to me that part of growing up was accepting the fact that on this earth, you would always face disappointments and letdowns from mortal men, even fathers. But he used to assure me that although my biological father had let me down, I had another father, a heavenly father, who would never let me down, and that he would always be there for me, no matter what."

She sighed. "So I shifted my faith to my other father. He became my rock, my strength, and like Poppa Paul said, he has never let me down."

Clayton clenched his teeth, angry at the disappointments she'd had to endure as a child. He couldn't help but admire her spirit. She'd been a fighter, a believer, a survivor.

Syneda continued. "And I made up my mind that I would never give my love and trust blindly to any man like my mother did. Over the years, I've learned that only a few people are blessed with sharing that special love and the unwavering trust that goes with it. Mama Nora shared it with Papa Paul before he died, your parents, your sisters and their husbands, Lorren and Justin and Dex and Caitlin have all shown me that it's possible for some people."

"But not for you?"

"No, not for me. I'll never fall in love. It's not for me. I don't need it."

Clayton's hands closed over Syneda's shoulders and the feel of his strong fingers soothed her. He leaned down and brushed his lips to her neck. "No, baby, I think love *is* for you," he said huskily. "You just don't know it yet."

"Clayton, you don't understand."

He met her eyes, his expression suddenly serious. "Yes, I do, Syneda. I really do." He understood more than she realized, he thought. He understood what her lifelong insecurities about love were, which had been so much a part of her childhood and evidently remained a part of her adult life. And because of how she felt, he knew he couldn't tell her that he loved her. Love would be the last thing she would want from him.

Knowing that he could never rid her of all the sadness and loneliness she had endured over the years, Clayton inwardly vowed to bring some happiness and pleasure into her life. Love was about more than being wanted. It was also about understanding, time and patience. He would do battle to have all those things with Syneda. First, he would be understanding whenever she would try keeping him, like she'd done other men, at arm's length. Second, he realized she needed time. Although she thought she had fully healed from the pain caused by her father, he sensed that deep down she really hadn't. And last, but above all, he would have to have patience. No matter what, he would not give up on her or his love. He was in it for the long haul.

He slowly got out of bed. "It's lunchtime."

Syneda smiled up at him. "Will we really get to eat this time?"

He laughed. "Yes, this time we will."

After lunch Clayton had gotten dressed and gone to a video store and rented a number of movies. They had ordered pizza for dinner and after watching the movies had decided to go to bed early.

In bed Clayton had held her in his arms. He refused to make love to her any more that day, knowing her body was still tender.

"Thanks for protecting me last night...and this morning,

Clayton. You must carry packs of condoms around with you," Syneda said with a teasing glint in her eyes.

Clayton chuckled. "Shut up, Walters, and go to sleep," he said, pulling her closer to him.

Syneda laughed as she snuggled closer. Her last thought before closing her eyes was that if she weren't too careful, she could get used to Clayton sleeping in her bed.

"This weekend was wonderful, Clayton."

Clayton stood by the door. His traveling bag was packed, and he was ready to leave. That morning she was the one who had awakened him to make love. Again they had skipped breakfast and ended up eating leftover pizza for lunch.

"Was this weekend wonderful enough to get me an invitation for another visit?"

Syneda hesitated before answering. "Do you think that's a good idea?"

"Yes."

She frowned up at him. "This weekend was to be a lust-purging experience to get you out of my system, and me out of yours."

He pulled her closer to him. He felt the soft warmth of her skin, and inhaled her arousing feminine scent. He wanted nothing more than to take her back to bed and make love to her for the rest of the day. "Then we failed miserably, because you're definitely still in my system."

Syneda stared up at him, becoming increasingly uneasy because he was still definitely in hers, too. "Another weekend will be a mistake."

"No, it won't."

A warning voice whispered in her head. She had let her guard down more with Clayton this weekend than with any other man. She needed time to think, to regroup. "I'll be busy next weekend."

Clayton nodded, recognizing her attempt to put distance between them. His gaze lowered to her body. She was wearing his dress shirt. It was the only stitch of clothing she had worn all weekend.

He reached into the pants pocket of his jeans and pulled out a key and placed it in the palm of her hand. "This is a spare key to my apartment." He didn't add that he had never given the spare key to any woman other than members of his family on occasion. "That shirt you're wearing is one of my favorites. How about personally returning it to me. Soon."

Syneda nervously bit her bottom lip as she gazed at the key she held in her hand. She then raised her eyes to meet his. "If you'll wait a minute, I'll change and you can take it with you."

"No. I want you to return it to me. In Houston. This coming weekend."

"Clayton, I can't do that. Don't you realize what you're asking of me?" He was suggesting that they continue their affair beyond this weekend. There was no way she could do that. Tossing aside common sense for a wild, reckless and passionate weekend with him once was enough. Considering doing it again would be asking for trouble.

"What do you think I'm asking of you, Syneda?"

Syneda closed her eyes momentarily. Clayton's voice, sexy and warm, wrapped about her like silken honey. Suddenly, sanity returned with full force and she opened her eyes. "To continue what we started this weekend."

Clayton reached up and tipped her chin up so their eyes could meet. "You're right, sweetheart. I'm not ready to end things. I still want you."

He lowered his head and kissed her tenderly. His lips slanted over hers, moving softly yet boldly, making circular motions. His tongue, smooth as velvet, teased her own tongue in a taunting yet provocative play. When he lifted his head, he gazed deeply into her eyes. The heat of them scorched her, and took her breath away.

Gathering his baggage in his hand, Clayton opened the door and walked out. Syneda stared at him, her mouth still feeling the pressure of his gentle but heated kiss as she remembered his parting words.

Chapter 9

Monday morning over breakfast, Syneda was still fighting the state of rhapsody she had found herself in. Clayton's departure yesterday had done little to bring her senses and mind back to reality. She had refused to take off his shirt until her bath late Sunday night.

His masculine scent had been drenched in the material, and an acute yearning for him had welled up inside her so strongly that at times she couldn't breathe. She had gone to bed wearing her nightgown and missing the aroma of his masculine skin the shirt had provided.

Not even the sore muscles she had encountered upon waking that morning or the marks of passion that Clayton's beard had left on various places over her body had dampened her spirits. That weekend they had soared to passionate, exhilarating heights, and her body was still tingling from the memories of it.

Taking a sip of her coffee, she realized that in order to make it through the coming weeks and months, she would have to get Clayton off her mind. The last thing she needed was to become involved with a man who had the ability to make her hot all over with just one look, and whose lovemaking surpassed anything she'd ever imagined.

On her way to work, she dropped Clayton's shirt off at the cleaners. She had made up her mind that the shirt would be returned to him but not personally as he'd requested. It would arrive at his place via FedEx overnight delivery.

Joanna looked up at Syneda when she stepped off the elevator. "Whoever is trying to impress you, Ms. Walters, is doing a darn good job. I'm definitely impressed with him."

Syneda raised a brow at her secretary's comment. "What are you talking about, Joanna?"

"There was a delivery for you first thing this morning."

Upon opening the door to her office, Syneda halted, shocked. Vases of flowers were everywhere.

"These are for me?" Syneda asked. She stood there, blank and amazed.

Joanna giggled. "Yes, they're all for you."

Joanna's response hit Syneda full force. "You're kidding."

"No, I'm not kidding. It took four guys to deliver them all. All these flowers make your office look like a flower shop. The guy definitely has great taste."

Syneda walked farther into the room. "They are beautiful, aren't they?"

"That's an understatement. Whoever sent these is definitely my kind of guy."

Syneda turned and faced her secretary with a smile on her lips that she couldn't contain. "Do me a favor and have another table brought in. Also, Joanna, I have a meeting with John Drayton. Please set up conference room B for our use. It will be a little too crowded for us to meet in here."

Joanna glanced around the room. "You think one table will do it? I think we need a couple of tables in here," she said teasingly, as she headed for the door. "The card that came with the flowers is in the middle of your desk." She left, closing the door behind her.

Syneda's hand shook nervously as she picked up the envelope and pulled out the card.

This weekend was more special to me than you'll ever know.
Clayton

Smiling, Syneda slipped the card back in the envelope and placed it in her desk.

"Ms. Walters?" Joanna's voice came through the intercom on her desk.

"Yes."

"Mr. Drayton has arrived. I have him settled in conference room B."

"Thanks, Joanna. I'm on my way."

Syneda looked at the distinguished-looking man sitting across the desk from her. His daughter, a young woman of twenty, had made a mistake and, being from a well-respected and wealthy family, they were not eager to share her mistake with the world. Nor did they want to make her pay for it for the rest of her life.

"Why didn't your daughter come with you? Are you sure she wants to give her child up for adoption, Mr. Drayton?"

"She'll do what's best for the family."

Syneda sighed. The man had said earlier that his daughter would not consider an abortion, and Syneda couldn't help wondering if perhaps Cassie Drayton was giving up her child under duress. "What about the child's father?"

"What about him?" John Drayton did not try to disguise his annoyance with her question.

"Even if your daughter is willing to give her child up for adoption, we'll need the consent of the father, Mr. Drayton."

"Consider it done. He won't oppose it," he replied with easy, smug confidence.

"I take it marriage has been ruled out as an option?" Syneda asked pointedly.

"Of course it has." His curt response held a note of impatience. "All I want is for your firm to arrange a private adoption. I'm sure there's some childless couple somewhere who would love to—"

"Adopt your grandchild?"

Mr. Drayton did not flinch at her words, nor did he seem remorseful when he answered. "Yes."

"We'll have to meet with your daughter, of course."

"That can be arranged."

"And the father?"

"Prepare the required papers. I'll see that he signs them."

Syneda angled her head and noted how John Drayton basked in the knowledge of his power. "Yes. I'm sure you will."

Restlessly, Syneda paced through her apartment that evening. Every room she went through reminded her of Clayton. Memories of their weekend together assailed her at every turn. He had spent less than seventy-two hours in her apartment and already his presence was missed.

It's not the quantity of time but the quality of time, her mind screamed. *And Clayton gave you top quality time.*

She stood in the doorway of her bedroom, remembering Clayton in it. A part of her wished he was there in it now. Another part of her knew that it was best that he wasn't, and that the best thing for her to do was to forget a weekend that she knew deep down she never would.

She had not even called to thank him for the flowers. She couldn't risk the sound of his sexy voice unnerving her. So she had chosen the coward's way out. During lunch, she had gone into a card shop and picked out a cute thank-you card, which she had signed and included in the box with his shirt that she'd sent back to him.

Taking a deep breath, she entered her bedroom. For the first time, it felt lonely to her. The bed was neatly made and looked nothing like the untidy and much-used bed it had been during Clayton's visit.

Syneda felt her resolve wavering as she sat on her bed. For a smart woman, she was completely stupid about sex. She had felt so savvy when she had entered the drugstore during lunch on Friday for her condom purchase. Determined to be on the safe side, she had purchased three packs of condoms, one for each day of Clayton's visit.

It was a good thing he was an expert at practicing safe sex because not only had she not purchased enough of the darn things, she had not given thought to using them until Clayton had discreetly pulled out his own foil packet before they'd made love; not only that first time, but every single time.

She couldn't help but appreciate his care and concern for her welfare. He never made a big production out of using them, nor had he tried to analyze her reaction. It did, however, make her feel comfortable to know he was a man who believed in a simple, direct approach to being careful, and who took the thought of AIDS or an unwanted pregnancy seriously. The last thing she needed was to have a child out of wedlock from a man who didn't love her, the way her mother had done. She and Clayton had made love enough times for that to happen, had it not been for him taking the necessary precautions.

Thoughts of him and their lovemaking suddenly made her feel as if her skin was on fire. Never would she have thought she would have spent the better part of a weekend making love to a man she considered a friend, at times an adversary, and at others a mentor. A man who was also a freewheeling bachelor, a sexual predator, a man who never made promises or hinted at the possibility of never-ending devotion and fidelity.

She didn't want to kid herself; Clayton was smooth and experienced. He was a man she could lose her heart to and get hurt if she was not careful. More than anything, she must not get love confused with great sex. She must not forget her own rules.

With that thought firmly embedded in her mind, Syneda's resolve became a little stronger than before.

"Ms. Walters, you have a call from a Mr. Clayton Madaris."

Syneda bit her lower lip. She had been expecting Clayton's

call. Evidently he had received the package she had sent to him. "Thanks, Joanna, I'll take it."

A few minutes later the connection was made. "Clayton?"

"Yes, Syneda. Thanks for the card, but no thanks for returning the shirt. I wanted you to return it in person," he said disappointedly.

Syneda smiled as she put her paperwork aside. Evidently he wasn't used to women not following his requests. "You can't always have what you want, Clayton. Thanks again for the flowers. You really shouldn't have."

"I couldn't help myself." What he had just said was the truth, Clayton thought. Upon arriving at the airport he had gone into a florist shop and ordered the flowers be delivered to her first thing Monday morning. There had not been one particular arrangement that had suited him, so he had ended up ordering several. Although he was disappointed that she had not personally returned the shirt, at least she had not returned the spare key to his apartment with the shirt.

Clayton couldn't help being plagued with vivid memories of her wearing nothing but his shirt. Never could he remember wanting a woman so much. The incredible hunger he had for her suddenly made his body go taut. He had to make love to her again and soon.

"I want to see you, Syneda. This weekend," he said huskily.

Syneda took a deep breath. "I've told you, I'll be busy."

"What about next weekend?"

"I'll still be busy."

"We need to talk, Syneda."

"No."

"Yes. Just what are you afraid of?"

"I'm not afraid of anything, Madaris."

"Then we'll talk. We either talk tonight on the phone, or I'll fly up this weekend and we'll talk in person."

"Don't do that, Clayton," she said shakily. She wasn't ready to see him again. He had a way of making her come utterly unglued.

There was a pause. "Okay then, I'll call you tonight at eight. Goodbye, Syneda."

Syneda hung up the phone without saying goodbye.

Clayton called at exactly eight o'clock. He didn't waste time on pleasantries. He had preplanned his strategy and went straight to the heart of the problem.

"Okay, Syneda, you talk and I'll listen since there seems to be something bothering you about the idea of us continuing to see each other."

Syneda sighed. Something bothering her was an understatement. "All right, Clayton, since you insist upon forcing the issue, I think you've forgotten there was to be only one weekend for us. All we shared was satisfying a case of lust and a little bit of curiosity. We've gotten both out of our system."

"Can you honestly say we did?"

"Yes, you're out of my system," she lied.

"Well, you're not out of mine."

"Too bad, Madaris. You don't get a second try."

A grin appeared on Clayton's face. She was following just where he had wanted to lead her. "Does that mean we go back to being just friends?"

"Yes."

"Then there's no reason for me not to come visit you in two weeks, as nothing more than a friend. I'll even check into a hotel if you want me to."

Syneda heard the challenge in his voice. It was something she could not ignore. Her first instinct was to tell him in unladylike words just where he could go, but she thought better of it. In this situation, the age-old saying "actions speak louder than words" would have to be proven. It was obvious he did not believe they could go back to being just friends without anything sexual between them.

Syneda balled her hands into fists. She would jump to the challenge to contradict his beliefs and show him that he was out of her system. She only hoped that in two weeks he really and truly was.

"Okay, Clayton, I'll see you in two weeks. And it won't be necessary for you to check into a hotel. My sofa converts into a bed, and I have plenty of room here at my place."

"Are you sure?"

"Yes, I'm positive. Just as long as you remember my position."

Unfortunately he *was* remembering her position, and the one that stuck out uppermost in his mind was the one of her Sunday morning lying flat on her back, pinned beneath the heated weight of his aroused body.

"Yes, Syneda, I'll remember your position," he said in a deep husky voice. *At the present time, I can't seem to think of anything else.*

"I wasn't aware you'd be working late tonight, Braxter."

Braxter Montgomery looked up from the papers he'd been reading. "I really hadn't planned to stay this late, Senator, but I'm picking up my date from work. I decided to stick around here and go over the guest list Jacob Madaris faxed today."

Senator Lansing smiled. "Ahh, yes. It's almost that time, isn't it? I thought it was pretty nice of Jake to give me a kickoff party for my reelection campaign."

"Yes, it was." Braxter knew that Jacob Madaris was a personal friend of the senator, and a loyal, longtime supporter. He owned a large cattle ranch called Whispering Pines.

Whispering Pines was located several hundred miles from Houston. In addition to the cattle business, Madaris also owned stock in many business investments, including being a major investor in his nephew's oil exploration company. Last year, Madaris Oil Exploration made national headlines when they had located a rich oil basin near Eagle Pass, Texas for Remington Oil Company.

"How's the list coming?"

Braxter smiled. "It's growing by leaps and bounds. There's quite a number of impressive names on it. People are coming from as far away as Hollywood and Miami."

The senator laughed. "That doesn't surprise me. Everybody knows Jake Madaris seldom throws parties. But when he does, it's a good one, and most people don't want to be left out."

Braxter glanced down at the list. "Yes, I can believe that. How did you meet Mr. Madaris?"

"I met Jake through his brother Robert who was six years older than Jake. Robert Madaris and I served in Nam together and became good friends. Unfortunately, Robert never made it back home."

"How awful."

"Yes, it was for the Madaris family. They're good people. Well, good night, Braxter."

"Good night, sir."

After the senator left, Braxter checked his watch. It was almost time for Celeste to be closing her shop. She'd told him this was her busiest time of the year, the first weeks of June. During this time most people began making summer travel plans.

He smiled, remembering how they had begun seeing each other. It was right after he had repaired her car that day in the parking lot. That had been almost two weeks ago, and they had dated steadily since then. She was witty and fun to be around. He thoroughly enjoyed her company.

Braxter pushed his papers aside. He stood and began putting on his jacket. He was looking forward to seeing Celeste again.

Chapter 10

"If there's some doubt in your mind about giving up your child for adoption, Miss Drayton, then why are you doing so without first exploring other options?"

Although Syneda tried remaining emotionally detached, she couldn't stop her heart from going out to the young woman sitting across the desk from her. She didn't fit the image of a wealthy and spoiled woman who had gotten herself in trouble and had run home to Daddy for help.

Syneda was assaulted with a terrible sense of wariness. Her earlier thoughts when she'd first met with John Drayton appeared to have been correct. Cassie Drayton, the only child of the wealthy New York clothing magnate, was giving up her child not because she wanted to but because she felt she was being forced to.

Glossy blond hair fell like a shimmering curtain over both sides of the young woman's face as she began sobbing into an embroidered handkerchief. "I have no other choice and neither does Larry."

"Larry?"

"Yes. Larry Morgan, my baby's father."

"Have you spoken to Mr. Morgan about any of this?"

"No. It's best I don't. He wants to marry me but that's impossible."

"Why?"

"Because I love him too much," she replied brokenly. "And my love may end up destroying him."

Syneda raised her brows in surprise. She had assumed the relationship between Cassie Drayton and the father of her child had not been a long-standing one, but one where sex and not love had been a factor. Evidently she'd been mistaken.

Syneda rose and rounded her desk. She laid her hand on Cassie Drayton's shoulder. "You're not a child, Miss Drayton. You're a twenty-year-old woman who has the right to make her own decisions. If you really don't want to give up your child for—"

"You don't understand, and why should you care, Ms. Walters? My father is obviously paying you a big fat retainer to quickly find a solution to my problem, especially since I refused to have an abortion. Your job is to place my baby with a couple who love each other and who'd love my child. But what really hurts is knowing that couple could just as well be me and Larry. We love each other deeply, and no one would love our baby more than the two of us."

The crack in Syneda's heart widened another degree. The young woman was totally distraught, and Syneda was at a loss as to what to do. She wanted to help without stepping beyond the boundaries of her role as an attorney. But right now Cassie Drayton didn't need an attorney, she needed someone she could talk to, and most important, someone who would listen.

"Cassie, I owe the couple who may be adopting your child complete peace of mind that one day you won't show up demanding the child back. I'm presently working on a case such as that, and all it's done is cause pain for both sides. So, if you're having doubts about going through with this, I suggest we discuss them now. You mentioned you and the baby's father love each other, yet you said marriage is out of the question. Could you please explain why you feel that way?"

"Why should it matter to you?" the young woman asked, sniffing.

"Because besides being an attorney, I'm also human. I have an ethical obligation to do more than just represent you. I want to hear you and listen to what you have to say."

"Are you in love, Ms. Walters?"

The question caught Syneda by surprise. "No," she replied gently.

"Have you ever been in love?"

Syneda met the young woman's curious tear-stained stare. "No, but that doesn't exempt me from understanding or trying to understand. And how about calling me Syneda."

Cassie Drayton hesitated only briefly before replying. "And I'm Cassie." She paused then spoke slowly. "I met Larry at college. He's a few years older and was obtaining a master's degree in accounting. He's brilliant," she said proudly.

"I fell in love with him the moment I saw him. We dated three months before I took him home to meet my family. As soon as my father discovered Larry's parents weren't a part of New York society's best, he forbade me to see him again."

"I gather you continued seeing him anyway."

"Yes. By that time Larry had completed his studies and had gotten a really good job with a prestigious accounting firm here in the city. He encouraged me to finish school and our plans were to marry after I graduated. Everything was going fine until we goofed and I got pregnant. Although a baby was not in our plans, we were happy about it anyway."

"What happened?"

"My father found out. He paid us a visit and made a lot of threats. Within twenty-four hours, he had carried them out. When Larry reported to work the next morning, he was told he no longer had a job. We later discovered that my father had also made sure Larry wouldn't find decent employment in this city or anywhere else as long as he continues to see me."

"What's Mr. Morgan's reaction to all of this?"

"He's furious. He tried telling my father that he loved me and would make me happy, but my father told him that he was not good enough for me and as long as he planned to include me in his future, he would make sure he didn't have one."

"So he gave in to your father's threats?"

"No, Larry would never do that. I'm the one who gave in. I know more than anyone what my father is capable of, Ms. Walters. He would destroy Larry's career completely without a moment's thought. I couldn't let him do that to Larry. I love him too much. I moved back home with my parents. I'm now back to being their puppet, letting them pull all the strings. But it doesn't matter as long as Larry isn't harmed."

"Where's Mr. Morgan now?"

"I don't know. He tried contacting me but I refuse to see him. It's for the best."

"Your father is so sure Larry will sign the forms to give up your child," Syneda said quietly.

"My father overestimates himself and underestimates Larry. He'll never sign those forms. Larry would never agree to give up our child."

A confused frown covered Syneda's features. John Drayton seemed so confident the man would do exactly the opposite. That was interesting, especially judging by Cassie's distress and opinion of her father's capabilities.

"Cassie, I suggest you give yourself a few weeks to think this over some more, then come back to see me."

"But what will I tell my father? He expects me to sign the papers today."

Syneda reached for a business card and pressed it into the young woman's hand. "You have time to make a decision, Cassie. This is something you should be absolutely sure about. If your father has any questions, just tell him to give me a call. If what you say is true, and Larry refuses to sign the papers, there's nothing your father can do."

Cassie nodded. "Thanks for listening, Syneda."

"You're welcome. And Cassie, I have a feeling that somehow things will work out for you and Larry."

Cassie looked doubtful of that. She said goodbye and left Syneda's office.

Syneda returned to the chair behind her desk and propped her head in her hands, suddenly feeling extremely tired. It seemed all her cases this week had been either difficult or in some way mind draining. Or maybe she was in a poor state of mind to deal with them. Knowing Clayton would be flying in this weekend was making her a basket case.

She had berated herself numerous times over the past two weeks for inviting him to stay at her place. She had been so sure she could handle it but now she seriously had her doubts. All it took was a few moments to think about their weekend together to know the man still was not out of her system.

She let out a deep sigh. This would be a rather interesting weekend.

It was Friday and not quite noon, Syneda noticed, glancing at her watch. Her right arm felt numb and she was positive that at any minute it was going to fall off. Also, her stomach was more than mildly protesting her lack of providing it with nourishment.

A doughnut and a cup of coffee were all she'd had for breakfast. She had too much work to take time to eat anything. Especially if she wanted to leave the office on time to be at home before Clayton arrived. He had phoned earlier in the week and indicated he would be arriving around six.

The smooth voice of Joanna on the intercom broke into Syneda's thoughts. "Ms. Walters?"

"Yes, Joanna, what is it?"

"I know you asked not to be disturbed but there's a gentleman here to see you. He doesn't have an appointment. He says he's a friend of yours by the name of Clayton Madaris."

The frown of annoyance on Syneda's lips was suddenly

replaced by one of complete surprise. *Clayton was here in New York already!*

"Ms. Walters?"

Syneda could tell by the strain in Joanna's voice that she was getting frustrated with her lack of cooperation. "All right, Joanna, please show Mr. Madaris in."

Nervously gathering the scattered papers in a neat pile, Syneda placed them in a folder on the corner of her desk. Then she stood to face the man who had plagued her mind for the past couple of weeks; especially this morning before she had become totally absorbed in her work.

The door swung open and Syneda managed to place a friendly though strained smile on her lips.

Clayton entered her office escorted by Joanna. It was obvious Joanna was completely enthralled by the tall, dark, handsome man dressed impeccably in a dark suit.

"Thanks for showing Mr. Madaris in, Joanna. That will be all for now."

"All right," Joanna replied, not taking her eyes off of Clayton. "If you're absolutely sure there won't be anything else."

A slight frown of annoyance covered Syneda's face. Joanna appeared to be in a daze. She hadn't moved an inch. It bothered Syneda that Clayton had this effect on women. "I'm positive, Joanna. You may leave us alone now. And make sure I'm not disturbed."

Clayton raised a dark brow at the harsh tone of Syneda's voice.

"All right, Ms. Walters," Joanna replied, not ignoring the curtness of Syneda's words. She gave Clayton a warm smile before leaving.

"I wasn't expecting you until late this afternoon, Clayton. You're early."

"My case this morning was canceled, so I caught an earlier flight out. I had my secretary phone you a few times, but she couldn't get through to speak with you. She did leave a message though. I hope you don't mind me showing up like this, but I need the key."

A confused frown covered Syneda's features. "The key?"

"Yes, the key to your apartment."

"Oh," Syneda said, as understanding dawned. She went into her desk for her purse. "You need the key to get inside my apartment." She handed it to him. "Just make yourself at home. I should leave here by five. What would you like to do tonight? How about dinner someplace?" She had already decided it would be best if the two of them spent as little time as possible at her apartment.

"What do you usually do on Friday nights?" Clayton asked, taking the key she offered.

"Usually, I just grab something on the way home, then watch my favorite television program." As an afterthought she added, "That's if I don't have a date for the evening."

"Do you have a date for tonight?" Clayton asked quietly.

"No."

"Then you shouldn't change things just for me. However, since I'll have nothing to do until you get there, how about letting me prepare us something to eat."

"Clayton, that isn't necessary."

"I'd enjoy doing it. I'm not a bad cook, you know."

Syneda knew that was an understatement. Thanks to their mother, who was superb in the kitchen, all three Madaris brothers were great cooks. "I just hate for you to go to all that trouble. You'll be showing up my insufficiencies as a hostess again."

As soon as the words had left her mouth, Syneda regretted them. They could dredge up memories of their last weekend together, and by the sudden silence in the room it appeared they had.

Clayton captured her eyes with his. "Trust me. You were a good hostess. You took very good care of me that weekend," he replied huskily. "I'll have dinner prepared by the time you get there. Don't work too hard."

Before Syneda could utter a response, Clayton had turned and walked out of the door.

"Clayton, I'm home."

Around five hours later, Syneda entered her apartment using the spare key. Her plans to leave work early had been aborted when she'd received another unexpected visitor. This time Larry Morgan.

He had told her in no uncertain terms that he would not agree to give his child up for adoption no matter what John Drayton did to him.

Syneda's thoughts came to a sudden halt when her nose picked up the aroma of food. She was starving. She'd skipped lunch to finish an important report only to have the completion delayed because of Larry Morgan's visit. Then, not long after he had left, she'd gotten a call from John Drayton. He had not been pleased with her decision to give his daughter more time to make a final decision. As far as he was concerned, the decision had been made. Therefore, he'd stated, he wanted to be represented by another attorney in the firm. That suited Syneda just fine.

"I was wondering when you'd get here," Clayton said, coming into the living room. He had changed into a pair of jeans and a white chambray shirt.

Syneda's mind began reeling as she eyed him from head to toe. He was an incredibly sexy man whether he was dressed in a suit, jeans…or nothing at all, she thought. She noticed he was holding two filled wineglasses. He handed her one of them.

"I thought you could probably use this. I take it you've had a bad day."

Syneda graciously took the drink he offered. "That's putting it mildly." She took a sip. "Thanks. Something smells wonderful. What is it?"

Clayton smiled. "It's a surprise. I just hope you're hungry."

Syneda laughed. "Clayton, I could eat a horse about now."

"Well, dinner is ready when you are. Would you like to take a warm bath to unwind first?"

"That's not a bad idea. I'll be back in a few minutes."

Clayton watched as Syneda rounded the sofa and went into her bedroom, closing the door behind her. He had found incredible hunger raging through him upon the sight of her. He only hoped his plan would work. He didn't want to push her into anything, but with Syneda, some things had to be forced on her, and accepting a relationship between the two of them was going to be one of them. She was so certain she didn't want or need the love of a man in her life that she was overlooking the obvious. A man who loved her was already in her life.

Over the past few days, he had done a lot of thinking about what she had told him the last night they had spent together; specifically, the information she had shared about her father. Whether she was willing to admit it to herself or not, the pain of her father's rejection and abandonment was clouding the way she thought about love.

He knew she had some deep-rooted fears. The first being her fear of ever becoming dependent upon anyone, especially a man. And for that reason he understood her need for more space than normal. She would never agree to a relationship that would be confining.

She was also a private person, and she thought she couldn't become seriously involved with a person for that reason. She didn't know that the key to that problem would be for her to become involved with someone with whom her privacy wouldn't be threatened.

And then there were her biggest fears, rejection and abandonment. It was plain she had decided the best way to avoid the heartache of both was by not getting close to anyone.

He could only imagine the pain, anguish, and disappointment she'd endured when her father had not shown up for her. In his mind, Clayton could envision her at the age of ten standing at the window peering out, waiting day after day after day.

Having been involved with Big Brothers of America, he'd always taken pleasure in watching a fatherless boy who'd been patiently waiting for a Big Brother finally get one. The joy, excitement and happiness on the kid's face was priceless. But because Syneda's father had never shown up for her, she had been cheated out of experiencing any of those emotions.

Clayton expelled a deep breath and walked back into the kitchen. He had a big job on his hands. He was deeply in love with Syneda and was determined that in time, she would put the past behind her and return his love. What she needed was time to heal, and he had found a way to give her the time she needed while still sharing a relationship with him.

He hoped she would go along with what he would be proposing to her. She was a strong-willed woman, but he'd have to be even stronger to get her to do something she would be totally against doing. But he was determined that before he left on Sunday, she would have accepted the fact that there could never be a platonic relationship between them again.

The warm bath was a wonderful idea, Syneda thought. Turning on the faucet she added a generous amount of her favorite bubble-bath gel to the flowing water. Closing her eyes, she inhaled deeply as the fragrance of a flower garden began filling the steamy room.

Removing her clothes, Syneda sank to her neck in the bubbles a few minutes later. She felt somewhat guilty about how much Clayton had done since his arrival. From the smell of things in the kitchen, undoubtedly he had prepared quite a feast. There was no way he could have found the ingredients he had needed to cook with in her kitchen, which meant he had gone grocery shopping. That thought made her feel even more guilty. He was her guest, she was not his. It seemed Clayton was always going out of his way to take care of her.

Getting out of the bath some time later, she toweled herself dry before lotioning her body. She liked the way the fragrance of the lotion lingered on her skin. After changing into a pair of slacks and a top, she entered the living room.

Syneda found Clayton sitting on her sofa, finishing the rest of his wine. He looked up when she entered and smiled.

"How do you feel now?"

"A lot better, but my problem will still be there to haunt me on Monday."

"Is it a case you're working on?" Clayton asked, handing her another glass of wine.

"Yes and it's a bummer. My client is—or I should say was, since it seems I'm no longer representing her—the daughter of one of the wealthiest men in New York. She's unmarried and pregnant, and her father wants her to give the child up for adoption."

"What does she want?"

Syneda sat down on the sofa. "She wants to keep her baby and marry the father of her child. He wants to marry her, too."

"Then what's the problem?"

"John Drayton doesn't think Larry Morgan is good enough for his daughter. And he's determined to ruin the young man's career unless he agrees to give in and sign papers giving the child up for adoption."

"Unless the woman is a minor, Syneda, there's really nothing the father can do, however, it's understandable why he would want to."

Syneda raised arched brows. "And just what does that mean?"

"It means that although the man is playing his role of father a little too thick, I can understand him wanting the best for his daughter."

Clayton's response rankled her. "Wanting the best for his daughter? That has nothing to do with it, Madaris," Syneda snapped. "He just wants to control her life."

"A life she undoubtedly couldn't control on her own. If she could, then she wouldn't be pregnant now, would she?"

Syneda gave him a hostile glare. "Accidents *do* happen, Clayton. Everyone isn't as overly cautious as you are. I can't believe you've taken the father's side in this."

Clayton heaved an exasperated sigh. "I'm not taking anyone's side. For Pete's sake, I don't even know these people. All I'm saying is that sometimes parents think they know what's best for their children. You can't hang the man because he thinks he's doing the right thing."

"But that's just it. He isn't doing the right thing. Cassie Drayton and Larry Morgan love each other. Their baby is a part of that love. But you wouldn't understand something like love, would you?"

"I guess not. But I suppose *you* do." Clayton could tell by her expression that his comment had nearly infuriated the life out of her. No doubt she felt like slapping him silly.

"I only know what I saw today, Madaris," she said after having stared at him for a long moment with angry eyes. "And today I met a man who desperately wants to be with the woman he loves."

"Ah, well now. It's good to know some men who say 'I love you' aren't just feeding women 'lines,'" he said sarcastically with a sweetness that he knew probably pushed Syneda beyond the boiling point. He hoped she was beginning to realize she couldn't judge every relationship in life based on what had happened between her parents.

Syneda's eyes narrowed. "Yes, but what you've failed to—"

"Let's just drop the subject. I don't want to argue with you."

"We aren't arguing. I just don't like—"

Before Syneda could finish what she was saying, she found herself lifted from the sofa and into Clayton's arms. "This is the only way I know to shut you up."

Before she could react, his mouth was opening over hers. Her struggles to free herself were useless. Clayton had her pinned in his arms while his mouth took over hers.

Syneda could not identify at what point she stopped resisting him as streaks of pleasure exploded deep within her. It seemed every desire she had tried to suppress since Clayton's last visit came pouring out. She couldn't help responding to the powerful sensual chemistry sizzling between them, and was unprepared for the sudden rush of hot passion that swept over her. She was a fool to have thought she had gotten this man out of her system.

She pressed herself against him, needing to feel his hard body and the strength of his arms holding her. She locked her arms around his neck and returned his kiss, wanting his taste to fill her mouth. Their kiss grew hotter, wilder, longer.

The sound of Syneda's stomach growling echoed in the

room. Clayton slowly lifted his head to first stare down at the sea-green eyes glazed with passion before moving lower to her full, inviting lips.

"You're hungry," he said huskily.

Syneda gazed into dark eyes that were starkly sexual. "Yes, I am," she replied, her words coming out soft as whipped cream.

Clayton wanted nothing more than to carry her into the bedroom. But he knew he couldn't. When they made love again, it would be on his terms. Terms he hoped she would agree to.

"Come on," he said, taking her hand. He led her to the kitchen and sat her down at the table. After placing various casserole dishes before her, he sat down across from her. "First, we eat."

Syneda's throat suddenly felt dry. She should not have let him kiss her. The last thing she wanted was for him to think her position had shifted and they could be more than just friends. "After we eat, then what?" she asked in a curious whisper, looking into his eyes.

Clayton's gaze held hers. The look in his eyes was intent, clear and challenging. "Then I'll make you an offer I hope you can't refuse."

Chapter 11

At first Syneda pretended not to have heard Clayton's statement. She went about spooning the baked chicken, macaroni and cheese, okra and tomatoes and rice pilaf onto her plate. She put down her first mouthful, savoring the taste of the well-prepared meal. Finally the strain of curiosity was too much for her.

"What kind of offer are you talking about?"

Clayton smiled. He'd known her nonchalant attitude wouldn't last long. She was an inquisitive person by nature. Most attorneys were. "I prefer we discuss it after dinner."

"Why can't we discuss it now?"

"I want to do it later."

Syneda sighed. Experience had taught her Clayton did things when it suited him. Evidently this would be one of those times. "All right, suit yourself, but I may not want to hear anything you have to say after dinner."

"I'll take that chance."

She frowned. She also knew from experience he enjoyed getting in the last word.

"How does everything taste?"

"Good. You're an excellent cook."

"Thanks."

They ate in silence for several minutes, and then Clayton spoke. "Mom should be giving you a call in a few days."

Syneda lifted her brow. "Why?"

"Uncle Jake is giving Senator Lansing a kickoff party for his reelection campaign at Whispering Pines sometime next month. More than likely Mom will be contacting you to make sure you come."

Syneda smiled. "I'd love to come. You know how much I admire Senator Lansing. I've never met him, but I'm a big supporter of his."

Clayton nodded. "The day after Senator Lansing's party is Gramma Madaris's eightieth birthday. We'll be having another party to celebrate that, too. Knowing Mom she'll want all of us to spend the night at Whispering Pines so we'll all be accounted for on Sunday."

"Okay." Syneda knew that sleepover also included her. Ever since Lorren had married into the Madaris family, they had not held any family gatherings that had not included her. She knew Clayton's mother, Marilyn Madaris, considered her more than just Lorren's best friend. The entire Madaris family thought of her as part of the family and she really appreciated that. Now that Mama Nora spent a lot of her time traveling with a group of other widows from church, Syneda enjoyed the rather close relationship she had developed with the Madaris family.

After dinner together she and Clayton cleared the dishes off the table and cleaned up the kitchen. Syneda couldn't help noticing Clayton had taken all the dishes out of the dishwasher and had stacked them neatly in the cabinets.

"Now we'll talk." Taking her hand, Clayton led her into the

living room where he motioned for her to sit down on the sofa. He sat next to her.

"All right, Clayton, what is it?"

He took her hand in his, and gave her an engaging smile. "I propose that we become lovers," he came right out and said in a very controlled voice.

Syneda looked at him. He was serious! "That's out of the question."

"Why? Have you changed your mind about love and commitment?"

His question startled Syneda. "Of course not!"

"You still don't want anything to do with either?"

"That's right," she answered quickly, wondering where Clayton's line of questioning was leading to.

"Then we're perfectly suited for each other, and becoming involved will have a lot of advantages for the both of us," he said.

"Advantages like what?"

"Neither of us wants to get involved in any sort of permanent relationship. I live in Houston, you live here, so there won't be any crowding. We'll both get the space we need. Then there's the stability of a steady relationship, which means there won't be any risks since we won't be dating other people."

Clayton quickly searched her face to see if any of what he was saying was sinking in. When all he saw was an unreadable expression, he continued. "We're both private people but a relationship won't threaten our privacy because we trust each other. We enjoy each other's company, we're friends, we respect each other's profession, and we enjoy being together in every way a man and woman can be together. But most importantly," he murmured softly, "becoming lovers is the perfect solution to our problem."

"What problem?" Syneda looked into Clayton's dark eyes and felt the heat displayed in them with every nerve in her body.

"The fact that you want me as much as I want you. And no matter how much we try to convince ourselves otherwise, last weekend was not enough for either of us. What we shared was very special, but it only made me want you that much more. I want you more than I've ever wanted a woman in my life."

Syneda frowned. "That's impossible. You've had lots of women. Most of them a whole lot more experienced than I am. Why me, Clayton? And why are you even considering limiting yourself to dating just me? You've always enjoyed having lots of women."

Clayton didn't think she was quite ready to hear how much he loved her. So instead he answered, "I'm getting older, wiser and more cautious. There's no longer such things as 'safety in numbers' and 'no risk, no pleasure.' Now the present climate is more like 'unsafety in numbers,' and 'no risk, live longer.' And although I'm a careful man, I don't like the chances I take sleeping around. It's time for me to make some lifestyle changes. Therefore, you and I getting together is the perfect solution. Like I said, we're perfectly suited for each other. Besides, you're all the woman I need."

He lowered his head and touched his lips to hers. He deepened the kiss when he felt her immediate response. He heard himself release a groan of pleasure when her mouth began opening beneath his.

Syneda's hands slowly slid up his chest, wrapping themselves around his neck. He reveled in her fire, her heat, her scent and her trembling warmth in his arms.

Clayton slowly broke off the kiss and looked deeply into her eyes. The passion he saw glittering in them was a mirror of his own. He then rested his forehead against hers, his breathing unsteady.

"You don't have to give me your answer tonight, or even this weekend if you need time to think about it," he said huskily, stroking her shoulder. He lifted his head to again look in her eyes. "I don't want to rush you into anything. Just promise me that you'll at least consider the idea."

Syneda nodded, unable to say anything. It wasn't too often she was at a loss for words. If anything, she usually had too many of them. But as usual, Clayton's kiss had zapped her of all logical thought.

Clayton heaved a deep sigh as he stood. "I think I'll go out for a while."

"Go out? Where?"

"No place in particular. I'll just take a walk."

"Take a walk? In New York? This late?"

Clayton grinned. "Yeah, I'll be all right. I might stop by that video store and pick up a movie or something." He reached up a hand and rubbed the back of his neck. "I just need to get out of here or I won't be responsible for my actions. I told you I would visit as a friend this weekend, and until you say otherwise that's all I'll be."

Syneda drew in a shuddering breath. He had left the decision in her hands. What did or did not happen between them this weekend and any weekend that followed would be her choice.

"I'll be back later."

She watched as he turned and walked out the door.

Alone, Syneda walked across the room, her arms cradling her middle. It was an instinctive protective action, and she needed all the protection she could get from Clayton Jerome Madaris.

How dare he suggest they become lovers! She didn't want to be *that* involved with any man. Men had a tendency to get too possessive, too domineering, too crazy. Her life was just fine without a man in it. She liked being in control of her life and not having to answer to anyone. And most of all she hated feeling vulnerable.

And with Clayton she felt vulnerable.

Even with the confrontational tension that usually surrounded them, lately there had been an increase in physical tension between them.

Syneda sighed, acknowledging the effect Clayton had on her. She was intelligent enough to know it wasn't based on love but on something for which she really didn't have a clue. Neither Thomas, Marcus, nor any of the other men she'd dated had made her feel the way Clayton did. None of them had even come close.

Her palms felt strangely damp. The neat, tidy case Clayton had presented to her was in no way a weak one. Like the brilliant attorney that he was, he had presented all the advantages of their becoming lovers. He had stated them so eloquently that there was no way she could even poke holes in his opening argument.

A cross-examination of the facts he'd presented would have been useless. He had, beyond a reasonable doubt, cited all the reasons she had avoided an intimate involvement. He had then used those very reasons not in favor of the defense, but to further the prosecution.

There was no way she could deny there would be some real benefits in becoming his lover. She would have the space she liked, the stability she wanted and the privacy she craved. But most importantly, she would have relief from the intense combination of passion and desire Clayton had stirred up within her. She had become trapped in the depths of her own sensuality. It was a state that only Clayton could rectify. At least with him, she didn't have to worry about being fed a line. There would be no "I love you" and no promises of "forever after." With him she could enjoy the present without the pain of the past or the worry of a loveless future.

"It's all about mutual satisfaction," she said softly to herself. "Mutual satisfaction and nothing more."

Syneda nodded, her decision made. She would agree to become Clayton's lover only if he was willing to accept her conditions.

Nearly an hour had passed before Syneda heard the key rattle in the lock. Tossing aside her legal pad, she stood. She didn't care that the expression on her face clearly showed she'd been worried. When Clayton hadn't returned in what she had considered a reasonable amount of time, she had begun pacing the floor, peeking through drapes and gnawing nervously at her bottom lip.

The nerve of him to make her worry!

"Where have you been?" she demanded the moment he walked in.

Clayton gave her an inquiring glance before calmly saying, "Out."

Syneda felt a surge of renewed anger. Here she had been driving herself crazy wondering if he had gotten mugged or run over by a speeding cab. And all he had to say regarding his whereabouts was "out."

"I know you've been out, Clayton. But you've been gone for over an hour. Did it ever occur to you that I was worried?"

Clayton shook his head. "No. That thought never occurred to me."

Infuriated, Syneda walked up to him. Heaven help her, but she wanted to grab him and shake him one time. "Well, I was."

A hint of a smile played around Clayton's mouth. His hand slipped to her waist and pulled her closer. "I'm sorry that I made you worry about me. I stopped by that arcade shop around the corner and played a couple of games."

Syneda frowned at him. "Look, Madaris. If we're going to be lovers, we need to have an understanding about a few things. I don't believe in disappearing acts."

Clayton's heart almost stopped beating with Syneda's words. He cupped her face in his hands, smiling brightly. "Are we going to be lovers?"

With a gentle smile she said, "Yes."

Clayton pulled her closer to him. "Does this mean you've decided to accept my proposal?"

"Yes, Counselor. You presented a pretty good argument, but I do have two conditions."

Clayton studied her eyes, noting the determined set in them. He knew that whatever her conditions were, there would be no negotiations. "What are they?"

"First, I want you to agree that at any time if either of us wants to end this relationship we can do so without any questions asked. Other than dating each other exclusively, we are not bound to each other."

Clayton didn't like that condition at all. More than ever he was determined to make sure she never wanted to end the relationship. "All right," he finally said.

"The next one involves your family."

Clayton raised a brow. "My family? What about my family?"

Syneda stepped out of the circle of his arms. "I don't want them knowing about us, Clayton. I don't want them to know we're involved."

He frowned. "Why?"

"I don't want to become one of those women they constantly tease you about—the kind they think you only date. I don't want to lose their love and respect."

"Syneda, that would never happen."

"I can't take that chance. I won't take it."

Clayton pulled her back into his arms. Although he didn't like what she was asking of him, he understood why she was doing it. Because of her deep-rooted doubts and fears, she needed an attachment to people she could count on and trust. His family had become that to her. They were her surrogate family, and she would never take the chance to be rejected and abandoned again. But what she failed to realize was that his family would always be there for her, no matter what. They would always love her. Nothing could or would ever change that. If anything, they would love her even more for finally opening his heart to love. But he knew nothing he said would convince her of that. Only time would prove it.

"Okay, Syneda, if that's the way you want it, I won't mention it. Justin and Lorren are the only ones that will know. But I want you to know up front that I don't care who knows. We're adults and don't have to answer to anyone. I won't ever be ashamed of what we'll be sharing, and I don't want you to be, either. You're very special to me."

The manly scent of Clayton filled Syneda's nostrils as he embraced her. She liked being held in the comfort of his arms. "And you're very special to me, Clayton."

Clayton's tongue traced the outline of Syneda's lips. He then moved his mouth from her lips to her neck and began kissing her there.

His caress on a sensitive part of her neck aroused her, setting her body on fire with desire. He lifted his head.

"Where do we go from here?"

Syneda smiled up at him. "How about the bedroom."

Smiling, he gathered her into his arms and took her to the very place she'd requested.

Late Sunday evening Syneda walked Clayton to the door wearing his white dress shirt. She looked down at herself. "This is becoming a habit."

He smiled as he pulled her into his arms. "But it's one I like. You look good in my shirt. I want you to return it to me in New Orleans."

Syneda's eyes widened. "New Orleans?"

"Yes. Let's meet in New Orleans two weeks from now. Will you do it?"

She looked at him for a few minutes before saying, "Yes."

Clayton smiled. "I can't come back to New York this coming weekend. I promised Dex and Caitlin I'd babysit Jordan while they attend Caitlin's high school reunion in San Antonio. I would invite you to keep me company, but Jordan would love telling her parents when they returned that Aunt Neda spent the weekend with her, too."

Syneda grinned. "Yes, I can just imagine Jordan doing that."

They looked into each other's eyes, momentarily becoming lost in the memories of the weekend. Clayton had been right. Somehow this weekend had far surpassed the last. The last time they had spent together was due to a mixture of curiosity and hormones. This time they had become closer friends, as well as lovers.

On Saturday morning over breakfast they had again discussed the Drayton case. And this time although they still didn't agree completely, they had respected the other's opinion.

"Waiting two weeks to see you again will seem like forever," Clayton said. He pulled Syneda into his arms giving her a good-bye kiss that was destined to be the longest on record.

Chapter 12

Clayton Madaris's slow-paced walk and relaxed smile reflected an extremely happy man. As far as he was concerned he was on top of the world. What man wouldn't be when he had found the woman of his dreams?

He could barely contain himself as he walked through the doors of the Remington Oil Building. The only thing that would make him any happier, he thought as he scribbled his name on the clipboard the security guard had handed to him, was for him and Syneda to have a Christmas wedding. But first he would have to make sure the future bride had fallen in love with him by then.

He shook his head, grinning. Very few people would believe that he, a man who'd always avoided any serious involvements, would be contemplating something like marriage. At times it was hard for him to believe, and he would find himself spending a very long time in the shower doing some serious thinking.

Then all it would take was for him to remember some of the reasons why he had fallen in love with Syneda to bring him back to reality. From the start, although they'd been at odds with each other, there had always been very good open communication between them. He liked the fact she was a very up-front person. She didn't believe in sugarcoating anything. And the truth of the matter was that he'd found her combustible nature absolutely irresistible. He still did.

Before, when he'd dated a lot of women, he'd had to date quite a number of them to obtain all the qualities he had found in the one he considered as the ideal woman: Syneda.

His thoughts drifted to the weekend they had spent in New Orleans a few weeks ago. He had been to New Orleans several times before, but never had he enjoyed the city the way he had done with her. They had wined and dined in the French Quarter, had been entertained at a number of hot spots, and had made love in the heat of the night in their hotel room. He had fallen even more hopelessly, madly and passionately in love with her.

As Clayton stepped on the elevator, his thoughts turned to his brothers. Although they were now happily married to the women they loved, he could remember them going through some really tough times in the name of love. In fact, he of all people had had to intervene to keep them from making a complete mess of things. If it hadn't been for him, Justin would not have had the good sense to accept Lorren as his fate, and poor, pitiful Dex would still be on the "pain and suffering list," working himself to death at Madaris Explorations trying to forget Caitlin.

Clayton was glad he wasn't going through any changes over a woman like his two brothers had. Things were progressing smoothly between him and Syneda. For most people, love didn't grow in a short time as it had done with him. That was the reason why he would give Syneda a little bit more time before springing his true feelings on her. By then, hopefully, she would be in love with him so much that she would agree to marry him right away. Nothing would please him more than coming home to her each and every night.

When the elevator stopped on the executive floor, he got off, checking his watch. He was right on time for his meeting with the president and CEO of Remington Oil, S. T. Remington.

He had gotten the opportunity to work closely with Mr. Remington last year when Dex's wife, Caitlin, owned a piece of land that Remington Oil had been interested in buying. Caitlin hadn't wanted to sell the property and instead she had leased it to Remington Oil. He had represented Caitlin as her attorney in the contract negotiations.

S. T. Remington, Clayton had soon discovered, was a sharp but fair businessman. He had taken an immediate liking to the man whose family's blue-blooded lineage could be traced all the way back to Texas's beginning when his great-great-great-grandfather rode alongside Sam Houston. Although Remington had been born to wealth and was considered to be a private person, he was caring and concerned for all aspects of human life. That was evident in his generous contributions to numerous charities.

"Good morning, Mr. Madaris," the secretary greeted. "Mr. Remington is expecting you. You can go right in."

"Thanks." Clayton entered the plush office and watched as the tall, distinguished-looking gentleman in his late forties stood to greet him.

"Madaris, how are you?" S. T. Remington said heartily, extending his hand to Clayton.

"Fine," Clayton responded, accepting the man's warm handshake. "And thanks for seeing me on such short notice. I hope it wasn't a problem."

"None whatsoever," the elder man said, gesturing toward the chair next to his large oak desk. "You mentioned something about a job referral."

"Yes," Clayton said, taking the seat.

"You didn't have to have a special meeting with me to refer someone for employment with Remington Oil. Stephen James is the manager of my Human Resources Department. He's always looking for energetic, career-minded individuals to bring on as part of our management team."

"Yes, but I thought it best to talk with you first. It's only fair that you know that if your company determines the person I want to refer is suitable for employment, and decides to hire him, there may be possible repercussions."

Remington lifted a brow. "I don't understand."

"Do you know John Drayton?"

"The John Drayton of Drayton Industries?" At Clayton's nod he said, "Yes, but not personally. Why?"

Clayton told Mr. Remington about the problems Larry Morgan was having finding employment because of John Drayton. He was careful to leave out confidential information or to reveal his source for the information he was sharing. "So, as you can see, no one will hire him."

"Is Morgan a friend of yours?"

"No, in fact, I've never met him and he knows nothing of me, and I prefer to keep it that way. I know of him and the problems he's having through an acquaintance whose identify I prefer not disclosing. It's a rather complicated story."

Remington nodded. "You don't know him, yet you want to recommend that we hire him?"

"I've checked into his employment history. It's apparent he's an excellent employee. The only reason he was released from his former job, and the reason he can't find employment now is because of John Drayton."

Remington smiled. "If Larry Morgan is as good as you say he is, then there's no reason we can't call him in for an interview. And if he meets all of our qualifications, we will consider him for employment with us."

"Thanks."

"You're welcome, and I think it's commendable that you're taking such an interest in someone you really don't know."

Clayton smiled. "I have my reasons."

"I'm sure you do. And don't worry about John Drayton. If he wants to start something with Remington Oil let him. I'm just the person to finish it for him."

Clayton laughed as he stood. He liked Remington's grit. It reminded him of someone else he knew. The beautiful, feisty woman he was in love with. "Thanks. I appreciate it."

Go ahead and be daring, a devilish little voice droned in Syneda's ear.

Don't even think it, the voice of reason shot back, *Clayton may not like it....*

Syneda closed the book with a thump. Why was she beginning to care what Clayton might or might not like? Why was she remembering that he'd once said he liked the way she wore her hair?

"Sorry about running off like that," Deborah, her hairdresser, said, coming back to her. "But Ms. Jones claimed the relaxer was stinging, and God knows she can't afford to lose another strand of hair."

Syneda smiled. She liked Deborah and had been coming to this hair salon for over five years. The hairstylist was good at what she did.

"Did you see a style in that book you liked? You're long overdue for a new look," Deborah said, working quickly and efficiently as she applied the conditioner to Syneda's hair.

Syneda thought for a moment, then said, "Yeah, I saw a couple that I liked."

"Well?"

"Well, what?"

"You haven't done anything drastic to your hair since you went from curly to straight over a year ago. How about a short cut? I think it'll look good on you."

Syneda frowned. "Why do you want to cut my hair? Is this one of your scissor-happy days? I saw what you did to Carla Frazier's head."

Deborah shrugged as she continued to work the conditioner into Syneda's hair. "Carla got just what she asked for. She wanted her hair cut off like that. And you have to admit, she looks good with short hair. Some people wear short hair well, some do not. That's why I'm thankful for such a thing as weaved hair."

Syneda grinned. She could always count on Deborah to lighten her mood. Although the woman could be a chatterbox at times, she enjoyed coming to the full-service salon.

"Well, are you gonna get a cut?"

"Not this time. Let me think about it some more."

After getting home and settling in for the night, Syneda thought back to her conversation with Deborah and her decision not to make any drastic changes to her hair. For the first time in her life, she had taken into account what a man might or might not like about her. Specifically, she had not gotten her hair cut because she had cared how Clayton would feel about it. When she'd changed from the curly look to the straight look last year, he had complimented her several times about her hair and had told her how much he'd liked it.

She frowned, not liking the way her thoughts were going. In fact, she hadn't liked the way her thoughts had been going for quite some time. All she had to do, at anytime and at anyplace, was to close her eyes to pick out one of several memorable moments she and Clayton had shared over the past couple of months. Even now, she could clearly remember their weekend together in New Orleans, especially that first night.

Vivid memories of their room, a romantic suite, filled her thoughts. It had been large and spacious with a king-size bed. The room had been cool, supported by the air-conditioning that had provided relief from the already hot "Nawlins" afternoon. But even the air conditioner had not withstood the powerful heat that began surging to unbearable degrees once Clayton had closed the room door, locking them inside.

He had ordered room service and the food had been delicious. But it was the things that had happened after the meal that still had her nearly groaning aloud at the memory. It was when he had scooped her up into his arms and had taken her into the bedroom, making beautiful, passionate love to her.

The ringing of the phone startled Syneda so much that she jumped. A part of her became angry at the intrusion. She picked up the phone.

"Yes?"

"Hmm, I like a woman who says yes right off the bat," a husky masculine voice said.

Syneda smiled as she stretched across her bed. "I was just thinking about you."

Clayton smiled. "Were you? Good thoughts I hope."

"The best."

"Enlighten me. And be specific," he said mildly.

Syneda closed her eyes and blushed as her mind did a sort of instant mental replay. However, this time it zeroed in on more things in detail. She could see herself, how she had been that night in New Orleans, naked, languorous, in his arms. She could feel the silk bedsheet against her bare back and the weight of his body, hard as a rock, upon hers. She could conjure up the taste of him in her mouth as he kissed her senseless.

"Syneda?"

"Hmm?" She refused to open her eyes just yet. She could visualize more that way.

"You're moaning into the phone, baby."

Syneda's eyes snapped open. "I'm not."

"Yes, you were. Did you enjoy our time together in New Orleans?"

"Oh, yes. Tremendously," she whispered.

"How would you like to meet me again next weekend?"

Syneda felt her mouth arrange itself into a smile. "Where?"

"Atlanta."

"Atlanta? What's happening in Atlanta?"

"We'll be what's happening. How about it?"

Syneda began to tremble at the thought of being with Clayton again. It had already been two weeks since they had last been together. A part of her wanted to say yes, just name the place and the time, and I'll be there. But then another part of her, the one that had always kept her levelheaded where men were concerned, wanted her to call time-out and take time to examine the feelings and changes slowly taking place within her.

She heaved a sigh, rolled onto her stomach and buried her face into the pillow.

"Hello? Syneda? Are you still there?"

"Yeah, I'm still here."

"Well, then, what about it?"

Syneda sighed. The "I don't need a man" part of her was tempted to tell him no, but the "I enjoy being with Clayton Madaris" part of her overruled.

"Yes, Clayton. I'll meet you in Atlanta."

"Celeste?" Braxter whispered.

"Hmm?" she answered, her voice sleepy.

"Do you want to spend the night?"

She opened her eyes and smiled up at him. "Since it's past midnight and I'm still in your bed, I think that's not a bad idea."

Braxter grinned. They had just finished making love. She was everything he wanted in a woman and more. "I'm going to have to leave town for a while."

She came awake and sat up in bed. "Why?"

He got out of the bed and stretched. "Reelection time. It's time for the senator to take his campaign on the road, back to his home state of Texas, and I'll be going with him."

Celeste frowned. She was clearly not happy with this news. She had spent one month with Braxter already, and had not been able to find out anything of particular interest about his employer. As far as Braxter Montgomery was concerned, Senator Lansing walked on water. The only thing she had stumbled on was the fact that around the same time of month in May of each year, Senator Lansing cleared his calendar for a few days and went back to Texas. She took a deep breath. There could be a number of reasons for him doing that. She would be the first to admit that everyone needed to get away by themselves once in a while.

"Does that mean you're breaking things off between us?" she asked poutily, not really caring one way or another. The person who had hired her had paid her in full up-front. And although she didn't have anything against Braxter personally, in fact, she thought that under different circumstances, she could have found herself very much attracted to him. He was indeed handsome and was definitely a terrific lover. But she had learned a long time ago not to mix business with pleasure.

"Breaking things off?" Braxter asked, laughing. "Of course not. I'll be coming home most weekends."

He got back in the bed and pulled her into his arms. "I've got an idea. How would you like to be my guest at the senator's kickoff campaign party three weeks from now? A friend of his, this wealthy cattleman named Jacob Madaris, is giving a huge party for the senator at his ranch. The guest list is pretty impressive."

Celeste arched a brow, feigning disinterest by yawning. "Really? How impressive?"

He smiled. "Not that I think you'll really be interested," he teased. "But I know for a fact that Sterling Hamilton is coming."

She bolted out of his arm. "Sterling Hamilton! The actor Sterling Hamilton?"

Braxter laughed, pulling her back to him. "Yes, but before you get overly excited, you may as well know that Diamond Swain is coming, too."

"Oh," Celeste said disappointedly. Anyone who kept up with the lifestyles of the rich and famous knew that Sterling Hamilton and the leading lady in most of his movies, Diamond Swain, were an item.

"Disappointed?"

"Crushed is more like it."

Braxter smiled. "Does that mean you don't want to be my guest at the party?"

She smiled up at him. "I said I was crushed, not crazy. Of course I'll attend the party with you."

She snuggled closer to him, smiling, pleased with the recent turn of events.

Chapter 13

Clayton glanced around the room, taking in the well-dressed, affluent people in their expensive suits and gowns. Around him the crowd swirled happily amid the soft, jazzy sound of Kenny G as he entertained a group on the other side of the huge room. As usual, Clayton thought, his uncle had spared no expense for his good friend, Senator Lansing.

He stopped at a table laden with food and helped himself to a little cracker covered with rich, dark caviar. Being at a party was the last thing he wanted. Especially a party where Syneda would be in attendance and the two of them would pretend to be only friends. The thought of seeing her again inflamed him with desire.

He hadn't seen her since their romantic rendezvous in Atlanta three weeks ago. Because of the important court appeal she'd been working on, and a couple of business trips he'd taken to California, they had not been able to hook up. Although they had talked frequently on the phone, their conversations had been short and as far as he was concerned, unfulfilling.

Clayton searched the crowded room with a steady, sweeping glance, recognizing various members of his family, business associates, friends, as well as a number of unfamiliar faces. He continued to scan the room for the one person he wanted to see. Syneda.

A group of people shifted from the crowd surrounding Kenny G, and for a moment he had a clear view across the room. And then he saw her.

She was dancing with Lloyd Jones. Clayton frowned. Although he didn't know Jones personally, he knew of him. He knew that the man was in his early thirties, single and considered by some to be a brilliant neurosurgeon.

"Don't look now, man, but you're glaring. And for some reason jealousy doesn't become you," a familiar voice said in a deep Texan drawl at his shoulder.

Clayton turned to face his brother Justin. "Am I that obvious?" he asked drily.

Justin took a sip of his wine. "Right now only to me because I know a little more than most. But if you keep it up, everyone in this room will know, especially Lloyd Jones. Do me a favor and behave yourself. I don't want to repair any broken bones tonight."

Clayton shrugged. "You won't have to," he said smoothly. "I promised Syneda that I would not give anything away."

"That should be interesting."

"If it was left up to me, everyone would know."

Justin chuckled when he saw Clayton's annoyed features. "I gathered as much." He took another sip of wine. "Give her time, Clayton. Things will work out."

"That's what I keep telling myself."

Justin stared long and hard at his brother. An amused grin touched his features. "You really have it bad, don't you?"

"No worse than you had it for Lorren," Clayton shot back, his eyes narrowing.

"I think there's a major difference here, though," Justin said, smiling, thinking of his wife and the love affair they'd shared before they had married.

"What?" Clayton asked, reaching for another cracker from the table.

"I was in love with Lorren. My intentions were honorable."

Clayton put a hand on the sleeve of his brother's jacket, claiming his full attention. "So are mine. I'm in love with Syneda."

Justin stared at him, openmouthed. "Impossible. You would never allow yourself to fall in love," he finally managed to say.

"Then that should say a lot for Syneda's abilities, shouldn't it?"

Recovering from the initial shock, Justin eyed his brother thoughtfully, not knowing what else to say. A grin spread across his face. "Care to hang with me for a while?"

"Where's Lorren?"

"She's upstairs. She wanted to get the kids tucked in bed before coming down. Well, well, well, take a look at who just walked in."

It took all Clayton's strength to tear his gaze from Syneda and Lloyd Jones to the person who had apparently caught Justin's attention.

"It's cousin Felicia Laverne. And take a look at her outfit."

Clayton's lips lifted in an amused smile. His attractive cousin was dressed in a silk leopard jumpsuit with matching short leopard boots and carrying a leopard clutch bag. Her face lit up in a warm smile when she saw them. She began walking their way.

"Justin, Clayton. It's good seeing you guys," she said, giving them both a quick peck on the cheek. She glanced around the room. "Where's Dex?"

"He's around here someplace," Justin answered, scanning her from head to toe. "What's with this outfit?"

Her eyes darkened. "My man's been acting like a dog so I've decided to begin acting like a cat. I'm on the prowl tonight and would love to purr to any man for attention. So you better warn your rich friends to stay away from me. You know how much I like men with money."

Justin chuckled. "None of my friends can afford you. After husband number two, maybe you should consider marrying a poor man."

"Not on your life. I'm sure there's some man out there with both honey and money."

Clayton shook his head. He and Felicia were first cousins and had been born in the same year. Their grandmother said the moon must have been out of orbit that year, given his womanizing ways and Felicia's inability to keep a husband.

"Well, I'll see you guys later. I understand there are a lot of men here tonight, and I want to check them out."

"Yeah, see ya," Clayton said, turning his attention back to Syneda. Sometime during his conversation with Felicia, the dance had come to an end, and Syneda now stood across the room talking to his aunt Delores. He sighed. At least Jones wasn't hanging around.

Clayton knew there was no way Syneda hadn't seen him, so why hadn't she come over and at least said hello? There would have been nothing conspicuous with her doing that. So why was she avoiding him?

Delores Brooks's happy chattering seemed to recede into the distance as Syneda's eyes drifted to Clayton. She had known the exact moment he had entered the room. Although the room was crowded, she had known.

Like a soft caress, his mere presence had touched her even while she had danced in the arms of another man. She frowned, getting annoyed with herself. Long ago she had made up her mind that getting deeply involved with a man was a personal complication she didn't want or need in her life.

But now, in a way she could not define, she was getting deeply involved with Clayton. And he was becoming a complication. She had picked up on that fact weeks ago, right after their trip to New Orleans. But she had convinced herself that he was the one man she could handle. She had believed an intimate relationship with him would not mean losing control over her emotions. After all, all she'd wanted to share with him was passion, and the man certainly was full of that.

But somewhere, somehow, for a little while, she had allowed herself to forget the promises she had made to herself, her goals, and her own personal established agenda. If she wasn't careful, she would forget the reasons she could never trust love. She had known firsthand the pain of believing that someone loved you and then being disappointed.

She met Clayton's glance across the room. The look in his eyes was heated, seductive, arousing. Memories of their weekend in Atlanta flowed between them and she read the message in his eyes. He had said nothing, he hadn't even bothered to move his lips. But then, he didn't really need to say anything. The message he was sending to her was plain and clear. He wanted her and sometime later tonight, family or no family, he intended to have her.

Shakily, Syneda took a deep breath. Even when she wanted to struggle against the sensual pull he had on her mind and senses, she couldn't. And she knew that deep down, tonight of all nights, she wouldn't. She wanted him, too.

Only when Clayton's aunt touched her arm to regain her attention did she drop her eyes from his. When she looked back in his direction moments later, he was gone.

I need to start mingling more, Clayton thought, when Justin disappeared after being beeped by one of his patients.

Clayton moved in the direction of the bar that had been set up. Frustrations were beginning to overwhelm him. He wanted to take Syneda and go someplace private, where the two of them could be alone. As usual, she looked good. His eyes had completely surveyed her sleek teal-colored gown. He had long ago accepted the fact that anything Syneda wore, she wore well, including his dress shirt.

Tonight her gown was totally alluring. The silky material fitted fluidly over her body, emphasizing her shapely figure. He not only wanted to hold her in his arms, but wanted to touch those familiar places that only a lover would be allowed to touch.

Glancing around, he noticed his sister and brother-in-law had just arrived. He walked over to them. "Good evening, folks."

"What's so good about it?" Traci answered with a pout on her lips.

Clayton met his brother-in-law's gaze and detected his well-hidden grin. He couldn't help but like Daniel Green, the man who had taken his sister off his parents' hands nearly ten years ago. Any man who could handle Letracia Madaris Green's raving-mad buying sprees definitely rose a notch in his eyes.

Everyone in the family knew that Traci lived to spend money and that the shopping malls were her second home. "Shop till you drop" was her motto in life. Clayton smiled. No doubt Traci's state of unhappiness had nothing to do with PMS. Daniel must have pulled the plug on her buying power.

"Have Mom and Dad arrived yet?" Traci asked, interrupting Clayton's thoughts.

Clayton's smile widened. He wondered why she'd be looking for their parents. She definitely wouldn't get any pity from them. They were probably still paying for the things she had charged while in college. "Yeah, they're here someplace."

Traci walked off. And without having the decency to excuse herself, Clayton thought. "I take it she's not a happy camper tonight," he said to Daniel.

Daniel chuckled as he nodded. "That's putting it mildly. But she'll get over it."

"Yeah, but I'd hate to be at your house while she's in the process of doing so. Should I guess why she's ticked off?" Clayton asked, leaning against a column post. His arms were folded across his chest as he eyed Daniel with amusement.

"You think it's funny, don't you, Clayton?"

"Hell, yeah, I think it's funny because Justin, Dex and I tried to warn you, but you wouldn't listen to us."

Daniel laughed, remembering. "Being in love makes you do foolish things. But you'll be spared ever finding that out."

Clayton lifted a brow. "Why do you say that?"

"Because you're one of those men who'll never fall in love."

If only you knew, Clayton thought.

"You like hit-and-run relationships."

Not anymore, Clayton wanted to say.

"And speaking of relationships, Clayton, I may as well warn you that, thanks to Traci, the buzz word is that there may be a special woman in your life."

That got Clayton's immediate attention. He began wondering if somehow he had given something away for Traci to pick up on. That couldn't have been possible since he hadn't seen her a lot lately. "What gave her that idea?"

"I don't know, but it sounds crazy, doesn't it? Everyone knows you don't believe in getting serious about a woman."

"What makes Traci think otherwise?"

"I overheard a conversation she was having with Kattie. They're trying to figure out what's going on with you, and why you're going out of town so much. They're curious about all of your weekend trips—especially since you're being so secretive. No one knows where you go or who you're seeing. It's driving them nuts."

"Serves them right for trying to get into my business." He looked thoughtfully at Daniel. "And I guess they have their own ideas of just who the woman is."

Daniel laughed. "Yep. They figure it's someone you met while attending that attorneys' conference some months back."

"Is that a fact?" Clayton said, slightly annoyed but relieved. He grabbed a glass of wine off a passing waiter's tray and took a sip. At least his two nosy sisters hadn't put two and two together and come up with him and Syneda.

"Do me a favor, Daniel."

"What?"

"Put a muzzle on your wife's mouth, and I'll have a talk with Raymond about putting one on Kattie's."

Clayton strolled off, hearing his brother-in-law's laughter follow him. He headed back to the main area of the house, intent on at least saying a few words to the honoree. While making his way to the other side, he noticed a deep silence spread across the room. He glanced toward the door and understood. The actor,

Sterling Hamilton, had arrived, and just like the rumor mill had predicted, the very beautiful woman who appeared as his leading lady in a number of his films, Diamond Swain, was with him.

Clayton chuckled. Once again Hamilton and Swain's appearance together would start tongues wagging. There were already reports circulating around the country that the two of them were secretly married. He knew if that was true, it would cause the heartbreak of quite a few women.

Clayton shook his head. He had enough to deal with regarding the woman in his life. He didn't have time to speculate about the woman who was supposed to be in Sterling Hamilton's.

Senator Lansing was pleased with the turnout. As usual, Jake Madaris had outdone himself. He glanced around the room and caught Braxter Montgomery's eye and smiled at him and the lovely young lady he was with. He had been introduced to her earlier. He was glad Braxter had finally gotten interested in someone. He thought the young man worked a tad too hard at times.

The senator's smile faded when, for the second time that night, he noticed the attractive young woman in a teal-colored gown making her way around the crowded room. He couldn't put his finger on it but there was something oddly familiar about her. There was something about her that captured his attention, not in a sexual way, but in a way he couldn't explain. It had something to do with her smile, her mannerisms, and the way she tilted her head when talking to someone.

He continued to regard her with interest. She reminded him of someone. But who?

Only a man as close to the senator as Braxter could have picked up on the senator's troubled expression, even from across a crowded room. "Celeste, please excuse me for a second."

He walked over to the senator. "Sir? Is something wrong?"

"I don't know," Senator Lansing said, his words barely a thread of a sound. He continued looking at the young woman across the room. "That woman, the one in the teal-colored gown. Do you know her?"

Braxter followed the senator's gaze. "Not personally, but I know who she is. She's Lorren Madaris's best friend."

"Lorren Madaris? Justin Madaris's wife?"

"Yes."

"What's her name?"

"Syneda. Syneda Walters."

Shakily the senator reached out to steady himself with a hand on the edge of an oak table. "Did you say Wal…Walters?"

Braxton frowned, clearly worried by the shocked expression on the senator's face. "Yes, Walters. Sir? Are you all right?"

"I need to get out of here for a moment, Braxter. I'm going up to my room for a while. Please make the necessary excuses."

Before Braxter could respond, Senator Lansing turned and went up the stairs.

Celeste stood on the other side of the room, grateful she had taken a lip reading class as an elective in college. She took a quick glance at the woman who had made the senator lose some of his color.

The attractive woman appeared to be around her age. Was she someone with whom the senator had once had an affair? Well, whoever she was, the sight of her had shaken up the old man. She smiled. She would have to find out the woman's name, and more about her. There might be something about the senator's reaction to the woman that was worth checking into.

Chapter 14

Clayton glanced around the crowded room, his gaze seeking out Syneda. He saw her dancing again, this time it was with his uncle Jake.

He relaxed, not concerned about competition from his uncle, who was the youngest of the seven Madaris brothers. Although Jacob Madaris was still a strikingly handsome man at the age of forty-four, everyone knew Jake was married to the Whispering Pines ranch. While in his early twenties, he'd married a woman who had left him after less than a year. She had been a city girl who had hated the rural life Jake loved.

"Where have you been?"

Clayton turned toward the sound of the familiar voice, and came face-to-face with his brother Dex. "I've been around."

Dex Madaris shook his head. "No, I don't mean tonight. I mean where have you been for the past couple of weeks? Caitlin and I haven't seen you since that weekend you kept Jordan for us. And you've been missing Sunday dinners at Mom's. It's not like you to pass up a free meal." Dex flashed him a grin. "Although with you not being there, there's more food to go around."

"Funny, Dex. Real funny. You're turning into a regular comedian," Clayton said, grabbing a handful of mixed nuts from the table.

"So, where have you been?"

Clayton frowned slightly. "Why is it that everyone wants to get in my business?"

Dex smiled. "Because you're usually in everyone else's."

"You can't deny that, Clayton," Justin said, coming to join them.

Clayton stopped munching for a moment and looked at the two brothers he loved and respected. But at the moment they were annoying. "Your opinions of me are touching," he said drily.

Before the brothers could respond, an old acquaintance of Justin's walked up. Introductions were made and conversations began. But Clayton tuned out all the talk around him, although he forced a smile and nodded his head occasionally. His real interest was in the woman across the room. The dance had ended and she stood talking to Caitlin, Lorren and Corinthians Avery, a woman who was the head geologist for Remington Oil.

"I see she has caught your interest, as well."

"Who?" Clayton asked the man standing beside him who had been engaged in a conversation with Justin and Dex moments earlier.

"The woman in the teal gown. She's gorgeous. I've had my eyes on her all night."

Clayton tried to keep his features expressionless. "Really?" He searched his memory for the name of the man Justin had introduced him to just minutes ago. Ahh, yes, his name was Bernard Wilson, and according to Justin he owned a large pharmaceutical company in Waco.

Clayton balled his fists at his side. A part of him wanted to smash the man's face for even noticing Syneda.

"So what do you think of her?" Bernard Wilson asked.

On a long breath, Clayton fought back the anger consuming

him. As nonchalantly as he could, he simply said, "She looks all right."

Bernard Wilson raised a brow. "I think she looks better than all right. I love the color of her hair, and the color of her eyes is so sexy. And look at the size of her waistline. I just love slender, well-built women." He then turned to Justin. "I understand she's a good friend of your wife, Justin. You'll have to introduce us."

Justin flicked a quick glance at Clayton, then back to Bernard and said, "Sure."

Clayton looked at his brother in disbelief, ignoring Justin's "what else could I say" expression. He then decided to take matters into his owns hands. If Wilson thought he was interested in Syneda, he may as well get disinterested.

"You like slender, well-built women, huh? Then you may want to think twice about asking Justin for an introduction."

Bernard Wilson frowned in confusion. "Why?"

"Because less than six months ago, Syneda was almost a hundred pounds heavier."

Dex, who had been quietly listening, and who had just taken a sip of wine, nearly choked when he heard Clayton's blatant lie. He coughed a few times to clear his throat.

Clayton gave Dex a few whacks on the back. "You shouldn't drink your wine so fast, Dex," he said calmly, as Dex tried to regain his composure.

"She used to weigh over a hundred pounds more?" Bernard asked incredulously.

So as not to get caught in the middle of Clayton's lie, Justin simply shrugged and said nothing.

When Dex started to deny it, the look Clayton gave him clearly said he'd better keep his mouth shut.

"Yes, it's hard to believe, isn't it," Clayton answered smoothly. "I understand she went on one of those quick-weight-loss programs. She was determined to get in that particular dress tonight. And you're right, she does look good in it. But you know what they say."

"What?" Bernard, Justin and Dex all asked simultaneously.

Bernard asked out of curiosity. Justin asked because he was eager to see just how far Clayton would go with this farce. And Dex asked because he was clearly in the dark and didn't have a clue as to what was going on. He cast Justin a curious glance, and all he got was a shrug for an answer.

"They say it never stays off when you get rid of it that fast. In a few months she'll be looking like her old self again. Plump."

Justin thought Clayton had gone a little bit too far and decided to step in. "There's more to a person than looks, Clayton."

"Yeah," Dex agreed, still clearly lost.

"I agree. And I'm sure Syneda feels her colored eye contacts will—"

"Colored eye contacts?" Dex asked, not believing what he was hearing. Clayton knew green was Syneda's real eye color.

"But I thought they were hers," Bernard said, his frown deepening.

"They are," Clayton answered him. "She bought them didn't she?"

Dex took a huge gulp of Jack Daniels from the glass he held in his hand. Justin suddenly became preoccupied with brushing off a nonexistent speck of lint from his suit.

"And her hair color?" Bernard asked drily. His interest in Syneda was clearly fading.

"From a bottle." Seeing Bernard's sullen expression Clayton added, "With all the enhancements available to women these days, you never know what's real and what's not."

Bernard nodded. "Thanks for leveling with me, man."

Clayton smiled. "Hey, don't mention it. We players have to stick together." He put his arm around Bernard's shoulder. "Don't look so down. I think there's a woman here tonight that's probably just what you're looking for. And I do believe you're just her type."

Bernard's mood brightened some. "Really? Where?"

"She's around here someplace. Her name is Felicia Laverne Evans. You'll know her when you see her. She's dressed in a leopard outfit."

Bernard smiled. "Hey, thanks, you're an all right guy." He turned to Justin. "Forget about that introduction, Justin. I'll see you guys later." Then he walked off.

"I don't know why you did what you just did," Dex said, glaring at his brother. "And maybe it's best that I don't know. All I have to say is that when Syneda finds out about those lies you just told Wilson, she's gonna give you hell."

Clayton smiled and calmly resumed eating his nuts. "Won't be the first time she's given me hell about something."

"No man should look that good," Kattie Madaris Barnes said to the other women standing with her. They were all staring at the man across the room, Sterling Hamilton. He and Diamond Swain were talking to Oprah.

"Don't forget you're a married woman," Lorren Madaris teased.

"I'm married, but I'm not blind," Kattie replied, grinning.

"I heard he and Diamond Swain are secretly married," Caitlin Madaris said.

"She's not wearing a ring. I've already checked that out," Traci replied.

Syneda hid her smile as she reached for a cracker covered with cheese. She had to admit Sterling Hamilton was indeed a very handsome man. But then, so was Clayton, she thought to herself. She could have pointed that out to Traci and Kattie, but they might get curious as to why she even thought so. As Clayton's sisters, they wouldn't see their brother through the eyes of another woman.

She glanced across the room where Clayton, Dex and Justin were involved in what appeared to be a deep conversation. In her opinion, and she knew Lorren and Caitlin would agree with her, the three Madaris brothers were three *fine* men. They gave true meaning to the words tall, dark and handsome. And although they were different in personality and temperament, she didn't know any men more loving, considerate and loyal to their families.

She glanced at her watch. It was getting late. She had hoped to have gotten the opportunity to meet Senator Lansing by now.

During most of the evening, he'd been constantly surrounded by people, and now she didn't see him anywhere.

"Syneda, are you all right? You haven't had much to say all night," Kattie said with concern in her voice.

Syneda smiled. "I'm fine, just kind of tired. I've been keeping late nights working on a case I'm appealing. I think I'll turn in early tonight."

"All of us should turn in early. Especially you two," Traci said to Lorren and Caitlin. "Although it's been a long time since I was pregnant, the one thing I do remember is needing plenty of rest." She grinned. "And don't forget Gramma Madaris expects all of us in church tomorrow, bright and early, beginning with Sunday school."

"Sunday school starts at nine o'clock," Kattie said. "Boy, is she asking for a lot."

Traci smiled. "I know, but with tomorrow being her birthday, I guess she feels she can ask her children, grandchildren and great-grands for anything."

"Where will her birthday party be held?" Syneda asked.

"It will be right after the services tomorrow in the church dining room. Gramma Madaris has been a member of that church for over sixty years. In fact, she and Grampa got married there when she was seventeen."

"Good evening, ladies," Justin said, coming over to join the group with Dex and Clayton with him. "I think you ladies are the most gorgeous ones here tonight. Don't you agree, Dex?" he asked, placing a soft kiss on Lorren's lips.

"Absolutely," Dex said, smiling. His arms went around Caitlin protectively, gently pulling her against him. "All Madaris women are beautiful, and they're all Madaris women."

Syneda smiled. It was on the tip of her tongue to remind Dex she wasn't a Madaris but thought better of it. Like everyone else, Dex considered her as part of the family.

She liked Justin and Dex. Justin had been there for Lorren when she had needed someone to help her through a difficult time in her life. And for that reason he was very special to her. With Dex, there was such tenderness in him, as well as stubbornness and pride. He was the type of man who protected his own. Last year Caitlin's life had been threatened, and Dex had made it clear that no one messed with his wife unless they were willing to face his wrath.

Her gaze went to Clayton. He took another sip of his wine, watching her with dark eyes. A part of her came to life under his steady gaze. It was silently reaching out to her, touching her, making her want him and bringing forth memories she could never forget. Not being able to handle his gaze any longer, she looked down.

"Clayton, you've been scarce lately. I've heard you've been taking quite a few trips out of town. Any reason why?" Kattie asked, her dark eyes twinkling.

Clayton's eyes narrowed. His gaze went first to Kattie and then to Traci. "What I do does not concern the two of you. Remember that."

Syneda's stomach was in knots. *Had Kattie and Traci figured out what was going on between her and Clayton? Did they suspect anything?*

Clayton glanced at Syneda and couldn't help but see the worried look in her eyes. He wanted to go to her and take her in his arms and wipe away that look. He decided to do the next best thing when he heard Freddie Jackson step to the microphone to sing. "Syneda, could I speak to you for a minute?"

"I hope the two of you aren't going to start arguing about anything," Caitlin said, smiling.

"Not tonight. I just want to dance." He knew that dancing provided a socially acceptable way to be close to her. And he desperately needed to hold Syneda in his arms.

Not giving Syneda a chance to refuse, he reached out and took her hand in his and led her to the area where people were dancing. He took her in his arms as Freddie began singing, "You Are My Lady."

Clayton's arm tightened around Syneda and he whispered, "I missed you."

Syneda relaxed in Clayton's arm. She knew the members of his family wouldn't think anything of them dancing together. They usually danced together at all the family functions. His family had commented several times on how well they danced together. "And I missed you, too," she said truthfully.

"I'm coming to your room tonight, Syneda."

She looked into his eyes. "No. Don't. Someone might see you."

"I'll make sure I'm not seen, but I'm coming, so don't ask me not to. I have to come. I want you so much I can barely stand it."

She lifted her face upward seemingly to invite the kiss he wanted to give her, but both knew he couldn't. "Don't tempt me, Syneda."

Syneda smiled and placed her head against his chest. Clayton pulled her closer to him. He wondered if she was listening to the words Freddie was singing. Syneda was indeed "his lady" and he would never let her go. *She is my lady,* he whispered in his heart. *She is everything I need and more.*

Dex was walking across the room to get another glass of punch for Caitlin when he glanced at his brother dancing with Syneda. He stopped walking. He had seen them dance together several times before, but never like this. It seemed they were so in tune to each other. There was such a look of possession in Clayton's eyes as he held Syneda while they danced. And there was another emotion on his face, the same emotion he and Justin wore whenever they looked at their wives.

He had never seen that look on Clayton before. He glanced around the room to see if anyone else had noticed and found that no one else seemed to be paying any attention to them. Then he remembered the scene earlier with Clayton and the lies he had told Bernard Wilson. Now it all made sense.

A smile tilted Dex's lips. He hadn't thought he would ever live to see the day Clayton fell for a woman. And of all people, Syneda. He wondered how the two of them had stopped arguing long enough to connect. His smile widened. Apparently they had enjoyed more than the beaches in Florida.

Clayton saw Dex across the room watching him and Syneda dance. He had seen the exact moment when the truth had hit Dex, and he'd put two and two together. Their eyes met and the shock he'd noticed in Dex's features gradually disappeared. He nodded to his brother and pulled the woman he loved closer into his arms.

Senator Lansing heard the knock on the door. "Yes?"

"It's me, Senator—Braxter."

Senator Lansing opened the door. "Come in, Braxter. I was about to go back downstairs."

Braxter entered then closed the door behind him. He studied the senator curiously. "Are you all right, Senator?"

"I don't know. I may have overreacted just a little. It's just that that young lady reminded me of someone. And then her last name is Walters. It may all be a coincidence." He sighed. "Do me a favor, Braxter, find out everything there is to know about her."

"I'll talk to Jacob Madaris and—"

"No, I don't want to involve Jake in this. I want this handled discreetly. I don't want anyone to know I want information on her. Use an investigative agency, and make sure it's one we can trust. I want the report on my desk as soon as it's received."

Braxter frowned. "This sounds serious, sir."

"It may not be. I may be getting myself worked up for nothing. But until I see the report, I won't know for sure."

Braxter nodded, wondering who the young lady could possibly be and what part she played in the senator's life. Unfortunately, Senator Lansing wasn't saying. He hoped there was nothing he really needed to worry about. There had never been any sort of scandal linked to the senator before, and now was not the time for one to happen.

"I have this friend from college who has an investigative company. I'll talk to him on Monday."

Senator Lansing nodded. "Do you know whether the young lady is still here tonight?"

"I saw her leave just before coming upstairs. She left with some other members of the Madaris family. It's my understanding that Jake's putting them up for the night in the various guest cottages around the ranch. Tomorrow is their grandmother's birthday and they're all staying overnight, including Ms. Walters. She's considered a member of the family."

Senator Lansing nodded, remembering that tomorrow was Jake's mother's birthday. His friend had mentioned that to him months ago. "Then there's a possibility that I'll see her at breakfast before I leave. I'm going to make it my business to meet her."

Chapter 15

Clayton followed the path that led to the guest cottages. The party for Senator Lansing had ended over an hour ago, and after engaging in polite conversation with the senator, he had quickly cut across the wide lawn and headed in the direction where the cottages were.

"Where are you going in such a hurry?"

Clayton turned quickly at the sound of the familiar voice. "Mom? What are you doing out here so late?"

Marilyn Madaris's face split in a smile. "I wanted to check on your grandmother. She was determined to sleep in the old house tonight, and Christy is staying with her."

Clayton nodded. The old house had been the original ranch house. It was the one his grandfather had built for his grandmother and where they had raised their seven sons.

"I was wondering why Christy left the party early," Clayton said.

Marilyn Madaris studied her son. "You never answered my question about where you're going in such a hurry."

"I'm not in a hurry. I thought I'd walk around a bit."

"Oh, I see."

Clayton couldn't help but notice his mother was giving him a strange look. It was one of those looks he recalled all too well from when he was a kid. It was a look that made you think you couldn't fool her about anything, no matter how hard you tried.

"Well, I'll see you in the morning, Mom."

"All right, Clayton, and don't forget your grandmother expects everyone to be in Sunday school in the morning, nine o'clock sharp."

"I won't forget. See ya."

Clayton waited until his mother was no longer in sight before climbing the porch to the row of cottages that sat off in the distance.

Syneda had just closed the book she'd been reading when she heard the faint knock on the door. The rapid beating of her heart, and the heat settling in the pit of her stomach told her just who her late-night visitor was.

Pulling her robe together, she crossed the room. She paused within a few feet of the door, knowing she should send Clayton away. She shouldn't take the risk of his family finding out about them. His sisters had already begun questioning his frequent weekend trips.

She sighed. As much as she knew she should send him away, she couldn't. She'd been under a lot of work-related stress the past couple of weeks, and she needed to lose herself in the kind of passion only Clayton could stir within her. "Yes?" she finally answered.

"It's me and turn off the lights before opening the door."

Syneda darkened the room then opened the door. She looked past Clayton into the velvety darkness that was lighted by only a few stars and a quarter moon.

"No one saw me come here," he said before she had a chance to ask. He stepped inside, closing the door behind him. He turned on a lamp near the door and the room became bathed in soft light.

Syneda studied him. Tonight he appeared as suave as always, but more unyielding and with less control. He reached out and tilted her chin up with his finger, and looked deep into her eyes.

Syneda's senses were piqued by his closeness and the desire she saw in his eyes. She could feel his heat and literally tasted his passion. An essence of electric tension was sharp and vibrated in the air between them. He reached out and took her hand in his, rubbing his thumb over the softness of her palm. The erotic touch sent her over the edge. He had first done that to the palm of her hand in Saint Augustine. And later when they began seeing each other, that had always been his silent code to her that he wanted her in the most intimate way.

Clayton leaned down and his lips brushed lightly over hers. He lifted his head and their eyes met for a brief moment before he was kissing her again, molding her mouth to his, covering it fully.

Syneda shivered and his arm tightened around her. "Are you cold?" he asked, breaking their kiss.

She shook her head. "No, actually I'm hot. I'm burning up…for you."

That was all Clayton needed to hear. He pushed the robe from her shoulders, and soon her short gown followed, falling to the floor by her feet. His eyes roamed slowly over her, and even in the dim light Syneda could see the appreciation shining in their dark depths. Then he lifted her in his arms and carried her into the bedroom and positioned her on the bed.

He stood back and without his eyes leaving hers, he began removing his own clothes. Then he took the time to protect her. When he rejoined her on the bed, he began kissing her again, bestowing feathery kisses to her ear, her temple, the tip of her nose and the corner of her mouth. His kisses then moved down her neck, and from there to her shoulder. "I love tasting you," he whispered huskily.

Syneda held on to him, the force of the passion she felt over-whelming her. It nearly took her breath away. His mouth claimed hers again. Her lips parted under the onslaught of his kiss. Her breath came in short gasps as his fingers touched her intimately, driving her to the point of total madness.

She softly moaned his name when she felt him ease into her, fusing their bodies together as one. They made love in a rhythm as old as time, but still as new as the early-morning dew. With infinite tenderness and passion, he loved her. She bit her lip and tried to control her groans of pleasure, but she didn't have to. Clayton kissed the sounds from her lips. She arched her hips, bringing him deeper inside her. What they were sharing felt so good and so right she thought her body would surely shatter from the force of it.

Moments later she did shatter when she reached the peak of total fulfillment and felt Clayton's body trembling with his own release, the sensations were extremely satisfying. Their pleasure built higher and higher, taking them both over the edge. Clayton's muffled groans combined with her own, as they both tumbled into pure ecstasy.

In a guest cottage not too far away, someone else was receiving a late-night visitor. The actress, Diamond Swain, quickly crossed the room after hearing the knock. She flung open the door and a smile spread across her face.

"Jacob. Oh, Jacob, I missed you so much." She reached for him. Her arms slid around his neck as their mouths met in a fierce, demanding kiss.

With their mouths still intimately joined, Jake Madaris's firm hands wrapped securely around her waist, lifting her higher in his arms and he closed the door with his foot.

"I missed you, too." And then he was kissing her again, more fiercely and more passionately than before.

"Jacob," Diamond murmured against his moist lips moments later. "I hate to tell you this, but we have company."

"Yeah, remember me, cowboy?" a masculine voice asked from across the room.

Jake spared the man a brief glance before gathering Diamond

closer into his arms. "Get lost, Sterling. Go find a woman of your own."

Sterling Hamilton threw back his head and laughed. "Good suggestion, and I would do that in a heartbeat if I hadn't promised a particular stubborn rancher that I would go around pretending his woman was really mine."

Slowly, Jake's eyes narrowed at his friend. "And from what I read in the papers, you're doing a pretty good job. Maybe too good a job. The last rumor I heard said the two of you were secretly married."

Sterling Hamilton smiled. "Jealous?"

"No, just cautious. Just don't forget who she belongs to."

"All right, stop it you two." With a half laugh Diamond pressed her head against Jake's chest. "And, Jacob, leave Sterling alone. He and I are doing a real good job fooling everyone. Besides, how can I be married to Sterling when I'm already married to you?"

Sterling chuckled. "Your wife has a valid point there, Jake. And with that bit of logic, I'm out of here," he said walking to the door.

"I put you up next door," Jake said to Sterling.

"Thanks," he said, turning back to the man who still held Diamond in his arms. He smiled. "Oh, yeah, Jake, your faith in me is touching."

"I wouldn't trust my wife with just anyone, Sterling. Remember that."

Sterling chuckled. "Believe me, I will. And by the way, Garwood sends his best regards. He couldn't make it tonight because he, Kimara and the kids are spending a few weeks at Special K."

"How is Kyle?"

"He's doing fine. Kimara is pregnant."

"Again?"

With a throaty laugh Sterling opened the door. "Yes, again. Some people enjoy making babies." He gave Jake and Diamond a wide smile. "And others just like to practice. I'll see you guys later." He left, closing the door behind him.

Chapter 16

The sun was shining brightly through the bedroom window when Syneda awoke the next morning. She stretched lazily and rolled over only to discover she was alone in the bed. Clayton had left sometime before daybreak.

She sucked in her breath sharply as memories of their night together descended upon her. Each time they came together was better than the last. Their passion for each other had driven them to new heights, making their hunger more demanding, and making their wanting of each other more urgent.

She took a quick glance at the clock on the nightstand near the bed. It was after eight already. There was no way she could make breakfast and still get to Sunday school on time. She would just have to skip breakfast, she thought, quickly getting out of the bed. She just hoped that she and Clayton would not be the only two people missing at breakfast.

* * *

The first thing Clayton noticed when he entered the sanctuary of the Proverbs Baptist Church was the fact he was late. Not only had he missed Sunday school, but the morning service had already begun. The second thing he noticed was that the church was packed with Madarises. They sat shoulder to shoulder, hip to hip, crowded in a church whose air-conditioning, as usual, wasn't working very well.

"Don't worry about the heat in church," his grandmother had told him once as a kid when he had complained about it.

"Why not?" he'd ask her.

She had turned to him and calmly said. "The heat in here isn't so bad. Just remember it's even hotter in hell. Just make sure, Clayton Jerome Madaris, that you never have to find that out."

After hearing that bit of news, he had never complained about the heat in the church again. His grandmother's words that day, as far as he'd been concerned, had been the gospel.

Clayton sat on the last pew, hoping no one would notice his late arrival. No such luck. His grandmother's eyes met his, all the way from the front row corner pew where she sat as the oldest member and official mother of the church. He didn't mistake the frown she gave him.

He shrugged. He had had all intentions of making it to Sunday school, but a night spent making love to Syneda had practically drained him. It had taken all his strength to get out of her bed and make it back to his own before he'd been discovered missing. He didn't like this sneaking around stuff and was determined more than ever to bring it to an end very soon.

He glanced around the church, looking for Syneda. He spotted her a few pews up sitting with Justin, Lorren and their kids. Jordan, Dex and Caitlin's daughter, was sitting in her daddy's lap and waved when she saw him. He smiled at his niece and waved back.

He also noticed his uncle Nolan. Clayton smiled. Nolan Madaris was determined to bring the leisure suit back in style. Clayton shook his head. At the last family reunion, he, Justin, and Dex had purchased an expensive suit for their uncle as a birthday gift. Evidently he hadn't taken the hint.

The choir members were singing out of their souls, and Clayton appreciated the songs that had the entire church electrified. As far as he was concerned, nothing uplifted a church service more than good singing.

"Today I want to welcome the Madaris family to our services," Clayton heard the minister saying as he began his morning sermon. His loud booming voice filled the sanctuary. "And since we have an unusual number of men in the congregation today," the minister continued, "I've selected as my subject, 'When a Man Loves a Woman.'"

This shouldn't put anyone to sleep, Clayton thought, shifting in his seat to get comfortable. Reverend Moss was a person who believed in seizing every opportunity to preach to anyone he felt needed it. Evidently after glancing over some of the Madaris men in the audience and seeing their bored, half-asleep expressions, he had felt there was a need.

"There has been a lot of talk lately about spousal abuse, and I've come to the conclusion that some men have forgotten just how to treat a woman, and that saddens me. I think it's fitting for us to go back and talk about the relationship between a man and a woman as dictated by the Word."

Clayton couldn't help but glance over at his uncle Lee who was notorious for going to sleep in church. He smiled when he saw his uncle's eyes drift closed. Evidently today wouldn't be any different from any other Sunday.

"First and foremost," Reverend Moss went on, "I want to point out that woman was created as a helpmate for man. I suggest all of you go home and *reread* the book of Genesis. Woman came from man. She was not taken from his feet for the man to walk upon her, like some men enjoy doing; nor was she taken from his hand for a man to knock her around."

Clayton grinned when he heard a hearty amen from his aunt Dora. Evidently his uncle Milton got heavy handed at times. He shook his head not seeing how that was possible. Uncle Milton was such a little man, and aunt Dora was a huge woman.

"And women," Reverend Moss continued, glancing around at the females in the congregation, "you were not taken from the man's head to place yourself above him." Several loud amens from the men in the congregation filled the air.

"The woman was taken from the man's side, from his rib, to walk beside him, and to be equal to him. She should be cherished by him, loved, honored and respected. The same thing applies, ladies, for the man."

The minister went further and spoke of several men in the Bible who cherished the women they loved. He told the congregation about Jacob and Rachel, Hosea and Goma, Boaz and Ruth, and a number of others. He wrapped up his sermon by saying, "When a man loves a woman, he places her above all else, and she becomes the most important person in his life. She becomes his queen."

By the time the sermon was over and the choir began singing again, Clayton was sure a good majority of the women in the audience were expecting overnight miracles from their husbands.

After the services were over, everyone was invited to the dining area for some of Mama Madaris's birthday cake and ice cream. The usher who had seated Clayton began leading members and visitors out of the church and toward the back where the dining area was located. When he passed the pew where Syneda sat, he thought about what the minister had said. Syneda was a woman to be loved, cherished, honored and respected. She had become the most important person in his life. And whether she accepted it or not, their destinies were entwined.

Senator Lansing took his seat on the plane and fastened his seat belt. If it wasn't for a meeting with the president back in Washington this afternoon, he would have extended this trip.

He'd been disappointed at breakfast that morning. Syneda Walters, like most of the younger members of the Madaris family, had slept late, skipping breakfast.

He had been tempted to ask Jake about her but hadn't. The possibility that she was Jan's child was a long shot, but he knew he wouldn't be satisfied until he knew for sure.

He would have to be patient and wait for the report Braxter was getting for him.

Celeste waited until Braxter had gone to claim their luggage before taking the cellular phone from her purse. She glanced around the airport terminal and when she no longer saw him she punched in a few numbers.

"Listen, I can't talk long. I want you to check out a woman by the name of Syneda Walters. She's an attorney in New York. There may have been something between her and Senator Lansing at one time."

Celeste frowned. "What do you mean he's a single man and has the right to date women? Well, how would the voters feel if they found out he'd been involved with a woman young enough to be his daughter?" She smiled. "Let me know if you find anything."

Chapter 17

Syneda had taken a break from work and stood at the office window staring down at the busy New York streets. It was hard to believe it was the end of September already. That meant she and Clayton had been seeing each other for almost five months.

Their relationship had fallen into a comfortable pattern for the both of them, proving that a long-distance affair could work in certain situations.

Not to overcrowd the other, they'd set a pattern of seeing each other every other weekend. Clayton either came to New York or they met somewhere in between. The weeks they were apart, he would send flowers, candy, balloons, cute stuffed animals or some other sort of "I'm thinking of you" gift.

Not once had she visited him in Houston for fear of running into members of his family. And although she talked with Lorren regularly, they never discussed her relationship with Clayton. However, Lorren had mentioned some family members were getting more and more curious about his frequent out-of-town weekend trips that he was not discussing with anyone.

Usually whenever Clayton came to town, they spent a quiet evening with dinner at her place or at a restaurant. Once in a while they would order out. Sometimes they rented videos to watch, and at other times they went to a movie or took in a Broadway play or concert. A lot of times they just stayed inside the apartment simply listening to music and talking. Although they still disagreed on a number of things, they were attuned to each other in their perceptions and attitudes of what they considered important.

Syneda drew in a sigh. Their time together seemed so natural and so right. She refused to question the changes that were taking place in her life; positive changes Clayton was responsible for. And she tried not to think about how much he was beginning to mean to her. Things were good between them and she wanted them to stay that way.

She smiled. Clayton was flying in this weekend and she couldn't wait to see him. She hadn't seen him in a couple of weeks and she missed him.

After his shower, Clayton returned to the living room and found Syneda where he'd left her over twenty minutes ago. She was still sitting Indian style on the sofa with a law book in one hand and a legal pad in the other.

Busy writing, she hadn't noticed his presence so he took the opportunity to study her. He always enjoyed watching her this way, intense and absorbed with what she was doing. She had no guards up around him and was totally relaxed with him being there, invading her space, or rather, as he preferred thinking, being a part of it.

When Syneda stopped writing a few minutes later, she arched her back, working out the kinks that had settled there. Then she looked up and saw Clayton watching her.

She released a deep sigh that was from the satisfaction of him being there with her as much as from finally piecing together a new argument for the Jamison appeal. Putting down the book and legal pad, she stood and slowly walked over to him, placing her arms around his neck. She knew the desire in her eyes revealed what she needed and what she wanted. No words had to be spoken. He gathered her up in his arms and carried her to the bedroom.

Sometime later, they lay together in the dark silence of the room, their bodies still joined in the torrid, sweet aftermath of their lovemaking.

"I can't seem to get enough of you," Clayton said, his voice thick and dazed. His heart was beating rapidly in his chest. The emotional force of their lovemaking was beyond anything he had ever experienced.

"I feel the same way," Syneda said drowsily. "You're special, Clayton. You're my friend, as well as my lover."

Clayton kissed her tenderly. "I know it might be a little early to ask, but are you planning to come to the big Madaris Thanksgiving bash?" he asked a few minutes later.

Syneda smiled up at him. "I wouldn't miss it for the world. In fact, your mom called last week just to make sure I was coming. She invited me to stay with them again this year."

"You turned her down, of course."

A bemused frown covered Syneda's features. "Why would I do that?"

Clayton reached down and gently pinched her nose. "Because, sweetheart, when you come to Houston, I want you sleeping in my bed, and not some bed at my mom's house."

Syneda's eyes widened in surprise. "Clayton, you know I can't do that."

"Why not?"

"Because your family doesn't know about us."

"Then it's time they found out."

"No."

"Yes," Clayton countered, rolling to his side, disengaging their bodies but still cradling Syneda in his arms. Over the past few weeks, he had given serious thought to finally telling his family about them. He felt he and Syneda were ready to take that next step. However, by the look on her face, it was obvious she felt otherwise.

"I don't want to treat what we're doing like some cheap backroom affair when it's not. It really makes no sense for us to continue sneaking around like being together is wrong."

"Don't do this to us, Clayton," Syneda said softly, caressing his arm. "You know how I feel about your family finding out about us. You said you understood."

Clayton tilted Syneda's chin up so that their eyes could meet. "Somehow you have this notion that me understanding certain things is the same thing as me endorsing them. You were wrong in believing that about Cassie Drayton and Larry Morgan, and you're wrong in believing that about us. I do understand your fears, but after spending the past months together, I would have hoped I'd helped put some of them to rest. Especially your misconceived notions about my family. They love you. Don't you know that nothing could tarnish that?"

Syneda's chin trembled. "I can't take any chances. Other than Lorren and Mama Nora, your family is the closest thing to a real family that I've ever had." She gazed into the depths of his dark eyes. "I can't risk losing that. Not even for you."

Clayton frowned. "I still don't understand why you think you would. My parents weren't born in the Stone Age, Syneda. They stopped being shocked about anything when they thought they would surprise Kattie at college in New Orleans, and showed up unexpectedly to find that she and Raymond were living together. They would understand us wanting to be together at my place."

"In other words, you want to openly flaunt our affair in front of them," Syneda said coolly.

"No, but I want them to know there's something special between us."

"Don't you understand what that will do? What happens next Thanksgiving when things have ended between us and you're dating someone else, perhaps seriously? How will they feel having both your old girlfriend and your present one there? It wouldn't be fair to place your family in a position of feeling obligated to continue to include me in the family gatherings, and it wouldn't be fair to your new girlfriend, who could possibly become your wife, to know you and I were once lovers. How do you think she would feel?"

"You don't have to worry about anything like that happening," Clayton snapped. "There won't be another woman."

"How can you be so sure of that?"

"Because I love you."

Syneda gasped and stared at him. It seemed her voice left her. "You can't mean that?"

This was not the way he had intended on revealing his feelings to her. "I do mean it," Clayton said curtly. "I love you and want to marry you."

Clayton's words hit Syneda with the force of a ton of bricks. Unable to lie passively in his arms any longer, she jumped out of bed. Glancing around the room, she noticed their clothing tossed carelessly about the room. Spying Clayton's dress shirt thrown on the floor, she automatically reached down and put it on.

Clayton watched Syneda through hooded eyes. She was not handling this the way he had hoped. "I really don't understand why you're trippin'. We've been seeing each other constantly for nearly five months, during which time I haven't seen any other woman. Why can't you believe that I love you?"

Syneda turned to face him. "I believe you may think you do."

"What's that supposed to mean?"

"It means that you see how happy and content Justin and Dex are, and think now is the time to try it for yourself."

"Don't try rationalizing my feelings for you, Syneda. I love you, plain and simple."

Syneda's eyes filled with tears. "No, Madaris. Nothing about love is plain and simple. Have you forgotten I can write a book on the word, or rather the lack of it? Sex is plain and simple, not love. My mom died not knowing the difference. But unfortunately, I had to find out the hard way that a night she spent in passion with some man, which may have been plain and simple love for her, was nothing but plain and simple sex for him."

"I'm not your father, Syneda. I love you and you're wrong. What we've shared these past months has nothing to do with sex. I fell in love with you in Florida. The reason I never told you was because I wanted to give our relationship a chance to grow gradually. You may deny it now, but I believe deep down you love me, too."

"No! I don't love you. I don't love any man. All I wanted to share with you was an affair. You broke the rules, Clayton, and I can't believe you've done that. I thought you'd be different from the others. You were supposed to understand." She turned and ran into the bathroom, slamming the door behind her.

When Syneda came out of the bathroom some time later, Clayton was dressed in a pair of jeans and a cashmere cardigan. His bags were packed.

They faced each other for a moment without speaking, then Clayton was the first to break the unnerving tension of silence. He walked over to stand before her.

"I felt it best that I leave, under the circumstances."

Syneda took a deep breath and lifted her tear-stained face to him. "I agree, you should leave. You're asking too much of me, Clayton. There can't ever be anything beyond what we've been sharing these past months."

"I want more, Syneda. I want an entire lifetime. I want you to be eternally mine."

"I can't give you that. When I accepted your proposal it was with the understanding that either of us could end it at any time. Well, I'm ending it."

"Don't do this to us, Syneda."

"I didn't do anything, you did."

"You think falling in love with you was wrong?"

"I don't want your love, Clayton. I didn't ask for it, and I don't want it."

Clayton flinched. Her rejection of his love hurt, and he felt his heart breaking into a million pieces.

Without saying a word, he picked up his baggage, turned and walked out of the bedroom. It was only after Syneda heard the sound of the door closing behind him that she gave in to her tears.

Celeste slipped out of bed when she heard Braxter singing in the shower. Moving quickly, she picked up the phone and began dialing.

"It's me," she whispered to the person who had picked up the phone. "What have you found out?"

She frowned. "What do you mean you haven't found out anything? It's been almost three weeks," she said angrily, her voice rising a little. "There has to be a connection. I saw the look on the senator's face every time he looked at her. Trust me, he knows Syneda Walters from somewhere, and I want you to find out where. I need to have—"

Celeste stopped talking when she heard noise behind her. She turned around. Braxter was standing in the bathroom doorway, his eyes a fuming dark as they locked with hers. There was no doubt in her mind that he had overheard her conversation. She quickly hung up the phone.

"Braxter, sweetheart, don't look at me that way."

"Who were you talking to on the phone?" he demanded in a loud voice. "And why is Syneda Walters of interest to you?"

Celeste backed up a little when he came toward her. His hand tightened on her arm when she didn't answer him. "I asked you a question, Celeste."

Celeste could feel his anger. "Let go of me, Braxter. I don't have to tell you anything that I don't want to."

Braxter's eyes blazed. "Who the hell are you and just what is your game, lady?"

"I don't have any idea what you're talking about, and I said let me go, or so help me, I'll scream so loud all of the occupants of this apartment building will hear me. I can just see tomorrow's headlines—'Senator Lansing's Top Aide Arrested for Manhandling a Woman in His Apartment.'"

When Braxter released her arm, she turned her face up to him and smiled. "I thought you'd see it my way. You're always mindful of shielding the senator from any negative publicity."

She walked around him and began getting dressed. "It was fun while it lasted, Braxter."

"Who are you working for?"

Celeste heard the pain in his voice and ignored it. "I work for no one."

Braxter walked over to the dresser and grabbed her purse, emptying the contents in the middle of his bed.

"What do you think you're doing!"

Braxter said nothing as he picked up her small appointment book and thumbed through it. He didn't see anything unusual, just little notations about what he assumed to be job-related appointments.

Then he flipped through her driver's license and charge cards, which indicated the name she had given him was her real name. He threw them aside and picked up her checkbook and began flipping through it. His eyes widened at the large amount she had deposited in her personal account a few months ago. It was exactly two days before they had met. He turned around and his eyes met hers.

Celeste trembled. He didn't say anything, but if looks could kill she would be on her way to the morgue. She hesitantly walked over to him and snatched her purse from his hands, placing the contents back inside. She knew she had pushed him to his limit and the best thing to do was to get out of there.

She walked to the door, then stopped before opening it. She slowly turned around and they stared at each other. She saw the pained and angered look on his face and a part of her almost shattered. For the first time, she felt her conscience pricking her. She actually regretted hurting him.

"It was nothing personal, Braxter. You're an all right guy," she said softly.

She turned and quickly hurried out of the apartment.

A physically and emotionally exhausted Clayton Madaris entered his office where he had come straight from the airport. He wasn't ready to go home just yet.

Sitting behind the big oak desk, he leaned his head against the back of the chair and stared into private space. He was in deep thought as he replayed the scene with Syneda over and over again in his mind.

Moments later he checked his watch for the time. He needed to call Alexander Maxwell. Alex was the brother of his best friend, Trask Maxwell. His and Trask's friendship went all the way back to touch football when they were kids growing up in the same neighborhood. Trask had gone on to become the greatest running back in the history of the NFL. Having retired from playing football a few years ago, he was now living in Pennsylvania and was a recruiter for the Pittsburgh Steelers.

Clayton picked up the phone and dialed Alex's number. At the age of twenty-six, Alexander was a top-notch private investigator. It was almost two in the morning, but he knew Alex was used to receiving calls at all times of night.

"Hello, Alex? I need your help. There's someone I want you to find for me."

Syneda woke slowly, and the first thing she did was listen for the sounds she had grown accustomed to hearing whenever Clayton visited. Things like the sound of him in the shower, or the sound of him moving around her kitchen while he prepared breakfast.

But there was no noise. All she heard was silence.

She rolled her head on the pillow so she could look at the gift Clayton had given her this visit, a huge stuffed teddy bear. He'd said it had reminded him of her, all warm and cuddly.

She slowly sat up and swung her legs over the side of the

bed. She stood and the first thing she noticed was that she had slept in Clayton's shirt. She had been so upset after he'd left that she'd cried herself to sleep and didn't undress. His scent was all over her and lingered in the bed where they had made love last night.

"I'll get over him," she said to herself as she went into the bathroom. She stopped and looked around. Clayton's presence was everywhere, even in her bathroom. A bottle of his favorite cologne was sitting next to her perfume, as well as a number of other toiletries he kept at her apartment.

She walked back into her bedroom and went to her closet and pulled out an empty shoe box. Returning to the bathroom she began placing Clayton's items in the box to mail to him.

I can do this, she kept thinking over and over. *No man, other than my father, has made me cry after him. I have to keep my mind focused on what I'm doing and why I'm doing it.*

After packing the items, she squared her shoulders and returned to the bedroom where she placed the box on her dresser. She opened the drawer and took out the key he'd given her; the one to his apartment that she had never used. She placed it inside the box with the other items. With that completed, she turned her attention to another task. She wanted to strip her bed and replace the linens. There was no way she could sleep in that bed again tonight where Clayton's scent lingered on everything.

A few minutes later, after taking her shower, she walked into the kitchen. The day was just beginning and already she was feeling tired. She was sure the cause was more emotional than physical.

She opened the dishwasher to get a bowl for her cereal and found it empty. As usual Clayton had placed her dishes nice and neat in the cabinets instead of leaving them in the dishwasher.

He's done nothing but disrupt my life, she thought. *Before taking up with Clayton, I kept things just the way I wanted them. I used to sleep late on Saturdays and I used to spend a quiet weekend alone doing the things I enjoyed doing.*

She slammed the dishwasher shut, suddenly no longer hungry.

She walked into the living room and sat down on the sofa. Clenching her hands together in her lap she tried pulling herself together. No man had ever made her lose her appetite.

Syneda looked down at her entwined fingers. There was no way she could deny the fact that during the past five months she and Clayton had bonded in a way she had never bonded with a man before. And deep down she knew she would never bond that way with another man.

She smoothed a hand back and forth across her forehead, feeling a headache coming on. Her apartment held too many memories of the times she and Clayton had spent together. She needed to get away. She didn't want to stay in the apartment all weekend alone.

Syneda stood and went into the bedroom to pack.

Braxter rose from the chair he had slept in all night. How could he have been so stupid? It had been nothing more than a setup. He had meant nothing to Celeste but a tool to gather the information she needed. But for whom?

He walked over to the window and looked out. He would have to contact the senator and tell him what was going on immediately. Someone was determined to ruin his credibility with the voters.

He thought about the portion of Celeste's telephone conversation he had overheard. Evidently she was trying to figure out what part, if any, Syneda Walters played in the senator's life.

For some reason, Braxter had a feeling when the answer came to light, all hell would break lose.

"I hope my unexpected visit won't throw the Madaris family schedule off balance," Syneda said jokingly as she entered the spacious and elegant ranch-style home of Justin and Lorren Madaris.

"Of course not," Lorren replied, giving her best friend a hug. "Your visits never throw anything off balance. Justin and the kids will be glad to see you. Just leave your bags here. Justin went to

Dallas and should be returning any minute. He'll take care of them when he gets back."

"Where are the kids?"

"They went with him so you came just in time. I was dying of boredom. Besides, it's about time you paid us a visit."

Syneda smiled. "I know and just look at you." She placed her hand on Lorren's stomach. "You're showing more now than you did at Whispering Pines last month. I'm so happy for you."

"Thanks." Lorren led them into the huge family room that was off the foyer. Syneda sat down on the sofa and Lorren sat across from her in a wing chair. "So, how have things been going with you, Syneda?"

"Fine," Syneda said flatly. "Work is lightening up somewhat, and I take the Jamison case back to court in a couple of weeks."

Lorren studied her friend who had been a pillar of strength for her during her divorce from her first husband, and later when her relationship with Justin was at a delicate point. She had known Syneda long enough to know when something was bothering her. "I wasn't asking about work, I was referring to your personal life."

"My personal life? Why, everything's great!" Syneda replied enthusiastically, and at the same time she tried to stop the quick rush of emotional tears she felt filling her eyes. She swallowed hard and tried blinking them away, but the gesture was too late. Lorren had seen them and had immediately come over and sat next to her.

"What is it, Syneda?" she asked softly. "You know you can talk to me about anything. I may not have any answers but I promise to be a good listener. We haven't had a chance to really talk in a long time. Does what's bothering you have something to do with Clayton?"

Syneda nodded, not trusting herself to speak.

"Do you want to talk about it now?"

"No, not now," Syneda replied brokenly. "But I will later."

"All right, we'll talk later."

* * *

Hours later after taking a shower and changing into a pair of slacks and white blouse, Syneda walked down the stairs to where everyone was. Justin and the kids were in the pool playing a game of volleyball, and Lorren was sitting in a chair nearby.

"I thought you were going to take a nap," Lorren called out to her.

"I was but decided not to. I'm ready to talk now."

Lorren nodded and stood. "Let's take a walk. You haven't been here since Justin had the airstrip installed for the Cessna that he, Dex and Clayton purchased together."

She then turned toward the pool. "I'll be right back. I need to let Justin know where we're going."

A few minutes later the two women were walking side by side along a narrow path that led to a clearing. Syneda spoke up. "It's over between Clayton and me."

Lorren sighed. Although she had never asked, she had been fairly certain Syneda was the mystery woman in Clayton's life. Apparently things had stretched beyond that one lone weekend Syneda had planned for them to have. Lorren loved both her brother-in-law and her best friend dearly, but she had felt their involvement with each other had been headed for trouble from the very beginning. Evidently, Syneda had taken the affair more seriously than Clayton had. She could feel her friend's pain.

"It lasted longer than I thought it would. I tried to warn you about him."

Syneda stopped walking and turned to Lorren. "You don't understand, Lorren. It's not Clayton's fault. It's mine."

A bemused expression covered Lorren's face. "Yours? You're right, I don't understand."

Syneda took a deep breath. "Clayton thinks he's in love with me and wants me to marry him."

Whatever Lorren had expected Syneda to say, those words were not it. Shock and disbelief covered her face. "Clayton loves you and wants to marry you?"

"Yes."

"Are we talking about the same Clayton Madaris?"

"Yes, Lorren, we are. He thinks he loves me and wants to marry me."

Lorren shook her head. "From the way you're talking, I take it that you don't believe him," she said. It was a little hard for her to believe.

"In a way I believe him, and in a way I don't know what to believe."

"If you're concerned about his past involving other women, Syneda, the one thing I've discovered about Madaris men is that when they do fall in love, they're hard-core lovers who are loyal, dedicated and sincere."

"That's not it, Lorren."

"Then what's the problem?"

"I can't give back to him the love he wants."

Lorren knew about Syneda's feelings about falling in love. "You have to let go of the past sometime."

"I've tried but I can't."

"Maybe you haven't tried hard enough because you've felt no man was worth the extra effort. Now you have to decide if Clayton is."

Syneda nodded. At the moment, she wasn't sure if perhaps Lorren's comment wasn't true. "I'm thinking about not attending the Madaris Thanksgiving dinner."

"Why? Because Clayton will be there? Unfortunately, there are going to be a lot of times when your two paths will cross. Have you forgotten you happen to be my best friend, Clayton is Justin's brother and the two of you are godparents to Justina, Vincent and our baby yet to be born? Avoiding Clayton will be impossible."

Syneda knew what Lorren said was true, however, she wasn't ready to accept that fact. "How about going shopping with me in Dallas?"

Lorren sighed as she accepted Syneda's hint that their discussion of her and Clayton was over for the time being. "I'd like that.

We can look at baby gifts for Caitlin. But I want you to promise me something."

"What?"

"Try to forget the past and follow your heart."

Chapter 18

"Ms. Walters, there's a couple here to see you. A Mr. and Mrs. Larry Morgan," Joanna announced over the intercom.

Syneda was sitting at her desk going over some notes she'd made on a case she was handling. She lifted her head in surprise. "Mr. and Mrs. Larry Morgan?"

"Yes."

She pushed the papers aside. "Please send them in."

Syneda stood when Joanna escorted the couple into her office. All it took was the smiles on their faces to let her know somehow things had worked out for them. "Congratulations," she said, returning their smiles and shaking both their hands.

"Thanks. We stopped by to do two things," Cassie said as they took the seats Syneda offered them. "First, we want to thank you."

Syneda raised a brow. "Thank me for what?"

"For taking the time to listen to me that day and for not trying to force me into giving up my baby for adoption," Cassie said.

"And I want to thank you for not throwing me out that day I

showed up here unexpectedly," Larry added. "You took the time to listen to what I had to say." He grinned. "And I had quite a lot to get off my chest."

Syneda nodded, clearly remembering that day. She and Clayton had almost gotten into an argument over the issue of Cassie's father's interference.

"I take it your father has finally come around."

Cassie shook her head. "Unfortunately he hasn't. And that's our second reason for coming here today. We want to say goodbye. We're moving to Texas."

"Texas?"

"Yes, Austin, Texas. Larry has received a job offer there. He'll be working for Remington Oil."

Syneda raised an arched brow. "Remington Oil?"

Larry grinned. "Yes, I'm sure you've heard of them. Who hasn't? They're a very good company to work for. They offered me a very good salary and the benefits are excellent."

Syneda nodded. Remington Oil Company was one of the largest oil companies in America. They had made history last year when they became the first oil company in over fifty years to locate a major oil field. Dex's company, Madaris Explorations, had been used for the job. Also, a piece of land owned by Caitlin had been instrumental in making that discovery possible. Clayton had handled the negotiations in both situations. Syneda couldn't help but wonder if it was just a coincidence that Larry Morgan had gotten a job with a company in which Clayton had close ties.

She cleared her throat. "Did you seek out employment with Remington Oil?"

Larry smiled. "No, and that's the funny thing about all of this. According to the personnel manager at Remington Oil, I came highly recommended, but he wouldn't say who recommended me. As far as I'm concerned, whoever recommended me is truly my guardian angel."

Syneda returned his smile. She had a funny feeling his

guardian angel was none other than Clayton. The words he had spoken that last night in her apartment suddenly came back to her. *"...Somehow you have this notion that me understanding certain things is the same thing as me endorsing them. You were wrong in believing that about Cassie Drayton and Larry Morgan, and you're wrong in believing that about us...."*

"Ms. Walters? Are you all right?"

Cassie's soft voice cut through Syneda's thoughts. "Yes, I'm fine. How did your father handle the fact that Larry has found a job? Especially when he'd gone to a lot of trouble to make sure he wasn't hired anywhere."

"Not too well. In fact, Larry and I found out that he called Mr. Remington personally and made threats. But believe it or not, he met his match."

"Really? What happened?"

Larry chuckled. "I heard Mr. Remington advised Cassie's father that he would be faced with a lawsuit if he tried anything. He further advised my father-in-law that he was considering diversifying Remington Oil and that the clothing industry would be the first avenue he looked at for a possible merger."

Cassie laughed. "I guess the thought of anyone attempting a corporate takeover of Drayton Industries was enough to make Dad think twice about carrying out his threats."

Syneda nodded in agreement. "Well, I'm glad things have worked out for you two."

"We're glad, too," Cassie said. "People in love deserve to be together. It's no fun being alone. Everyone needs someone to love and someone to love them."

"It's been a while, Clayton. Welcome to Sisters. You were missed."

"Thanks," Clayton said to the hostess. He leveled a long, hard look around the restaurant. Sisters was a place he used to frequent quite a bit. It was known for its good food, lively entertainment and, most important, its abundance of women. It was a place women came to hang out; some to cultivate sisterhood—so he'd been told—some to be noticed, and others to do the noticing because where there were women, you were sure to find men.

"Trevor's here and he's dining alone. Do you want to join him?"

"Yeah, that will be fine."

Clayton followed as she led the way to the table where his good friend, Trevor Grant, was sitting. Trevor was the head foreman for Dex's company.

As he was being led to the table, Clayton couldn't help noticing the number of women who called out a greeting to him or who were smiling openly at him. At any other time he would have made a clean sweep around the room, flirting with the women that he knew and getting ready to hit on those that he didn't know. But not now. He was only interested in one particular woman; a woman who had told him in no uncertain terms that she didn't want him.

"Well, well, well, aren't you a sight for sore eyes," Trevor Grant said, shaking hands with Clayton before he sat down. "This place hasn't seen the likes of you for months. Where on earth have you been?"

"Busy." He turned to their hostess. "Just give me the usual."

The woman nodded. "All right." A grin then curved her lips. "And by the way, Clayton. Kayla's been asking about you, but Evelyn hasn't. In fact, she's now taken up with Al."

Clayton gave her a dry look. "I'm happy for her."

The hostess shook her head and walked off.

Trevor laughed. "Losing your touch, Clayton?"

He gave his friend a grim smile. "Just my interest."

Trevor lifted a brow. "You not being interested in a woman will be the day they prepare you for burial."

Clayton smiled and didn't say anything. Instead he stood and pulled several quarters out of his pocket. Since this was Monday night, there was no live entertainment. Music was being provided by a huge jukebox that sat in the corner of the room. It contained a number of the latest hits, as well as quite a few of the oldies.

"Excuse me for a minute." He walked over to the jukebox and

after depositing his quarters, punched a couple of songs, "The Track of My Tears" by Smokey Robinson and "What Becomes of a Broken Heart" by Jimmy Ruffin. He walked back over to the table and sat down. The songs he had selected were all indicative of how he felt.

Trevor folded his arms and pinned Clayton to his seat with a curious stare. "What's wrong with you? You're acting like a lovesick puppy." Trevor chuckled. "But since I know that can't be the case, at least not with you anyway, what's your problem?"

"Don't have one. And what's so bad about falling in love?"

Trevor looked up and frowned, not believing Clayton had asked such a question. "What's wrong with it? Everything's wrong with it. That's when a man's troubles begin, once he falls for a woman."

Clayton cocked his brow. "And I take it you've never fallen in love."

Trevor shrugged. "Not voluntarily, no."

"And involuntarily?"

Trevor squirmed slightly in his seat. "I may have had a short moment of madness." Trevor thought about the woman he had met over a year ago, Corinthians Avery. She was head geologist for Remington Oil. Their initial meeting was anything but normal. There was no doubt in his mind that she'd disliked him on sight and he'd disliked her equally as much…or so he had thought. But the infrequent times he had seen her since their initial meeting, when they'd been thrown together due to work obligations, he had found himself wanting to seek her out and make hot, torrid, passionate love to her. He hadn't done that, of course. The woman hated his guts. But that hadn't stopped her from invading his dreams at night, or his thoughts during the day.

"What happened?" Clayton asked.

"Nothing happened. The woman doesn't like me. Besides, she's in love with someone else. She's in love with a married man."

Clayton arched one eyebrow. "You're kidding?"

Trevor shook his head. "Wish I was kidding. Can you believe

that, especially after what happened with my old man. I almost fell for the same kind of woman who destroyed my parents' marriage."

After almost emptying a bottle of hot sauce over his fried chicken then topping it off with ketchup, Trevor tilted back in his chair and eyed his friend. The second song Clayton had selected was now playing. "Are you or are you not going to tell me what's going on with you?"

Clayton exhaled a deep, drawn-out sigh. "I've fallen in love."

Trevor didn't say anything for the longest moment. He just stared at Clayton in disbelief. Finally he spoke. "Must be one hell of a woman."

A smile tilted Clayton's lips. "She is."

"Who is she?"

"Don't ask."

Trevor rubbed his hand over his jaw, thinking. "Man, she isn't married, is she?"

Clayton glared at Trevor. "Of course not! You know I don't do married women."

Trevor smiled. "I thought you didn't do falling in love, either, but you did."

Clayton couldn't help but return Trevor's smile. His friend had him there, unfortunately.

"So, what's the problem? Whoever the woman is I'm sure she's elated, since you're the biggest catch in Houston."

"She doesn't want me."

Trevor almost choked on his chicken. He grabbed his water to wash down the piece of meat caught in his throat. "A woman doesn't want you! Are you serious?"

"Yes, as serious as a heart attack."

Trevor pursed his lips. "She actually rejected you, man?"

"Yep."

Trevor shook his head. He then pushed his plate aside and tapped his thumbs together for a few seconds. "Do you have any more quarters?" he suddenly asked Clayton.

"Yeah. Why?"

"I want to play something on the jukebox."

Clayton stood and pulled out a couple of quarters and handed them to Trevor. He watched him cross the room to the jukebox, deposit the money and select a song. He then came back and sat down.

"I played this song for the both of us."

Clayton lifted a brow when the jukebox roared to life with Trevor's selection. He had chosen Toni Braxton's "Unbreak My Heart."

Senator Lansing looked up in surprise. "Braxter, you're early. I wasn't expecting you to come in until around nine."

"There's an important matter I need to discuss, sir."

The senator nodded, noting the seriousness in Braxter's voice. "Have a seat over there. Is something wrong?"

"That will be for you to decide."

At the lift of the senator's brow, Braxter continued. "The woman, the one I've been seeing, the one I took to Texas with me and introduced you to…"

"Yes, what about her?"

"She was using me to get information about you."

The senator sat straight up. "What? How do you know that?"

"Last night I overheard a conversation she was having with someone, a private investigator. Somehow she must have found out about our interest in Syneda Walters and is doing her own investigating into it."

"Who is she working for?" the senator asked calmly.

"I don't know. But whoever it is, that person wants to make sure you're not reelected."

The senator frowned. He was running against Noel Frazier. He couldn't believe the man would stoop to something so low. In fact, the two of them had vowed to run a clean campaign. "I want you to find out who's behind it."

"Yes, sir, and if you want me to, I'll turn in my resignation."

"Why?"

"Because I may have done more harm than good to you now. Because of me, the media may get ahold of something that you prefer kept private."

The senator smiled weakly. "When you're an elected official, Braxter, you don't have any privacy. I would have preferred getting the information on Ms. Walters before anyone else. However, if there's anything in the report that I need to be concerned with, I'll deal with it."

"But I let Celeste Rogers make a fool out of me. I can't believe I was so stupid, so inexcusably stupid."

"You weren't stupid, Braxter. You're a man who fell in love, and with love automatically comes trust. And the person you trusted betrayed you."

"So what will you do, sir?"

"Nothing. We'll just let the person who appears to be in control of things finish whatever game he or she is playing."

Syneda entered her apartment. She had gotten through the day…now if she could only get through the night. Then she would concentrate on the rest of the week.

The day hadn't been so bad with the visit from Cassie and Larry Morgan. An hour or so later, she had received notification of a date for the appeals court to hear her oral argument.

She had immediately called the Jamisons to give them the news. They had cried over the phone. Barbara and Walter Jamison had been without their little girl for almost six months. They were hoping and praying to win the appeal so little Kasey would be returned to them.

Later that night, when Syneda turned off the lamp and made herself comfortable in bed, she couldn't help but think of the Morgans and how Clayton had helped to change their lives. The more she thought about it, the more convinced she became that somehow he had been instrumental in Larry Morgan finding employment with Remington Oil.

Then there was the Jamison case. Although she had come up with the new argument to use with the appeal, it had been Clayton's expertise and experience as an attorney that had given her food for thought and ideas for different avenues to pursue. Numerous times during his weekend visits, he had brought a law book or two from his own personal law library. She had enjoyed spending time with him researching cases and digging for precedents she could use. A part of her knew if she won the appeal, it would be because of Clayton's help.

As Syneda shifted in bed, she thought about something else she missed in not being with Clayton—the intimacy they shared. Although she wanted to believe it had only been about sex for them, she knew they had shared a whole lot more. There had been the sharing of emotions and feelings, and that's what she missed most of all. He had opened emotions in her she hadn't wanted opened. He had made her feel, he had made her need—regardless of whether she had wanted those things or not. Clayton had made her experience them. And she had experienced them with him. Perhaps in the end that was the main reason why she had fought against it, and why even now she was still fighting against it. She was fighting the love she felt for him.

Syneda knew she had avoided the truth long enough and it was time to be honest with herself. She did love Clayton. She probably had always loved him. But even with that admission, she knew she would continue to fight her love for him. Her survival depended on it. As a child, her heart had not just been broken, it had been crushed. And it couldn't survive being crushed again. She couldn't take the chance.

No matter how much she loved him, she couldn't risk having her heart destroyed. She just couldn't.

Chapter 19

Justin Madaris pounded on the door a good five minutes before it finally opened.

Clayton scowled at Justin and then at Dex before rubbing a hand across his eyes that were clouded with sleep. "What are the two of you doing here? And what are you doing in Houston, Justin?"

Justin studied his youngest brother with an intensity that came from being the oldest and always having to look out for his younger siblings. He knew immediately that something was wrong. A quick glance at Dex indicated that he had picked up on it, as well. Clayton's robe looked rumpled and his ungroomed appearance made him look a little rough around the edges. His face had the look of a man who'd had a bad night. In fact, he looked as if he'd had quite a few bad nights. "What are you still doing in bed, Clayton? It's almost two in the afternoon."

Swearing, Clayton rubbed the top of his head and stepped aside to let his brothers in. "Maybe I wanted to sleep late."

"Clayton, you don't know how to sleep late," Dex said with a half smile on his lips.

Clayton glared at Dex. "Just what is this? Gang up on Clayton day?"

Dex shrugged as he sat down on the sofa. He glanced around the room. "This place is a mess. I never knew you could be so sloppy."

"So now you know," Clayton said, moving through the untidy living room and sitting in a chair. Dex was right. His place was a mess and it wasn't like him to be sloppy. If anything, he was known to be extremely neat. He hated disorder of any kind. But now he didn't care. Lately he hadn't cared much about anything.

Clayton gave Dex a hard glare. "For a man who makes a living playing in dirt, I hardly think you have room to talk. The biggest mistake Mom ever made was buying you that sandbox for your fourth birthday."

"Kids, behave," Justin said, chuckling.

Clayton's response was a grunt. "You never did answer me, Justin. What are you doing in Houston?"

Justin dropped in the chair across from Clayton. "And you never answered me. Why are you still in bed?"

"You go first since you're the oldest."

Justin grinned and then conceded. "I drove Lorren down for Caitlin's baby shower. Did you forget it was this weekend?"

"Yeah, I forgot," Clayton said, and felt annoyed that he had forgotten. During the past few weeks, his mind had been preoccupied with other things.

"So why are you still in bed?"

Clayton rose and went into the kitchen. Dex and Justin followed him. Ignoring them, he switched on the coffeemaker.

"We're not going away, Clayton."

Clayton turned to his brothers. "I can see that," he said, glaring at them, frowning. "The reason I was still in bed is because I had no reason to rush getting up this morning," he finally said, simply.

"I'm surprised to hear you say that, considering the fact that Syneda flew in for the baby shower today."

Clayton's eyes became hard like volcanic rocks. "That's all the more reason," he said coolly. "She's the last person I want to see."

Dex looked at his brother, surprised. The last time he had seen Clayton and Syneda together was when the family had been at Whispering Pines. At the time, Syneda had been the only person Clayton had acted like he wanted to see. He hadn't been able to keep his eyes off her. "I take it there's trouble in paradise."

Clayton turned toward him. "There is no paradise. There never was and there never will be. The only paradise was the one that I concocted in my mind. But the lady has set me straight. The only thing she's interested in is a surrogate family she can claim, and not a man who wants to love her."

Justin took a good look at his brother, hearing the deep pain in his voice. And there was also a coldness, a hardness within Clayton that had never existed before, and he immediately knew the cause—rejection. Syneda had done something to Clayton no other woman had done. She had rejected him. She had taken the love he had never confessed to another woman and had thrown it back in his face. And from the looks of things, he wasn't handling it too well.

"And the really funny thing about it," Clayton continued, "is that I watched the two of you go through your bouts of pain, and I used to think to myself that it could never happen to me. I used to tell myself I was above all that, that there wasn't a woman anywhere who could infiltrate my mind and my heart like that, and cause me that much pain, that much grief, that much anguish." With studied calmness, he sat down in the chair at the round oak table. He dropped his forehead to his joined hands, "Boy, was I wrong. I was so very wrong."

He then held up his head and looked at his brothers. The hurt and pain were evident in his eyes, plain for them to see. "How do you handle telling a woman for the first time in your life that you love her, only to have her tell you that she doesn't want you nor does she want your love. And that all she wants from you is a good time. And what's really hilarious is that that's the same thing I've been telling women for years."

He squeezed his eyes shut for a moment, then reopened them. "I guess it's payback time. And for me, payback came all nicely packaged in the form and shape of a woman by the name of Syneda Tremain Walters. And she got me just where it hurts the most— straight in the heart. How am I supposed to handle something like that? How am I supposed to handle the hurt and the pain?"

Justin and Dex watched their brother in silence, neither knew what to say but both were familiar with what he was going through. They had been there. Giving advice had always been Clayton's thing, even when the advice hadn't been wanted.

Justin shook his head. Clayton had done more than just given advice to him and Dex. He had deliberately undermined and manipulated their love life. He had done what he felt had been necessary to straighten out their problems with the women they loved. Now Clayton's own love life needed straightening out and Justin knew that his baby brother didn't have a clue as to how to help himself.

Justin finally spoke. "Give her time, Clayton."

Clayton's response was a quiet laugh. "I've given her time, Justin. Maybe that's the problem. I've given her too much time."

"Then try being more patient with her," Dex put in. "How you and Syneda even got this far without killing each other beats the hell out of me," he said, shaking his head in amazement. "Both of your analytical and strongly opinionated minds are enough to rattle any relationship. Just chill and be patient. You know how I almost screwed things up with Caitlin by not being patient."

Clayton took a long, deep breath. "I have been patient, Dex. I've been patient for over five months. But now I'm tired of fighting for what I want against what Syneda evidently doesn't want. You can't make someone love you, and I'm sick and tired of even trying."

He stood. "The hurt and the pain aren't worth it anymore." He took another deep breath. "The two of you can let yourselves out. I'm going back to bed."

He then walked out of the kitchen.

* * *

Clayton had lain across the bed for nearly an hour and knew from the sounds coming from the living room, Justin and Dex had not left. In fact, with the television blasting and the sound of his refrigerator opening and closing periodically, he could tell they had made themselves at home and were watching a football game and eating up his food.

Why on earth were they still hanging around? Did they think he was going to hang himself or something? He took a quick glance at the box that sat on his dresser. The package had been sent from Syneda and had arrived a couple of days ago. In it were items he'd made a habit of leaving at her place. She had returned all of his things along with the spare key he had given to her with a note that simply said, "It's better this way." The thought of it increased his anger. It might be better for her but it certainly wasn't better for him.

Clayton got out of bed and went into the bathroom to take a shower. Since it appeared Justin and Dex weren't going anyplace, he might as well watch the game with them.

Syneda looked out the window as the cab drove through Houston on its way to the airport. She had flown in that morning and, a little over seven hours later, she was flying back to New York. With her day in court for the appeal on Wednesday, she needed to be fully prepared.

Caitlin's baby shower had really been pleasant and she had received many nice things. Syneda smiled at the games they had played at the shower. She had really enjoyed herself, as she always did with the Madaris family.

She was glad that Clayton had not stopped by. She didn't think she could handle seeing him just yet. She knew that Justin and Dex had gone over to his place. Neither had returned before she'd left for the airport.

A part of her couldn't help wondering how Clayton was doing. Had he dismissed her from his mind already? Was he back to dating other women again?

She took a deep breath, irritated with herself for even caring. But she did care. She loved him and the thought of him with someone else…

But, she reminded herself, she had been the one to end things between them. She had sent him away. She'd had no choice. She could not start depending on anyone for her happiness. The only person she could always count on was herself.

As the cab continued to make its way through the city, Syneda couldn't help but think of Houston. This was Clayton's territory, his city. The city of his birth. In Houston, Clayton Madaris was a very well-known and successful attorney. But when he had come to her in New York, he had been her friend, her mentor and her lover. And deep down she knew she had lost all three. No matter what she wanted to think, there was no way they could ever go back and reclaim that special friendship they once shared. She was only fooling herself if she thought they could.

Later that night Clayton received a call from Alexander Maxwell.

"You don't believe in giving me easy jobs do you?" his friend said, chuckling.

Clayton smiled. "What can I say, you're the best. Do you have any information for me yet?"

"No, not yet, but I've stumbled onto something pretty interesting. I thought I'd better bring it to your attention."

"What?"

"There are two other investigators checking out Syneda's past. Seems like you're not the only one interested."

Clayton sat up straight, frowning. "Who are they?"

"Don't know yet. I picked up on them in my database. I know about them but they don't know about me. We have an advantage."

"Let's keep it that way, Alex. I want to know who they are and what their interest is."

When he hung up the phone a few minutes later, Clayton couldn't help wondering who else besides him would be interested in Syneda's past.

Chapter 20

Syneda won the appeal and Kasey Jamison would be returned to her adoptive parents by the end of the week.

She knew she should celebrate, but her win had also been the result of someone else losing. Kasey's biological mother.

Syneda left the courtroom after getting the ruling when it was released. She had spoken immediately with the Jamisons and shared their happiness.

Entering her apartment, the first thought that came to her mind was that she needed Clayton. She wanted to share her victory with him. She looked around her apartment. Although she had returned all of Clayton's things, his presence was still there. It was there in the living room where they had made love occasionally. It was in her kitchen where he had whipped her up a number of tasty meals. His presence was in her bathroom where they had showered together frequently, and it dominated her bedroom where he had made her his.

He had made her his. He'd been the first man to capture her

heart, making her irrevocably his. Syneda tilted her head back
and drew in cold air, feeling the tears sting her cheeks. Her apartment was cold from the freezing weather outside, not unusual
for New York the week before Thanksgiving. She quickly wiped
away her tears.

Her tears were for all she had lost, at her own hands, because
she hadn't been strong enough to take a chance on love—the kind
of love Justin had for Lorren, the kind of love Dex had for Caitlin.
Clayton had offered her that and she had refused it.

Cassie Drayton Morgan had been right when she'd said, "It's
no fun being alone. Everyone needs someone to love and someone to love them..."

Syneda had never believed that until now.

And Clayton had been right when he'd said that what happened with her father did not concern them. It was time she got
beyond that and moved on. And she was ready to do so. But first,
there was something she had to do before she could finally put
the past behind her. There was someone she had to visit.

Syneda had won the appeal.

Clayton leaned back in his office chair. He had just gotten
word from a fellow attorney who was working on a similar case.
He wanted to call Syneda and tell her how happy he was for her,
and how proud he was of her. But he didn't.

She had made it very clear things were over between them,
yet he still wanted to talk to her. He still wanted to hear her voice.
He picked up the phone and after hesitating a few seconds
slammed it back down. The words she had said to him the last
night they were together tore into him. "I don't want your love,
Clayton. I didn't ask for it and I don't want it."

Clayton rose from his chair, balling his hands into his pockets.
He was hurting in a way no person was supposed to hurt. He was
hurting everywhere, both inside and out, and all at once.

He knew that although Justin and Dex had tried being sup-
portive, they just didn't understand. The problems plaguing his

and Syneda's relationship would not evaporate with time and patience. It would take love and trust, and she wasn't willing to take a chance on either.

Clayton tugged at his tie, wishing he could rip it off and then do the same thing to his heart—rip it out. But something in him made him bite back both his anger and his frustration. He refused to let any woman make him lose his mind, his self-respect or his pride. In time he would get over her, he would make sure of that.

And no woman would ever get close to his heart again.

Syneda took a deep breath as she leaned against the huge wrought iron gate. Her plane had landed less than an hour ago and she had immediately taken a cab from the Dallas airport.

For the past eighteen years of her life she had avoided coming here. She used to tell herself that if she never came, her mother would never know the truth. Her mother would never know that the man she had died loving, trusting and believing in had let them down.

Syneda straightened and began walking across the stretch of velvet-green lawn. As she neared the area where the groundkeeper had instructed her to go, poignant memories of her childhood with her mother resurfaced.

The two of them had been close, almost inseparable, except for the time her mother was at work and she was at school. They had done a lot of things together. Although there hadn't been plenty of money, her mother had worked hard and had taken care of their needs.

The short walk was finally over and as Syneda stood before the headstone, she felt renewed pain followed by a deep sense of cleansing. She knew by the time she left to return to New York, a part of her past would be left here. It was the part she should have buried a long time ago.

She knelt down and placed the bouquet of flowers across the headstone. She squeezed her eyes shut against the mistiness that began clouding them. "Mama, I know it's been a long time, and your little girl is all grown up now. And I know in my heart you understand why I haven't come until now."

Syneda felt a momentary stab of pain when she thought of the man who had fathered her. "I never wanted you to know he didn't come for me, Mama, because more than anything I truly wanted you to rest in peace. And I knew you couldn't do that if you knew the truth. I didn't want you to worry about me."

Syneda's hands trembled as she wiped the tears from her eyes. "I'm okay now. I admit I wasn't in the beginning, the disappointment of him not coming hurt for a while, but I'm okay now. My heavenly father took very good care of me. He sent me to live with Mama Nora and Papa Paul. I know you would have liked them. They took me to church every Sunday just like you would have done. And I had Lorren. She's the sister I've always wanted."

Syneda took a deep breath as her fingers traced lazy patterns in the cold earth. "I made something of myself, Mama. I went to college and got a law degree. And I've met someone special by the name of Clayton Madaris. I know you would like him, too. He's kind, gentle, strong and caring. And he loves me. I didn't want to believe it at first, but now I do. And I love him. I love him very much and one day soon I'm going to tell him just how I feel. I want to marry him and if we ever have children, I'll tell them all about you. I'll tell them how you took care of me all by yourself. I know it must have been hard being a single parent and all, but you did it. I'll tell my kids how you used to read me stories before tucking me in at night and how you would wake me up by singing a beautiful song in the morning. I'll tell them all about our good times."

Syneda hesitated briefly before continuing. "But most of all, Mama, I'll tell them how much you loved me and how much I loved you." Tears that she had held for so long were released and she wept.

Syneda wept for the mother who had been taken away from her at the age of ten, and for the father who hadn't cared enough to come and claim her as his daughter.

A few minutes later she wiped her eyes and slowly stood.

"Goodbye, Mama," she whispered. "Continue to rest in peace. I love you."

She turned and walked out of the cemetery in the direction she had come in.

Chapter 21

How could he have let his mother talk him into coming here? Seeing Syneda was the very last thing he wanted, Clayton thought, walking toward the airport terminal. Passing through the entrance he moved in paced steps, ignoring the noisy sounds from the crowds. The airport was packed with people traveling to and fro to spend time with family over the Thanksgiving holiday. With a brief glance at the monitor, he checked the gate for the flight arriving from New York. Noting he was a few minutes early, he took a seat to wait.

He disregarded the attractive young woman sitting across from him who'd sent an inviting smile his way. Her eyes ran over him, and Clayton couldn't help but give her a half-amused smile before tipping his head back against the wall and resting his eyes.

When Syneda's flight was announced he stood and forced himself to relax. That brief moment of calmness came to an abrupt end the moment he saw her walk through the gate. She was dressed in a pair of white jeans that gracefully hugged her firm hips, and a peach-colored pullover sweater. She looked absolutely stunning.

Syneda's face registered surprise when she saw Clayton. His towering height made him quite visible over the crowd of people that were waiting for other passengers. She shivered slightly when she felt his hooded eyes on her.

He was dressed in a pair of faded, snug-fitting jeans and a burgandy pullover sweater that outlined every detail of his muscled body. A body she had come to know rather well during the past few months.

How could I have thought I didn't love him? How could I have thought I didn't want him? Taking a deep breath, she walked over to where he was standing. "Clayton, I'm glad to see you."

"Yeah, I bet you are," he replied coolly, his lips forming in a taut line. "Mom sent me." He took the flight bag from her shoulder. "She would've come herself, but didn't trust me or Dad to watch her sweet potato pies that were in the oven."

"Oh," Syneda replied. Her gaze met Clayton's and the eyes staring back at her were like chipped ice. There were so many things she wanted to say to him, but she couldn't say them in a crowded airport. They needed privacy.

"Are you ready, Syneda?"

"Yes."

"Let's go then," he said gruffly.

Together they walked down the wide, crowded corridor. Syneda was having a little bit of trouble keeping up with Clayton's long strides.

"It will only take a minute to claim your bags," Clayton said curtly upon reaching the area where the rest of her bags were.

"Am I the first to arrive?" Syneda asked, pointing out her bags to Clayton. Then she felt foolish for doing so. They had taken enough trips together over the past few months that he would have recognized her luggage easily.

"No. Traci and Kattie were over earlier today to help peel the potatoes for the pies, but they left before noon. They'll be back later today. Dex and Caitlin will probably be there by the time we arrive. They had to wait for Jordan to get out of preschool before coming over. And Justin, Lorren and the kids are flying in this afternoon."

"What about Christy?"

"She's been home from college since Monday."

For the first time since seeing him, Syneda couldn't help but notice the fleeting smile that somewhat softened Clayton's features. "Let me rephrase that," he said. "Christy's been in Houston since Monday, however, she's seldom at home. She's making her rounds visiting friends. She only pops in to eat and sleep."

"What about Jake?"

Clayton frowned. "I don't know what's going on with Uncle Jake. For some reason he's not coming this year. He called Mom earlier this week and said he had other plans. It's not like him to miss Thanksgiving dinner with us."

As they stepped out of the building, Clayton led her over to a car parked nearby. He set down the bags and pulled the key out of his pocket. "Mom suggested I drive her car," he said, as he loaded Syneda's things into the trunk of the sleek champagne-colored Seville. "I guess she figured all your things wouldn't fit in my two-seater."

Syneda nodded and again their eyes met. His eyes appeared colder than they had earlier. Suddenly, all the words she had wanted to say to him stuck in her throat. What could she say to undo what she'd done? What words could she use to make him understand she was ready to love him and she trusted him? She was the first to break the eye contact.

"Will my being here bother you, Clayton?" she asked, feeling a little unsure of herself and suddenly filled with self-doubt. His cold attitude toward her wasn't helping the situation.

"Not particularly," he said dispassionately, opening the car door.

"Maybe I should not have come."

The look Clayton gave her was as sharp as a broken piece of glass and as cold as the weather she had left in New York. It was definitely not filled with the warmth she was accustomed to. "Too late to think about that now. You're here, aren't you?" he said harshly, shutting the door. Then he walked around to get into the car.

His words had hurt, and when Clayton started the car, Syneda turned her attention to the scenery outside the car window. She couldn't help wondering if she had made a mistake by coming. What if he no longer had a place in his heart for her? What if he no longer wanted her? It had been over a month since they had been together, and she hadn't heard from him. The thought that he no longer cared for her sent her mind reeling in sheer panic.

When they arrived at Clayton's parents' home, Dex was in the driveway washing his father's pickup truck. Clayton brought the car to a stop and Syneda opened the door and got out of the car.

"Syneda's bags are in the trunk," Clayton told his brother gruffly, tossing him the keys. "Tell the folks that I'll be back later." He then got into his Mercedes and left.

Dex shook his head resignedly, then turned his handsome smile on Syneda. He came around the car and gave her a huge hug. His charcoal-gray eyes were filled with concern. "Are you all right?"

Syneda gave Dex a forced smile. She wondered if he knew about her relationship with his brother, but at the moment she didn't care who knew. "Yes," she replied softly. "I'm fine."

"What in the world has Clayton in such a bad mood?"

"I don't know. I'm glad I'm not the only one who's picked up on it."

Syneda went about her job of grating the cheese for the casserole trying not to listen to the conversation going on between Clayton's sisters, Traci and Kattie.

Soon after she had arrived, the two women had returned to help with all the cooking that had to be done. It was an annual Madaris ritual that the women in the family prepared the entire Thanksgiving meal the night before, and the men were responsible for getting up on Thanksgiving Day morning to fix the special dessert. Rumor had it that this year it would be a delectable peach cobbler.

Working by Syneda's side in the kitchen was a very pregnant Caitlin, whose due date was less than two weeks away. She was busy chopping onions, celery and bell peppers for the potato salad.

"I thought the two of you were convinced Clayton had a love interest," Caitlin said to Traci and Kattie without looking up from her task.

"All evidence seemed to lead that way," Traci replied as a smile touched her lips. "Especially all those weekend trips that he refuses to discuss."

"All right, girls," Marilyn Madaris spoke up. "Your brother has a right to his privacy. What he does and who he sees are none of your business."

"We know that, Mom. We're just trying to figure out what's bothering him."

Syneda was tempted to provide them with the answer they sought. She was what was bothering Clayton. He had been in a bad mood since picking her up from the airport.

"Has he mentioned bringing a surprise guest to dinner tomorrow?" Traci inquired.

Marilyn Madaris shook her head and smiled. "No, he hasn't."

"Where's Lorren?" Caitlin asked as she began peeling the shells off the boiled eggs.

"She's in the den with the kids, reading them a story. Bless her heart. How she can put up with all of them in her condition is beyond me," Kattie answered. "She has so much patience."

The conversation in the kitchen shifted from Clayton to other topics as the women continued working diligently on tomorrow's dinner.

"Are you all right, Syneda?" Caitlin asked a little while later when the two of them were left alone in the kitchen. "You've been rather quiet today."

Syneda liked Caitlin. She was a very likable person who was just as beautiful on the inside as she was on the outside. She and

Dex had married within two weeks of their meeting. What followed not too long after that was a long and bitter separation that had lasted for nearly four years. Love had reunited them, and when you saw them together, you would never have guessed the problems their marriage had endured. Problems that Caitlin was quick to admit had made their love and marriage stronger.

"I'm fine," Syneda replied, giving Caitlin an assuring smile.

At that moment the kitchen door swung open and Clayton walked in. A frown covered his features. "Where's Mom?"

"She's upstairs trying to find a place for all the kids to sleep. Your dad wants all his grands under his roof tonight," Caitlin replied, eyeing her brother-in-law warily. His handsome face had become brooding and a scowl clouded his features. Her sisters-in-law had been right. He was in a rather bad mood.

"I think I'll go upstairs and offer my assistance. Do you want to come with me, Syneda?" Caitlin asked.

Syneda shook her head as her gaze met Clayton's. "I'll be up later. I would like to talk to Clayton for a while."

In his present mood, Caitlin wasn't sure that was such a good idea but kept her thoughts to herself. "Okay. I'll see you guys later."

When the door closed behind her, Clayton walked forward, stopping in front of Syneda. He looked down at her intensely. "What do you want to talk to me about?"

Taking a deep, unsteady breath, Syneda stepped back. His towering height seemed intimidating. "Let's step outside."

"No."

"No?"

"That's what I said. Why can't you say what you have to say right here? Are you afraid we'll make a scene and the family will find out about us?"

She frowned. "That's not it at all. I thought—"

"And what did you think, Syneda?"

"I thought that maybe we could go someplace where we could be alone."

Clayton stared at her. She had a lot of nerve trying to offer him a chance to put things back the way they used to be between them. She was still only interested in an affair with no commitment or complications. Didn't she understand that he could have what she was offering with a number of other women? Didn't she know that with her he wanted more? Had she not gotten it through her head that he loved her with such a passion that even now his hands were trembling from just being near her, wanting to touch her, to love her and to keep her with him always? Just looking at her brought back memories he could very well do without.

"You're the last woman I want to be alone with, Syneda." He turned to leave.

His words hurt Syneda, but she was determined that he would hear her out. Moving quickly she blocked his exit. "You're going to listen to what I have to say, Madaris."

"Don't count on it. Now move your butt out of my way."

"No."

The stark coldness in his eyes made her shiver from the chill cast in the room, but Syneda didn't care. As far as she was concerned she was just as mad as he was. He could be so stubborn at times.

"You make me so mad, Madaris, I could just smack you."

"I wouldn't advise you to act crazy and do it," he said threateningly, glaring down at her.

"Act crazy? You mean like this?" she asked angrily before smacking him.

The swiftness of Syneda's action caught Clayton completely off guard. Enraged, he grabbed her hand and yanked her to him and glared down at her. Then all of a sudden he was kissing her, his mouth hard on hers, his tongue thrusting into her warm moistness, probing and caressing.

He had wanted to be brutal in his kiss, to punish her for hurting him. But he found he couldn't. Especially when he felt her response. So he continued to kiss her, letting all his needs and frustrations take over.

Soon an inner part of him told him this was not the way. He loved her too much to take less than a full commitment, less than her total love. Feeling disgusted with himself for his lack of control where she was concerned, he shoved her away from him and spun around and walked in the opposite direction.

"Clayton, please wait and listen to me."

He stopped walking and turned back around. The look in his eyes told her he had been pushed beyond his limit. "No, Syneda, *you* listen to me. You're here but that doesn't mean I have to like it. Just do me a favor and stay the hell away from me. You wanted my family so bad, well, you can have them, but that doesn't include me. All I want is for you to leave me alone." He turned and walked out of the kitchen.

Shaken by his angry words, Syneda sat down in the nearest chair. Clayton no longer wanted her. She had been so sure that once she saw him again and they had a chance to talk, and she told him how much she loved him, things would be all right between them. She hadn't expected his anger, and she never expected him to not want anything to do with her. He actually acted as if he hated her. She must have hurt him deeply for him to feel the way he now felt toward her.

Her shoulders drooped. There was no way she could stay here with his family knowing how he felt. Making a decision to find an excuse to leave first thing in the morning, she walked through the same door Clayton had walked through just moments earlier, almost colliding with Mrs. Madaris.

"We didn't mean to desert you, dear."

"You didn't. In fact, I was just about to find you. Something has come up and I'm going to have to return to New York first thing in the morning."

Syneda found herself under the warm charcoal-gray gaze of the woman, who gave her an endearing smile. "I'm sorry to hear that. I really enjoy you being here with us."

Marilyn Madaris's eyes were lit from some inner glow. "I've been in this kitchen since six this morning, and I think I'm more than due a break. I've started taking afternoon walks around the neighborhood. Would you like to join me?"

Syneda nodded. She always enjoyed Clayton's mother's company. Besides, her conversation with Clayton had taken a toll on her.

The two women walked outside the house. The treetops stirred with the whisper of a cool breeze. They were ten minutes into their walk before either woman spoke. Then it was Clayton's mom who broke their silence. "Have I ever told you how Jonathan and I met?"

The question surprised Syneda. "No, I don't think you have."

The older woman smiled. "I was fresh out of college and had landed my first teaching job. It seemed good fortune was on my side because the elementary school I was assigned to was within a block of my apartment. I was grateful for that because money was tight, and I couldn't really afford a car payment."

They continued walking. "My first day on the job I came face-to-face with the principal. He was a stern but very tall, dark, handsome man by the name of Jonathan Madaris. I think we were attracted to each other immediately, although I tried my best to fight it. I had my own set of plans for my future, and they didn't include getting serious about anyone for a long while."

Her laughter mixed with the sustained whine of an ambulance siren in the distance. "Lucky for me, the school board had a policy that stated school administrators could not date their teaching personnel. However, Jonathan Madaris had made up his mind that he wanted me, and would not let some school administration policy stop him."

Syneda's interest was piqued. "What did he do?"

"Without me knowing what he was about, and after I had worked only a few weeks at his school, he had me transferred elsewhere. I was assigned to another school that was out of his district and over fifty miles from my home. I was furious. Not once did he consider the fact that such a move would be an inconvenience, as well as a hardship for me. He was only thinking of himself. He had only one goal in mind and that was to have me, one way or another."

"And what did you do?"

"I rebelled and fought him every step of the way. But he didn't give up on me until I did something that's almost unforgivable to a Madaris man."

"What?"

"I injured his pride."

Syneda raised a brow. "How?"

"I filed a complaint against him with the district school superintendent. It was somewhat similar to a modern-day sexual harassment complaint. Fortunately, although I didn't know it at the time, the school superintendent was a good friend of Jonathan's. He called him in and told him what I'd done. By that time, I had cooled off and had regretted my actions and withdrew the complaint. But Jonathan was very upset with me. It took him a while to come around."

Marilyn Madaris stopped walking and Syneda also ceased her steps. She found herself caught under the older woman's soft gaze that seemed to probe deep within her soul. "My sons, especially Dex and Clayton, with Dex being the worse, are no different from their father when it comes to the issue of the Madaris pride. They can be stubborn men, but when they fall in love, it's forever, and nothing, not even Madaris pride, can destroy that. It just takes a very strong woman to work around it."

Syneda's eyes widened suspiciously. "Why are you telling me this, Mrs. Madaris?"

"Because I thought you should know."

Syneda nodded. "All right," she replied with sudden calm. "And I only think it's fair that you know that I'm in love with Clayton, and that we've been seeing each other secretly for almost six months. But you knew that, didn't you?"

Marilyn Madaris wore an open, friendly smile. "I had my suspicions, but I wasn't absolutely sure until that night at Whispering Pines when I saw the two of you dancing together. I knew then."

Syneda was operating on pure amazement as she took a much-needed deep breath. "You picked up on it just by seeing us dance together? But we've danced together a lot of other times."

Marilyn Madaris's eyes lifted. A smile touched her lips. "But never like that. It was somehow different the way he was holding you, the way you were holding him, the way the two of you kept looking at each other. It was like the two of you were the only two people at that party."

She laughed. "I may be getting old but these eyes of mine don't miss too much, especially when it concerns my children." She smiled again. "However, I don't understand why you and Clayton wanted to keep it a secret."

A lump formed in Syneda's throat and she moved her shoulders under Mrs. Madaris's concentrated gaze. "I asked him to. I didn't want the family to know that we had been seeing each other."

"Why?"

Syneda took a deep breath. She silently admitted she was relieved to bring everything out in the open. "I was concerned about what you and the rest of the family would think of me getting involved with him."

"We would think what we've always known—you're a level-headed young lady and a special person. Clayton's falling in love with you makes you that much more special. For so long, his father and I were concerned that he would never find someone special to settle down with. I see that he has, and I'm glad it's you."

Syneda stared at the older woman. "We're having problems."

"Somehow I picked up on that, but I'm sure the two of you will work things out."

"And you don't mind that Clayton and I are having an affair?"

"An affair?" Marilyn Madaris's face broke into a wide grin. "Since Clayton is his father's son, I have every reason to believe something permanent is forthcoming. That's another thing about Madaris men," she continued, "once they find the woman they love, they need commitment. They believe when people just live together, it's too easy to walk away and call it quits. Forever to them means just that. Forever."

She eyed the young woman standing before her. "What I don't understand is why Clayton is upset?"

Syneda blushed although the thought of confiding in Mrs.

Madaris didn't bother her. She had long ago learned that the woman was very understanding. As they strolled back toward the house, Syneda told her everything, including the fact that Clayton was upset with her because she was staying with them instead of at his apartment.

Marilyn Madaris said very little as she listened to Syneda tell her about her mother's death, and about the father who had rejected her and the resulting childhood insecurities that had followed her through adulthood, and how she had let it come between her and Clayton.

Talking about it with the older woman made Syneda realize what Clayton had said all along was true. You can't let the past dictate the future. Before long the two women were back at the Madaris family home.

Before entering the door Syneda turned to the older woman. "Thanks, Mrs. Madaris, for listening."

"You don't have to thank me. I enjoyed our talk, and I know you're just the woman for my son. I've known that since the first time I saw you and Clayton together and you were giving him hell about something the two of you had disagreed on."

An approving smile touched her lips. "I think Clayton is a very lucky man."

Syneda's entire face spread into a smile with her comment. "I think so, too, but only because he has you for a mother."

The two women embraced before entering the kitchen where they found Dex sitting at the table reading the paper.

"Where is everyone?" his mother asked. The house was un-usually quiet.

"Caitlin is upstairs taking a nap, and Jordan talked her uncle Justin and her grampa into pizza. They thought it would be nice if they took everyone out for pizza instead of having it delivered here. I think they were trying to give you a break from all the noise."

Marilyn Madaris laughed. "Pizza on Thanksgiving Eve? They better have room for turkey tomorrow. Did Clayton go with them?"

"No, he's left and said he won't be back until tomorrow. Why?"

"I hate to inconvenience him, but Syneda is staying over at his place tonight."

Ignoring the shocked and surprised look on Syneda's face, as well as that of her second-born son, Marilyn Madaris continued, "That way we can have plenty of room for the kids to sleep comfortably since your father insists they all spend the night."

She then turned to Syneda. "Go gather your things, dear. You may use my car," she said, placing her car keys in Syneda's hand. "I expect both you and Clayton here in the morning no later than eleven. Understood?"

Syneda nodded before rushing from the kitchen and up the stairs to grab her things.

Dex stood, his expression wary. He didn't know how much he could or should tell his mother about Clayton and Syneda's relationship. "I don't think that was such a good idea, Mom, to send Syneda over to Clayton's for the night. Caitlin and I have plenty of room at our place. She could have stayed with us."

He hesitated briefly before continuing. "You've probably been too busy to notice Clayton's mood today. It's been the pits. And I really don't think you want to subject Syneda to that. You know how disagreeable they are most of the time, anyway. And with Clayton's present mood, one little spark could cause a big explosion. Being together is the last thing they need tonight."

A smile touched his mother's lips. "Perhaps. And perhaps not."

Less than an hour later Syneda stood in front of the door to Clayton's apartment. She had come prepared for anything but his rejection. She would not settle for that. Taking a deep breath, she rang the doorbell.

A somewhat tired and angry-looking Clayton opened the door. He lifted his brow in surprise. "What are you doing here? I thought I made it clear that I wanted to be left alone." There was a sharp edge to his voice.

Syneda swallowed nervously, but she refused to back down. "I need to talk to you, Clayton. Please."

Clayton hesitated a moment before moving aside. Syneda stepped inside his living room and turned to face him. The look on his face was inscrutable, and he was so distant that a knot of uncertainty coiled within her. However, she refused to give in to her anxiety. She was determined to accomplish what she came to do.

"I came to return something to you, Clayton."

Clayton shut the door and leaned back against it. His hand remained on the knob as if he needed support. "What? I thought you sent back everything."

"Everything but this," Syneda said. She opened the coat she was wearing.

Clayton's full attention was drawn to Syneda's outfit when she completely removed her coat and dropped it to the floor. His white dress shirt was the only thing she was wearing. His breath caught in his throat when she began unbuttoning the shirt.

"What do you think you're doing?" His voice was harsh with no vestige of softness.

Syneda stopped and met his gaze. The eyes staring back at her were cold, remote and distant. "I had a long talk with your mom this evening, Clayton, after you left," she admitted quietly.

He stepped from the door and came to stand before her. She could tell he was seething with mounting rage. "So?"

"And she knows about us. I told her everything."

Clayton's mouth hardened. "And just what do you expect from me for doing that? Some sort of medal for bravery?"

His words infuriated her, and anger flared in Syneda's eyes. She lifted her chin. "I thought you would be pleased about it. Evidently, you're not. Coming here was a mistake." She snatched her coat from the floor and walked past him. She had just opened the door when Clayton's arm shot in front of her and slammed it back shut.

Grabbing her by the shoulders, he turned her around to face him. "What do you want from me, Syneda? The only woman I've ever loved throws my love back in my face, and you think all you have to do is strut your behind in here and I'm supposed to fall at your feet? Sorry, babe, it doesn't work that way. At least not for me. I'm a man with feelings. I can bleed just like the next person."

Syneda glanced up at him when she heard the pain in his voice and saw the hurt in his glare. Her heart squeezed in anguish when she realized what he'd been going through over the past month. And she understood what Marilyn Madaris had meant about the Madaris pride. She had trampled his pride by rejecting the love he had offered her.

She lowered her eyes, her long lashes fanning her cheeks. She stood nervously before him trying to find the right words to express just how she felt. She decided on the simple approach, to speak from her heart. She lifted her eyes slowly to meet his.

"I was wrong, Clayton. And I know that now. I do love you, and more than anything, I want your love in return. I know you offered it to me once, but at the time I was too scared and too unsure of myself to even consider accepting it. But now I know what I want, and if you'll offer your love to me again, I promise to take it in my heart and cherish it. And from this day forward, I will always and forever be eternally yours."

Clayton stared down at her. They stood transfixed, mesmerized by a sensual power that for the moment bonded them together in heart and mind.

Syneda saw his hands ball into fists at his side and knew he was fighting hard to resist her. But then, little by little, she saw the coldness leave him and watched as warmth crept back into his body, beginning with his eyes.

He slowly bent his head to kiss her, his mouth moist and gentle against hers, and she knew that love had won. When he lifted his head, a flood of warmth and love shone in his eyes.

Tears of happiness slowly found their way down Syneda's cheeks, and he tenderly kissed them away. With a raw ache in his voice he said, "I want more from you than my shirt, Syneda. I agree with what you said about there having to be more between us than sex. And I want more, a lot more."

He covered her hand with his and pressed her palm against his mouth. "I want everything you have to give and still more. I want you to marry me, to have my children, to be my partner in life and love. I want you to walk beside me, and to believe in me, and believe that I love you more than anything or anyone in this world. I need you."

Syneda's heart swelled with love for him. "And I love and need you, Clayton. I need a man in my life whom I can trust, a man whom I can believe in and depend on." Her lips quirked in a smile. "And I want a man who wants more than the shirt off my back."

Clayton laughed, pulling her gently into his arms. "You'll get everything you want and more."

Syneda pressed her face into his shoulder. "You'll never know how hard it was for me to get out of your parents' home unnoticed wearing my coat with only your shirt underneath."

Clayton grinned. "You're something else." He hugged her tighter. "How soon can we get married?"

Syneda laughed affectionately as she pulled back out of his arms. "I'm open to suggestions."

Clayton smiled. "How about tomorrow?"

"Tomorrow?" Syneda laughed. "That's kind of rushing things a bit, isn't it?"

"I don't know if I'll be able to let you return to New York. Besides, I don't want to run the risk of you changing your mind on me."

"I won't change my mind. I want all the things you're offering—marriage, children, trust, and most of all love, your love."

"I guess I won't cheat my parents out of witnessing their last remaining son's marriage. Especially since they weren't present at Justin's and Dex's weddings. Do you have anything against a big wedding?"

Syneda shook her head. "No. In fact, I think I'd like that. We may as well do it right. How about a June wedding?"

"How about December?"

"June."

"I'd like a Christmas wedding."

"Next Christmas?"

"No, this Christmas."

Syneda grinned, shaking her head. "That's too soon. I say June."

Clayton frowned. "June? I don't know if I can wait that long."

Syneda chuckled. "June's only seven months away, and believe me, time will go by quickly. That will give us time to really plan things. Caitlin and Lorren will have had their babies and Christy will be home from college for the summer. Then there are the cases I need to finalize or transfer to other attorneys, not to mention the fact that I need to look for another job here in Houston."

Clayton's hand moved slowly down her back as he stared down at her. "You'll have another job. I have plenty of room in my office to take on a partner. I like the sound of Madaris and Madaris, Attorneys at Law. Don't you?"

Syneda smiled up at him, her heart bursting with happiness. "Yes, it sounds wonderful, but I'm a little worried we might disagree on every case we take on."

Clayton smiled and folded her to him. "I'll take that chance." He silently pledged to love and protect her for the rest of her life. "I think," he rasped close to her ear as his hands came to rest on her smooth thighs, "that you can return my shirt now."

Syneda pulled away from him. "My things are in the car."

Clayton nodded. "I'll bring them in later. Right now I can think of other things I prefer doing. I've always thought that my shirts look better on you than they do on me," he said huskily as he continued the task of unbuttoning the shirt. He paused briefly to bend his head. His mouth claimed hers in a kiss of both violent tenderness and turbulent longing.

Syneda kissed him back with all her heart and with all of the love that she had accumulated through the years but had been afraid to give.

"Your mom expects us by eleven in the morning," she whispered shakily when Clayton lifted his mouth from hers and began removing his shirt from her body.

"Eleven?" He smiled down at her. "In that case, we shouldn't waste any time," he said moments before gathering her up into his arms.

"My sentiments exactly," Syneda said, returning his smile and pulling his mouth down to hers.

Chapter 22

"What do you mean the two of you are getting married? Is this some kind of joke?"

The living room of the Madaris family home was in a complete uproar as everyone began shouting questions at Clayton and Syneda all at once. When? Where? How? Why?

Clayton laughed at the look of surprise and shock on most of the faces staring at them. He and Syneda had made the announcement to the family after arriving a few minutes before eleven and finding them gathered around the breakfast table.

He pulled Syneda to his side. "When? Sometime in June. Where? That's for Syneda to decide. How? The usual way two people get married. And why? Because we love each other very much," he said, pulling her to him and placing a gentle kiss on her lips.

Kattie shook her head, still not convinced. "Okay, you two, the joke is over. April Fool's Day is months away."

Syneda chuckled. "Believe us, Kattie. This isn't a joke. Clayton and I are really getting married."

Traci rolled her eyes heavenward. "Be real. The two of you don't even get along most of the time. Besides, you haven't been romantically involved, and…"

Traci stopped talking in midsentence when a thought suddenly hit her. She gave Syneda a long, penetrating stare.

"You're her!" she exclaimed. "You're the one responsible for Clayton's out-of-town trips." She shook her head. "I don't believe it. Why didn't someone tell me?"

Dex chuckled. "Evidently they wanted to keep it a secret, and everyone knows you can't hold water, Traci."

Traci turned and glared at her next-to-oldest brother. "And I suppose you knew?"

Dex smiled at his sister. "Yes, but they didn't tell me, either. I figured it out at Uncle Jake's party for Senator Lansing. All anyone had to do was to take a good look at them dancing together and figure it out."

"I saw them dancing together and didn't notice anything unusual," Kattie piped in.

"Probably because like most of the women there that night, you were more into noticing Sterling Hamilton," her husband Raymond suggested, grinning.

The majority of the women in the room nodded. That was a good possibility. A very good possibility.

"But why the secrecy? Why did the two of you hide the fact you were seeing each other?" Caitlin asked. She frowned at her husband. The nerve of him knowing and not sharing the information with her.

Syneda glanced up at Clayton. He took her hand in his. "When Syneda and I went to Florida together, it was as two good friends. However, we discovered something special while we were there. The reason we didn't tell any of you about it was because we wanted to go slow. We needed time to see where the attraction was going and what it meant. And we needed time to sort out our feelings."

He pulled her into his arms. "We have them sorted out now. We love each other very much and want to commit our lives to each other. I've asked her to make me the happiest man on earth by becoming my wife and she has agreed."

Syneda's gaze held Clayton's. He had made it all sound so romantic. He had eloquently and smoothly presented his family with an understandable, convincing and acceptable reason why they'd kept their relationship a secret over the past months. Only the two of them knew things hadn't really been quite that way.

"We're happy for both of you." Jonathan Madaris's words to his youngest son and future daughter-in-law were followed by similar ones from the others as they crowded around the happy couple offering words of congratulations once the surprise had officially worn off.

A poll was taken to see who else had known about the couple's involvement beforehand. Marilyn Madaris admitted knowing and confessed to passing the information to her husband that weekend at Whispering Pines.

Justin and Lorren admitted to finding out about the couple when they paid them a surprise visit to Florida.

And, surprising his wife, Kattie, Raymond admitted to knowing. He recalled seeing them together in Atlanta during one of his business trips, although they hadn't seen him.

"The reason I didn't tell you, Kattie," Raymond said when she glared at him, "is because you don't hold water any better than Traci."

This was truly a day of Thanksgiving, Syneda thought hours later as she sat around the dinner table with Clayton at her side and his family around her. News of their engagement had quickly spread and the telephone calls from other members of Clayton's family—uncles, aunts and cousins, began rolling in.

Everyone was more than happy to hear that the man who had loved his freedom, who often boasted of having to answer to no woman, and whose credo in life for the longest time had been "all men are fools, except for bachelors" was finally tying the knot. They were very pleased with his choice of wife. And there was no need to welcome her to the family because as far as they were concerned, she was a member of the family already.

"Tomorrow is the biggest shopping day of the year, Syneda," Traci said from across the huge table in the Madaris family dining room. "If you like, we can go shopping for—"

"No!" It seemed the entire Madaris family echoed the single word at the same time. Traci turned and glared at them. "And what's wrong with Syneda going shopping tomorrow?"

Daniel gave his wife a serious look. "There's nothing wrong with Syneda going shopping. You just aren't going with her. You've been suspended from shopping, remember?"

Justin chuckled. "Suspended from shopping? That's a new one."

Daniel smiled. "When you're married to Traci, you have to do what you have to do." He held up his hand when Clayton opened his mouth to say something. "And don't you dare remind me that the three of you warned me, Clayton."

Traci gave her husband an imploring look. "But, Dan, I have to go shopping with Syneda. How else will I know what she wants me to wear in her wedding?"

"The wedding isn't until June. You have seven months to pay off your charge cards, Traci," he replied.

Syneda smiled. It had been decided that Lorren and Caitlin would be her matrons of honor, and Clayton's three sisters, and their cousin, Felicia Laverne, would be her bridesmaids. She thought of asking two good friends from college to be her bridesmaids, too.

The wedding would be held at Gramma Madaris's church near Whispering Pines, and the way the plans were shaping up, the guest list would be enormous.

"Syneda won't be going shopping with anyone but me tomorrow," Clayton said. He captured her hand in his and held it tenderly. "The first thing I'm going to do in the morning is to take her to the jeweler."

"Make sure you pick out the most expensive ring," Clayton's youngest sister, Christy, suggested. "By the way, Syneda, who's giving you away at the wedding?"

Syneda met Clayton's eyes and smiled. "No one is giving me away, Christy. I'm giving myself away."

Dex laughed. "That should be interesting. But knowing you and Clayton, I guess we shouldn't expect the norm, should we?"

Syneda smiled at him. "No. As you can see, we're full of surprises."

Clayton watched as the morning light shone through his bedroom window. Its rays highlighted Syneda, who still slept soundly in his arms.

He moved, shifting her closer to him, wanting to be a part of her again, but knowing that she needed to rest. They had spent the entire Thanksgiving Day at his parents' home. It had been after midnight before they had returned to his apartment.

His lovemaking last night, just like it had been the night before when she'd shown up at his place wearing only his dress shirt, had been aggressive, demanding. It was as though he couldn't get enough of her. And she had only added fuel to his fire by meeting him kiss for kiss, stroke for stroke, matching his demands with equal fervor.

He leaned over and whispered in her ear. "I love you."

A smile touched Syneda's lips as she struggled to open her eyes. "And I love you, too, Madaris. Now kiss me awake."

"My pleasure." His mouth found hers in a passionate kiss that she returned.

Moments later, after he had broken off the kiss, she rested against him, feeling like the luckiest woman in the world. All the past fears, doubts, disappointments and pain seemed to have left her under the onslaught of Clayton's love. And she knew that as long as he was a part of her life, she could deal with just about anything.

She sat up, ignoring the morning chill that was in the room. "I went to the cemetery to visit my mother last week, Clayton."

Clayton gently pulled her back down beside him. He understood that must have been an important undertaking for her. She had once told him that she had never visited her mother's grave, and had shared with him the reason why.

He raised himself up and looked down at her, concern on his face. "How did it go?"

"It went okay. I had to go there in order to close a chapter in my life forever. I knew I loved you and didn't want to deal with my father in my life any longer. I wanted to get rid of it once and for all."

"And did you?"

"Yes."

"I'm glad." He kissed her again, this kiss longer than before. Afterward when she lay in his arms snuggled close to him, he wondered if he should tell her about hiring Alex to find her father. It had been his original plan, right after she had broken things off with him, to find the man and beat the hell out of him for what he had done to her, and for being the cause of all their problems. But then, after rationality had set in, he had kept Alex looking for the man just out of pure curiosity. He wanted a name. He couldn't help but wonder what kind of man would do what her father had done to a child.

But now, there was a whole new element to everything with Alex's revelation that two other investigative agencies were looking into Syneda's past.

"Syneda?"

"Hmm?"

"Have you ever tried finding your father?"

He felt her tense. She looked up at him, frowning. "Of course not. Why would I?"

"And you know nothing about him?"

"Nothing other than the little bit I told you."

"So you have no idea how he looks? Your mother never kept a picture of him around the house?"

Syneda sat up again. "Why all the questions, Clayton?"

"Just curious. We don't have to talk about it if discussing him upsets you."

She shook her head. "No, discussing him doesn't bother me now." She lay back down in his arms. "I don't know how he looks, and I don't recall Mama ever having a picture of him. I assume he's some light-skinned brother with light-colored eyes since my mother's coloring was darker than mine, and her eyes were dark brown."

Syneda frowned. "Now, to think about it, I remember her telling me all the time when I was a lot younger how much I looked liked him. She stopped telling me that after I began asking questions about him."

Syneda shifted in his arms. "Now I want to ask you a question."

Clayton nodded, smiling. "What do you want to ask?"

"Do you know anything about Larry Morgan being hired at Remington Oil?"

He chuckled. "Why would I know anything about it, sweetheart?"

Syneda gave him a pointed look. "Because you do. I know it and you know it whether you admit it or not."

Clayton shrugged. "End of discussion."

She frowned at him, knowing he wouldn't fess up. But she had a way to make him talk and confess all. She smiled sweetly up at him. "Can I see that case of condoms you have in your closet?"

Syneda held her left hand out in front her. Tears misted her eyes as she looked at the three-carat diamond ring on her third finger that Clayton had just placed there. It was absolutely stunning.

It had been past noon before they had left Clayton's apartment. After showing her the case of condoms in his closet, he had proceeded to put a few of them to good use. The first place they had stopped on their shopping expedition was the jeweler.

"Oh, Clayton, this ring is absolutely gorgeous." She looked up at him. "Are you sure?"

Clayton glanced down at Syneda's face and saw the uncertainty lingering there. It was there in her eyes. Dear heaven!

How could she still doubt anything about him? But then he remembered she had had eighteen years of doubt and pain from another man she had wanted to believe in. Placing her complete trust in someone didn't come easy for her.

"Am I sure about what, Syneda? That I want to marry you or that I love you?" he asked her quietly.

"Both." She bowed her head, unable to meet the intensity in his eyes any longer.

"Syneda?" He waited for her to look up at him. Waited for the abundance of golden-bronze hair that fanned across her shoulders to fall back in place and frame her face.

When she lifted her eyes to him, her gaze was searching his for answers. "Yes?"

"I'm sure," he said, his voice low and soft. "I'm sure that I love you very much, and that you're the woman I've been waiting for all my life, even without knowing I was waiting. And I'm sure I want to marry you, to make you my wife. I want to give you my name and one day I want to give you my babies. I promise to be a good husband to you and a good father to our children."

She smiled through the tears that misted her eyes. "Babies? Meaning more than one?"

Clayton grinned. "Yes, babies, meaning more than one."

He tilted her chin up with a knuckle. His expression was serious. "Trust me, Syneda, and know that I would never deliberately hurt you." His tone suddenly became fierce. "Believe that I love you with all my heart and soul, and that I will love you for all eternity. And that I will always be here for you."

He stepped back and, ignoring the fact there were other shoppers in the store, some more curious than others, he opened his arms to her.

Syneda stepped into his embrace, and he drew her to him. Reveling in his touch, she clung to him. "Thanks for loving me, Clayton."

He tightened his arms around her. "Thank you for letting me

love you." After some moments had passed, he checked his watch. "We have a few more stores to hit before dinner."

Taking her hand in his, he asked, "Ready?"

She nodded.

"Then let's go, baby."

"Are you certain you don't mind having dinner here?"

Syneda smiled. "I'm positive. I know about your past reputation and that it included other women, lots of them. And since this was your hangout, it wouldn't surprise me to run into a few here tonight. That really doesn't bother me. I'm woman enough to get beyond that. Besides, we are here for a worthy cause."

"True," Clayton said as they entered Sisters. They were meeting Justin and Lorren and Dex and Caitlin for dinner. Each year on the day after Thanksgiving, the local chapter of the Delta Sigma Theta Sorority sponsored a tree-decorating event at Sisters. Each ornament was individually purchased and placed on the tree and came with the name and address of an underpriviledged child they would sponsor for Christmas. The place was packed and Clayton was glad for the turnout.

"Welcome to Sisters, and I understand congratulations are in order, Clayton."

Clayton smiled down at Netherland Brooms, the attractive owner of Sisters. "Thanks, and yes, they are. I would like you to meet Syneda Walters, my fiancée. Syneda, this is Netherland Brooms, but we all call her Nettie. She's the owner of Sisters."

Nettie took Syneda's hand in hers. "I'm glad someone finally hooked this guy on in," Nettie said to Syneda, grinning.

Syneda smiled at the woman's comment. "Yeah, and I'm glad I was fortunate enough to be the one to do it."

"The two of you make a lovely couple, and I wish you much happiness."

"Thanks."

Nettie turned to Clayton. "Your brothers and their wives are here. They have been quite busy this year, haven't they?"

Clayton laughed, knowing she was referring to the pregnant state of his two sisters-in-law. "Yes, it appears they have been pretty busy."

Clayton and Syneda followed Nettie over to the table where the Madaris party was sitting.

"We were wondering when the two of you were going to get here," Dex said, smiling. "Justin and I can't starve our ladies too long, don't forget they're each eating for two."

"Sorry," Clayton said, grinning. "We lost track of the time shopping."

"The ring!" Lorren suddenly exclaimed. "You got your ring!"

Syneda nodded, beaming happily and holding her hand out for the others to see. "Isn't it gorgeous?"

Lorren and Caitlin released oohs and aahs. Justin and Dex gave their brother nods of approvals.

The hostess came and took their order and within a reasonable time, their dinner was served. Afterward, Justin ordered champagne to toast the engaged couple.

"Well, well, well, look who just walked in," Dex said, slanting a grin in Clayton's direction. "And look who's with her."

Clayton turned and rolled his eyes to the ceiling, while muttering a silent curse. Why did his cousin Felicia have to show up now? And of all people, Bernard Wilson was with her.

"I'm sure she appreciates you sending Bernard her way," Justin said, grinning.

Syneda lifted a brow after seeing an uncomfortable look on Clayton's face. "Is something wrong?"

He shrugged. "No."

Clayton heard the sounds of Justin and Dex chuckling and glared across the table at them.

Syneda looked around her. Her attention focused on Clayton's cousin and the handsome man who was with her. They had seen them and were headed over to their table.

"Hi, everyone," Felicia said when she reached the table. "Glad to see everyone out for a good cause. Let me introduce Bernard. But I think he knows everyone already."

Bernard smiled as they sat down to join them. "I met everyone at that party for Senator Lansing, except for you," he said to Syneda. "We were never officially introduced," he said extending his hand to her. "Bernard Wilson."

Syneda took the hand he offered. "Syneda Walters."

"Soon to be Syneda Madaris," Felicia said, smiling. "And thanks for asking me to be in the wedding."

"The two of you are getting married?" Bernard asked Syneda in surprise, letting his gaze move from her to Clayton.

"That's right," Clayton said, sipping some of his champagne. "Why?"

"But I thought…"

He didn't finish his statement when the hostess came to take the newcomers' order.

They got into talking about other things. Dex and Justin began enlightening everyone about the small airplane the brothers had purchased together.

Bernard couldn't help noticing Syneda and the amount of candy and nuts she was nibbling on. And that was after she had finished eating a slice of coconut pie with vanilla ice cream.

Syneda felt Bernard's gaze on her and stopped munching. She lifted a brow. "Is anything wrong, Bernard?"

He smiled at her. "No, I was just noticing how much you're enjoying those nuts. You do know they're fattening, don't you?"

Syneda heard Dex and Justin clear their throats. She raised a brow to Bernard. "They're fattening?"

"Extremely fattening since they're filled with oil. I know how hard it is to lose weight and how it's even harder to keep it off. You've done an excellent job, and I admire you for it."

Syneda smiled at him. "Thanks, but you must have me confused with someone else. I've never had a weight problem. I can eat like a horse and never gain a pound."

He raised a brow at her before turning to frown at Clayton. The sly smile Clayton gave him let him know he'd been had. "And I guess you are not wearing colored eye contacts," Bernard said drily.

Syneda grinned, wondering why he would think she was. "No, I'm not. Why would you think I was?"

"Because I was deliberately led to believe you were. In fact, I was led to believe a number of things about you that evidently aren't true."

"Really? And who would tell you untrue things about me?"

Bernard laughed, shaking his head. "Someone who evidently felt a need to protect his interest."

Syneda raised an arched brow, then realization dawned. She turned to Clayton and glared at him. "Would you like to tell me what's going on?"

As if on cue, Justin and Dex stood and, turning to their wives, suddenly suggested they use that time to select their ornament for the Christmas tree. Felicia and Bernard quickly decided to do the same.

When the table had cleared, Syneda asked Clayton again. "Would you like to explain what's going on? What did you tell Bernard about me?"

Dark eyes looked at her. "He had plans to hit on you that night, so I decided to take action."

"By telling him I had a weight problem and wore contacts? And just what else did you tell him?"

Clayton shrugged. "I told him that wasn't your natural hair color."

"You did what! I don't believe you did such a thing." Syneda glared at him. "Why all the lies? I could have handled the likes of Bernard Wilson that night."

"I'm sure you could have. I just didn't want him near you, that's all."

Syneda shook her head at Clayton's admission. It was hard to believe he had been jealous. She then remembered his behavior in Florida. At the time it hadn't made sense. Now considering everything, it did.

After a few minutes, she couldn't help the smile that stole across her lips. She should be furious with him but wasn't. He was at times her nemesis, but mostly her friend. He was her lover and soon, in seven months, he would be her husband.

"What am I going to do with you, Clayton Madaris?"

"Love me."

She leaned over and kissed his cheek. "Heaven help me but I do that already." She took his hand in hers. "Come on, let's go purchase our ornaments and help decorate the tree."

Clayton's alarm went off at six o'clock Monday morning. He missed Syneda already. It had been hard putting her back on the plane for New York yesterday afternoon.

He got out of bed and went into the bathroom. He returned to the bedroom moments later when the sound of the phone interrupted his shower.

"Hello."

"I hear congratulations are in order."

Clayton chuckled. "Good morning, Alex. I see news travels fast."

"Yes, especially when a fellow bachelor defects. Trask called last night and I told him the news. He asked me if you had gone crazy or something."

Clayton laughed. "The next time you talk to Trask, tell him I said I'm not crazy. I just happen to be a man very much in love. His time will come one day, so will yours."

"I hope not. Besides, speaking for myself, I promised your kid sister on her thirteenth birthday I'd wait for her to grow up," he teased. "Congratulations, anyway. The only saving grace for you is I happen to think the woman you're marrying is first class. It's about time you noticed it."

Clayton couldn't help but agree.

"The reason I'm calling so bright and early is because I have that information you wanted. I have the names of the other two investigating agencies, as well as the identity of Syneda's father."

For some reason, Clayton felt uneasy. "And?"

"I've located him, Clayton, and you won't believe in a million years just who he is. And I prefer not having this conversation over the phone. Are you free for breakfast?"

"No. I have to be in court by eight-thirty. How about lunch?"

"Lunch is fine, and I prefer somewhere private."

Clayton frowned. "Sounds serious."

After a moment of hesitation, Alex said, "Depends on how you look at it. I'll let you decide."

"All right. We'll have lunch in my office. I'll order sandwiches."

"Okay, and remember I don't do mayo, and I do just a tad of mustard."

"Okay."

"And Clayton."

"Yeah?"

"I'm tired of turkey."

Clayton shook his head, laughing. "Got it."

Chapter 23

"I understand congratulations are in order."

Syneda lifted her gaze from the paper she was reading and saw Thomas Rackley standing in the doorway of her office.

An easy smile played at the corners of her mouth. "Thanks. I guess I don't have to ask how you found out, do I?"

He grinned, shaking his head. "Office gossip is at its best today."

She leaned back in her chair. "I assumed that it would be."

Thomas stepped inside her office and saw the radiance of her smile. He cocked his head to the side and studied her for a moment. "You're happy, aren't you?"

The smile on Syneda's face widened. "I think I'm happier than anyone has a right to be."

He weighed her answer with a critical squint before his eyes grew openly sincere. "I'm glad. You deserve to be happy. I'm glad you met someone and fell in love."

"It wasn't easy."

Thomas chuckled. "And no doubt you gave the poor guy pure hell."

Syneda tried suppressing the grin that crossed her face. "No doubt."

His smile deepened into laughter. "I'm glad he hung in there."

The amused look left Syneda's eyes when she thought about what Thomas had just said. Clayton had hung in there when most men would not have. "I'm glad he did, too."

Clayton gave Alexander Maxwell a long, penetrating stare. He was absolutely speechless and had been since Alex had provided him with the information he'd wanted, especially the identity of Syneda's father.

He stood and walked over to the window and looked out. His mind felt bruised by the bitter truths Alex had just hit him with. Of all the men who could have fathered Syneda, it was hard to believe the one man he would never have suspected in a million years was the one.

"So what are you planning to do with this information?"

Alex's question abruptly invaded his thoughts. Clayton shrugged heavy shoulders. He felt like the weight of the world was sitting on them. He turned to Alex. "I don't know."

"You're surprised, aren't you?"

Keeping Alex's gaze, he nodded, his breath feeling heavy in his chest. "Weren't you?"

"Sure, I was. When I decided to do a little further investigating, surprise isn't quite the word I would use with what I found out. Hell-shocked is more like it. This was one of the most challenging puzzles I've pieced together in a long time."

"I believe you," Clayton said, returning to his seat behind the desk. "Is there any way you could be mistaken about any of this?"

"No. That's why I went the extra mile on this one and located Syneda's mother's friend, that nurse, Clara Boyd, who conveniently disappeared after Jan Walters died. I knew there had to be a missing link someplace. And now when you really think about it, you'll agree that Syneda is the spittin' image of her father."

Clayton nodded as he absently traced the pattern of the wood grain across his desk. "Just for sanity purposes, let's go over all of this again."

Alex nodded, understanding completely. "All right," he said, stretching his legs out in front of him, trying to get comfortable in the chair. That wasn't too easy for his six-foot-four frame. "Those other two private investigators are based in Washington, D.C. That immediately told me something. Whatever was going on was somehow linked to the political scene. I just didn't make Syneda's connection until Senator Lansing's name popped up. Then I figured out that one of the investigators was trying to get the lowdown on the senator."

He stood when the chair became too uncomfortable. "Since it seems Senator Lansing was dating Syneda's mother during her senior year of college, the year Syneda was conceived, it appears he's her father. A father who didn't claim his child. It's my guess they plan to release their scoop to the media. When they do, all hell is going to break loose, and Syneda will be caught right smack in the middle. I can see the headlines now, and they definitely won't be positive for Senator Lansing. He'll have a lot of explaining to do."

"What about the other investigator?"

"I believe he's working for the senator. I think Senator Lansing somehow got wind of what was going on and decided to check things out for himself. Both investigators are turning in what they think are accurate reports."

Clayton rubbed his chin. "Accurate reports? That's a laugh."

"Yeah, and the only person who knows the truth, besides you and me, is Senator Lansing."

"Let's not forget Clara Boyd."

Alex's face hardened as he remembered his interview with the woman. She had broken down and told him the truth under his intense questioning. "Yeah, some friend she turned out to be." He sat back down after stretching his legs some. "So, going back to my earlier question, what are you going to do with the information?"

Clayton stood. "I'm going to do everything I can to protect Syneda. She's been hurt enough. The first thing I'm going to do is to see Senator Lansing." He leaned over his desk and punched the intercom button. "Serena, book me a flight to D.C. as soon as possible."

Senator Lansing looked up upon hearing the knock on the door. "Come in."

Braxter walked in. "The investigator's report is here, sir," he said, handing the senator the huge envelope he carried. "It was delivered a few moments ago."

The senator nodded, taking the packet Braxter handed him. "Have you read it?"

"No. I considered it a private matter."

"Thanks, I appreciate it."

"Just keep in mind, Senator, someone intends to ruin your reputation if they can with that same report."

The senator rubbed a hand across his face. "I haven't forgotten. And, Braxter, please hold my calls for a while. I want to go through this report immediately." He checked his watch. "It's almost closing time. You can go on home if you'd like."

Braxter shook his head. "There's something I need to work on. I'll be out front if you need me."

"Thanks."

"Oh, yeah. On Sundays I always buy newspapers from major cities in Texas to see how well you're doing in the polls. This article appeared in the society column of a Houston paper and caught my attention." He handed the newspaper clipping to the senator. "I thought you might be interested."

The senator scanned the article that announced Texas attorney Clayton Madaris's engagement to fellow New York attorney Syneda Walters. The wedding was planned for June of next year.

"It seems Syneda Walters will be marrying Jacob Madaris's nephew," Braxter said, breaking the silence in the room.

Senator Lansing took a deep breath. "Yes, it appears that way, doesn't it. I've known Clayton Madaris a long time. He's a fine young man and an outstanding attorney."

Once Braxton left, closing the door behind him, the senator pulled the papers out of the packet and began reading.

Laying aside the packet that had just been delivered to her, Celeste stood and walked to her bedroom and sprawled out in a chair next to her bed. She raked a hand through her shoulder-length hair, wondering why she felt so awful.

The job was completed. She was sure the packet in her living room contained information Senator Harris would be eager to get his hands on. Although Emery Fulton, her friend from college who had done the investigative work for her, hadn't told her exactly what was in the report, he had said it contained some information on Senator Lansing that if released to the media, could be damaging.

Standing, she walked back into the living room and picked up the packet. She should call Senator Harris and let him know that she had the information he'd paid her to get. But for some reason she couldn't make herself pick up the phone and do that.

For the past two years she had cultivated a pretty good life for herself. It was a life she enjoyed with the material things she had always wanted as a child but never had. Thanks to a mother who ran off and left her with an alcoholic father at the age of twelve, she had learned to survive without help from anyone. And she had never wanted or needed anyone.

She had met Senator Harris a couple of years ago when he had come into her travel agency to arrange a cruise for him and his wife. It didn't take long for him to figure out that in her profession, since she came in contact with a lot of people, especially by planning trips for those in political circles, she could be an asset to him.

At first he had only been interested in inside information on some of his supposedly close friends. She had passed information to him about Senator Mat Williams's affair with a woman young enough to be his daughter, Senator Paul Dunlap's daughter's abortion, and Senator Carl Booker's son's drug addiction.

He had paid her well for the information she had obtained with Emery's help. But this assignment involving Braxter had been the first that she had gotten personally involved with to the point of going so far as to sleep with someone to get information. And since the day Braxter had discovered the truth, her life had not been the same. Somehow his pain had become hers, especially knowing she'd been the cause of it.

She picked up the phone to make the call to Senator Harris and then slammed it back down. She just couldn't do it. The amount of money he had paid her no longer mattered. She would pay back every penny of it to him.

She went into the bedroom and slipped into her coat. Going back into the living room she picked up the packet, grabbed her purse, then walked out of the door.

Nedwyn Lansing leaned back against his desk chair as he released a long-drawn breath. Suddenly all the anger he had ever felt in his entire lifetime hit him with the force of a tidal wave.

How could this have happened? How could such a mistake be made? How could Jan's child be turned over to the authorities when her father was very much alive and would have wanted her had he known about her?

He shook his head to calm his temper. There was no doubt in his mind that Syneda Walters was Jan's child. The report clearly named Jan as Syneda's biological mother and gave the reason she'd been placed in a foster home after Jan's death. Her father had not come to claim his child.

He picked up the phone knowing the one person he had to call immediately. He paused when there was a knock on his door. He then remembered that Braxter had not yet left.

"What is it, Braxter?"

Braxter opened the door and came in. He immediately noticed the intense expression the senator wore. "I just got a call from security downstairs. Clayton Madaris is here to see you."

"Clayton Madaris?" The senator shook his head slowly,

glancing down at the report before him. He sat silently for a moment before saying, "Have security send him up."

Clayton frowned when he stepped into the senator's office and saw the other man standing there. "I was hoping to get a chance to speak with you privately, Senator."

The senator nodded. He then proceeded to introduce the two men. "Braxter is my top aide, Clayton, and we can talk openly in front of him. Besides, it's about time I let him in on what's going on, since I have a pretty good idea as to why you're here. Let's sit down."

Once everyone was seated, Clayton began. "I'm sure by now you're aware someone is trying to ruin your political career, Senator."

The senator's gaze didn't flicker from Clayton's. "Yes, I'm aware of it. What I would like to know is what's your connection, and how do you know so much about it?"

Clayton breathed an annoyed sigh but calmly contained himself. Although he had known the senator a number of years due to the senator's close relationship with his late uncle Robert and his uncle Jake, Clayton understood his need to be cautious in certain situations. This was one of those situations.

"My connection is the woman I plan to marry. Someone is planning to use her as a weapon in an attempt to destroy your credibility with the people. The reason I know so much about it is because I hired a private investigator to find her father for me."

"And you think you've found him." It was a statement rather than a question.

"I know I have."

The senator took a deep breath and stood. He paced the room several times before coming to a stop in front of Clayton. "And you believe I'm your man, don't you?"

Clayton's gaze never left the senator. "No. I know for a fact that you're not."

The senator raised a surprised brow. "Do you?"

"Yes. My investigator is a very thorough man who loves putting together puzzles. The only reason I came here before going to see her father is to get some answers about a few things."

"If you're going to ask me if he knew about her, the answer is a definite no. There's no way he would have known and not claimed his child. He was too deeply in love with Jan. In fact, he still loves her. Her dying changed nothing. The second week of May of each year, on the date they met, he tortures himself by first visiting her grave, then later he tries to erase the pain by drinking himself to death for two days. And he's not a drinker. I'm the only one he'll let see him that way. And I make it a point to go visit him every year in May to help him through that painful period."

Braxter had been sitting quietly listening to Clayton and the senator, trying to follow along and piece together what they were talking about. The only thing he understood was the explanation for the senator's mysterious trips each May.

"Excuse me," he interrupted the two men. "I'm trying to follow the two of you here." He turned to the senator. "Are you saying that report I gave you from the investigator indicates you're Syneda Walters's father?"

"After reading it, one would assume that, yes."

"But you're not?"

"No, I'm not."

Braxter shook his head. "I don't understand. Why would anyone assume you're her father if you aren't?"

The senator went over to the window and looked out. He could see the Lincoln Monument in the distance even in the dusk of night. He turned back to Braxter. "Most people thought Syneda's mother, Jan Walters, and I dated exclusively during our senior year of college."

"But that wasn't the case?"

"No. We just wanted people to think that we did."

A look of ungoverned confusion shone in Braxter's eyes. "Why?"

Sadness shone in the senator's gaze. "Because society wasn't ready to accept what they considered as forbidden love."

When Braxter looked even more confused, Clayton decided to intercede by asking him, "Have you ever heard the term 'jungle fever'?"

"Yes, of course." Braxter stared first at Clayton then back at the senator when understanding dawned. He paused for a moment before finally asking, "And just who is Syneda Walters's father?"

The senator hesitated briefly before saying quietly, "Syntel Tremain Remington."

Braxter was shocked into silence. "S. T. Remington of Remington Oil?" His voice was filled with disbelief.

"Yes, and I need to talk to Syntel as soon as possible. He knows nothing about any of this. The shock may be too much for him. Arrange a flight that will take me to Austin tonight."

"I'm going with you," Clayton spoke up.

"I think this is something he needs to hear from me personally."

"I agree, but I intend to be there when he hears it. Like I said earlier, there are a number of questions that I want answered. My main concern is Syneda and how she's going to handle all of this. For years she assumed her father abandoned her. Now from what I understand that's not the case. I want to know if he knew his father had intercepted a phone call meant for him and paid the caller good money not to give Syntel's name to the authorities as Syneda's father."

"Is that what happened?"

"Yes. We were able to find the woman, and she told us everything. She even admitted taking the money."

The senator shook his head. "He will never forgive his father for that. He loved Jan deeply."

At that moment there was a soft knock on the door.

"Yes, come in," the senator called out.

The door to the senator's office swung open and Celeste walked in.

"What are you doing here?" Braxter snapped. He was both surprised and upset to see her. His chest heaved with outrage at the sight of her. "Who gave security the approval to let you in here?"

Celeste nodded to the other two men in the room before answering Braxter. "I deliver travel packages to occupants of this building all the time. Security is used to seeing me."

"What do you want?"

She placed the packet on the desk. "I came to give you this and to say I'm sorry. I hope one day you'll forgive me for what I did." She turned to leave.

"Excuse me, miss," Clayton said, putting together what was transpiring between the two individuals. "Who hired you to get information on Senator Lansing?"

Celeste turned back around. She remembered Clayton from the party at Whispering Pines. She bit her lower lip. It had taken every scrap of courage for her to come here tonight to make amends. But she had to come. She had to do the right thing.

Her gaze left Clayton, then went to the senator, before finally coming to rest on Braxter. She knew he hated her and would never forgive her. The piercing dark eyes staring back at her did not show any signs of forgiveness.

She knew at that moment why she hadn't been able to go through with passing the report on to Senator Harris. She had fallen in love with Braxter. Her eyes closed momentarily, shielding his angry glare from her. When she reopened them, she shifted her gaze back to Clayton. "The person who hired me is Senator John Harris."

She then turned and quickly walked out of Senator Lansing's office.

Chapter 24

"Are you sure he's going to be here?" Clayton asked as he and
Senator Lansing stepped into the elevator of an elegant apartment
building near downtown Austin.

"I'm pretty positive," Senator Lansing replied, keying a
special code into the elevator door panel box. "During the week,
Syntel stays here instead of commuting back and forth to the
ranch. And he seldom goes out in the evenings."

Clayton nodded. Since discovering Syntel Remington was
Syneda's father, he had begun searching his mind for whatever
personal information he knew about him. It was a known fact that
he had never married. He also remembered reading somewhere
that he had taken over the running of Remington Oil fifteen
years ago, upon his father's death.

Clayton's thoughts came to an end when the elevator door
opened and they stepped into a plushly carpeted hallway and
walked toward the only door on the floor.

The door was opened on the second knock. A surprised expression lit Syntel Remington's face. He moved aside to let the two men enter. "Ned, I didn't know you were in Austin." He then turned questioning eyes to Clayton. "Madaris, this is a pleasant surprise."

For the first time since meeting him over a year ago, Clayton looked deeply into Syntel Remington's eyes. They were eyes so much like Syneda's in color and shape that he couldn't believe he hadn't noticed them before. But then he hadn't been aware that the man standing before him was her father. He also noticed that Syntel and Syneda shared similar smiles and the same well-defined features.

"I just arrived in Austin less than an hour ago," Senator Lansing said. "I flew in from Washington. We both did. There's an important matter we need to discuss with you, Syntel."

Syntel Remington's brow lifted. "This sounds serious, Ned."

"Trust me, it is."

"Let's go into the study. I was just about to settle down and get some reading done."

He led them to a brightly lit room where bookcases lined both sides. He gestured for them to take a seat. He then took a seat behind a large oak desk.

"All right, Ned, what is it? What's so important to send you racing to my door from Washington with one of Texas's most dynamic attorneys in tow?" he asked, managing a wobbly smile. He was confused and concerned with the expression his best friend wore.

The room fell silent, and a few moments later Senator Lansing spoke. "It's about Jan."

Syntel Remington's eyes suddenly became distant and pained. "What about Janeda?"

The senator's lips lifted in a faint smile. Janeda had disliked her birth name and in college she had shortened it to Jan. No one got away with calling her Janeda. No one except Syntel.

Syntel Remington stood, crossing his arms like a protective

shield. Clayton couldn't help but note it was something Syneda did occasionally.

"Ned, I asked you, what about Janeda?"

The room fell silent once more and before Senator Lansing could respond Syntel spoke again. "All right, I think I get it now. If the two of you are here to warn me that you've gotten wind that one of those slick and sleazy tabloids have somehow dug up information about my relationship with Janeda and plan to print it, don't concern yourselves with it. I will never deny ever loving her. You should know that, Ned."

Nedwyn Lansing nodded. "Yes, I know, Syntel, but that's not it. That's not why we're here. There's something else, something you should know. And I think you should sit back down before hearing it."

Syntel looked for a moment like he wasn't going to take the senator's suggestion, but then he took his seat again. "What is it, Ned?"

"Jan had a child. Your child."

Clayton watched the color drain from the man's face with Senator Lansing's words.

"What did you say?" Syntel's lips barely moved when he asked the question.

Senator Lansing forced himself to respond calmly. "I said Jan had a child. Your child. A girl."

Syntel jumped up out of his seat, nearly knocking a plant off his desk in the process. His face was filled with rage. "Who told you that lie, Ned? How could you believe such a thing?"

"It's true, Syntel. I checked it out myself. If you remember, Jan disappeared right after you'd left for the Air Force Academy. I think she did it because she knew she was pregnant."

"If what you say is true, why wouldn't she have told me? She knew I loved her. There was nothing I would not have done for her."

"I think she knew that, and that's the reason she left without telling you. She didn't see a place for her in your life. You and I know that society would never have accepted a marriage between the two of you. At least not back then. She knew it, too, and left."

Syntel slumped back down in his chair. He buried his face in his hands, shaking his head. "No, I don't believe it. I refuse to believe Janeda would give our child away."

"She didn't give the child away. She raised your child alone as a single parent until her death."

Syntel's head snapped up. "Are you saying I have a child somewhere? A daughter?"

"Yes. She was ten years old when Jan died."

Syntel shook his head as if dazed with disbelief. "What happened to her?"

"Because the authorities assumed she didn't have any living relatives after Jan died, she became a ward of this state and was placed in a foster home."

"No!"

Clayton watched as Syntel Remington's entire body jerked as if it had been struck. His face filled with rage. "Are you saying my child was raised by strangers?"

Clayton spoke for the first time. "That was the only recourse under the circumstances. But I can tell you that the Phillipses were good people and she was treated very well."

Syntel looked at Clayton as if he had forgotten he was there. His shoulders slumped. "So no one knew I was her father?"

With a sigh of resignation, Senator Lansing stood, knowing he had to tell his friend the rest of the story. During the flight from D.C. to Austin, Clayton had told him everything, including his investigator's personal interview with Clara Boyd. It had been a case of downright deceit and betrayal by Syntel's father.

"That's not true, Syntel. There were two others who knew you were the child's father. When Jan knew she was dying, she told someone she thought she could trust to contact you. In fact, she died believing you were contacted and were coming for your child. She even told your daughter you would be coming for her."

He wiped a film of perspiration from his forehead before continuing. "However, instead of getting you, the person who'd made the call for Jan spoke to your father instead. And…"

"And what?"

"Your father made the decision not to pass the information on to you and to make sure your name was never connected to Jan's child. Clayton hired an investigator who has located the woman. She admits receiving money from your father in payment for not revealing your identity to the Children's Services Department."

Syntel raked his fingers through his tousled hair. The expression on his face was pained, disbelieving, enraged. "That can't be true," he said in a strained voice choked with deep emotion. "My father would not have been that cruel, that heartless, that hateful. He would not have turned his back on his own grandchild, my child, my own flesh and blood," he said, as if trying to convince himself. But looking at the sympathy in his best friend's eyes and Clayton's, he knew deep down his father had done just that.

"Where is she? Oh, God, please tell me you know where she is now."

Clayton stood and faced the man. He had to swallow in an attempt to remove the lump in his throat. "She lives in New York."

"New York?"

"Yes." Pulling his wallet from his pants pocket Clayton took out a picture he'd had taken of Syneda when they had visited Atlanta. As she smiled for the camera, her sea-green eyes shone brightly, her golden-bronze hair flowed about her shoulders and highlighted her light brown complexion.

"This is your daughter, Syntel, the woman I love and plan to marry in June."

A wry smile touched Clayton's lips as he realized something. "I often wondered about the origin of her name since it's unusual. Now I know where it came from. Janeda was thinking of you when she named your daughter. It's a combination of both your names. However, her middle name is all yours. The woman in this picture is Syneda Tremain Walters." He handed the picture to Syntel.

Syntel nervously accepted the photograph Clayton handed to him. There was complete silence in the room as he looked at it. His eyes began filling with tears. Suddenly the only sounds in the room were the sounds of Syntel Remington's heartwrenching sobs.

After Nedwyn and Clayton had left, Syntel Remington sat slumped down in a chair. A spasm of pain flitted across his face when he thought of what his father had done.

Janeda had given him a daughter, and in the end she had believed in their love enough to want him to know about their child, to want him to take care of her, even when they had not seen each other in ten years.

But she had known that his love for her would have survived the test of time and that he would want their child, and that he would take care of her. Janeda had died believing in him.

He couldn't help but remember the last night he and Janeda had spent together. He was to report to the Air Force Academy the day after graduation. The Vietnam War was on everyone's mind, and it had been the main thing on his that night. Maybe if it hadn't been, he would have paid more attention to her mood and the words she had spoken to him. And maybe he would have sensed some sort of a change in her, and noted that something was bothering her.

She had been the joy of his life, his true love. To him the color of their skin had never made a difference. But to her it had. She'd always been afraid of what others would think about it. Interracial relationships had not been accepted during that time, and that was the reason Ned had been used as their go-between and their cover.

Syntel hadn't cared what others thought, and he had told her that countless times. His love for her was the only thing that mattered to him. But because she had cared, he had respected her wishes.

He closed his eyes remembering that night, their last one together, the night before graduation. They had just made love and he'd been holding her in his arms, never wanting to let her go...

***

Janeda snuggled closer to him. "We're so different," she said, looking deep into his eyes.

He smiled down at her. "No, we aren't. You just got a better tan than I do," he said jokingly.

She smiled back at him, then suddenly her expression became serious. "I'm afraid."

He pulled her closer. "Don't be. Everything's going to work out all right. I'll have six weeks at the academy and then I'll come back for you. It's not certain that I'll be sent overseas, but if I do, we'll get married before I go. You're the most important person in my life. I want to tell my parents about us so that if you need anything while I'm gone you can contact them."

"No. Please don't tell them anything, at least not yet. I'll be all right. Just be careful, and always know that I love you. No matter where you go or what you do, just believe that I love you, and will love you forever."

He pulled her closer into his arms. "And I love you. I always will. I will make you my wife one day, and I don't care who may not like it as long as I have you...."

Syntel opened his eyes. He had been at the academy only a couple of days when Ned had contacted him that Janeda had moved out of her apartment and hadn't told anyone where she'd headed. He had almost gone out of his mind with worry, and when days passed with no word from her, he'd almost gone crazy. The only thing that had gotten him through his days at the academy was the belief that sooner or later she would contact him.

She never did.

He was sent to Vietnam directly from the academy. His father had tried to stop the order but had soon discovered that the Remington name hadn't meant a thing to Uncle Sam.

Janeda never contacted him and when he returned to the States nearly twenty-four months later, he had tried finding her but couldn't. He'd tried forgetting her but had been unsuccessful in that attempt, too. Years later, he'd hired an investigator who had concluded his report within weeks. Janeda had died of a bad case of acute pneumonia at the age of thirty while living in Dallas, Texas. The report had not mentioned anything about the fact that she had been survived by a child. His child.

The lump in his throat seemed to grow larger. He stood and walked to the window and looked out into the darkness. He had a daughter. A twenty-eight-year-old daughter that he hadn't known about until tonight.

His child…Janeda's child…their child.

Syneda Tremain Walters.

Syneda recognized the smell of spaghetti the moment she entered her apartment. A broad smile covered her face.

Clayton was here!

She called out to him and moments later he walked out of the kitchen and swept her into his arms, kissing her with a need that she returned. Finally she lifted her head after he had placed her back on her feet. "What are you doing here?"

He leaned down and kissed her moist lips. "Aren't you glad to see me?"

"Yes, but it's Wednesday. I wasn't expecting you until the weekend."

"I missed you," he responded huskily, cupping her chin and leaning down and kissing her once more. It was a deep kiss, long and warm. His lips left hers then moved to her ear, her temple, and her nose before retracing the path back to her mouth. The sensual force about to explode between them was acute. He pulled her closer to him. "Do we eat first or make love?"

Syneda looked up and studied the face of the man she loved, the man she was going to marry. Desire-filled eyes stared down at her. She had missed him, too, and wanted nothing more than to lose herself in his arms, to lose her body in his.

Her hands slowly slid up his chest and around his neck. "Make love to me, Clayton. Now."

He kissed her again as he swept her into his arms and carried her into the bedroom.

"I'm hungry."

Clayton smiled at Syneda's words. He lowered his head and placed a kiss on her lips. "You could have eaten first. I did give you a choice."

"I know, but I preferred doing this first," she said, smiling against his lips. She eased up on her elbow and looked down at him. "At this moment I'm happier than anyone deserves to be."

He reached up and captured her face in the palm of his hand. "If there's anyone who deserves to be happy, you're that person."

Clayton kissed her, knowing he had to discuss the reason he had come to see her during the middle of the week. He would never forget how Syntel had taken the news of Syneda's existence. He had been filled with joy, sorrow and anger. Joy that Janeda had given him a daughter, sorrow that he had been cheated out of twenty-eight years of her life, and anger in knowing his father had been the cause of it.

A deep sigh escaped Clayton's lips. He had had to explain to Syntel why it was so important how they handled revealing his identity to Syneda. As best he could, he had told him about Syneda's rejection-and-abandonment complex, and how at first she would not accept a serious relationship between them because she had associated loving a man with abandonment and rejection. He had seen fresh tears cloud the older man's eyes when he had told him how confident Janeda Walters had been when she'd been told upon her death bed that he would be coming for his daughter and how Syneda had waited patiently for him to come for her.

"Clayton, I'm hungry."

Syneda's words cut into Clayton's thoughts. He smiled at her. "Then I guess I'd better feed you. But first I need to tell you something."

She looked up at him curiously. "What?"

"We've been invited somewhere this weekend."

"Oh? Where?"

Clayton reached up and traced his knuckle across her smooth skin. "To S. T. Remington's ranch."

Syneda's eyes widened. "Really? Why?"

"He wants to meet you."

She laughed. "Why would S. T. Remington want to meet me?"

He smiled, a slow, lazy smile. "He's eaten up with curiosity about the woman who nabbed me from the throes of bachelorhood. Trust me, he's dying to meet you." Dying to meet her was an understatement, Clayton thought. Syntel had been ready to fly to New York and claim his daughter.

"Well, what about it, baby?"

Syneda leaned up and kissed him. "I had relished the idea of spending this weekend here alone with you. But if you want us to go, I will. Is anyone else going to be there?"

"Yes. Senator Lansing will be there, too. They've been best friends since college."

Syneda nodded. "Then I'll finally get the opportunity to meet the senator. I never did meet him at Whispering Pines."

"Now you'll have your chance."

Syneda snuggled closer to Clayton. "Hmm, sounds like it will be a rather interesting weekend."

Clayton pulled her to him. "Yeah, I have a feeling that it will be."

"How did things go with S. T. Remington?" Braxter asked as he entered the senator's office.

Senator Lansing sighed raggedly, pushing his chair back from his desk. "No different than I expected. Syntel loved Jan very much and to discover he had a child he didn't know anything about because of the deceit of his father was a lot for him to take in."

Braxter nodded. "I'm sure it was. Has Ms. Walters been told anything yet?"

"No. Clayton strongly suggested we wait until the weekend. He's taking her to Syntel's ranch then."

"I hope things turn out all right. In their own way, both of them have suffered enough."

"I fully agree."

"Have you decided what you're going to do about Senator Harris?"

"Yes. I'm not going to do anything. He didn't get the report, and nothing has happened."

"But he tried to ruin you."

"And no doubt he'll probably try again. I can't go around worrying about people like him, Braxter. All I can do is continue to do the job I was sent here to do. I don't have time to play games like Senator Harris is inclined to do."

"So you're going to let him get away with it?"

"Thanks to Celeste Rogers, he didn't get away with anything."

"Yes, thanks to Celeste Rogers," Braxter said bitterly.

"Have you seen her since that night she brought the report here?"

"No, and I don't intend to, either."

"She apologized for what she'd done."

"How can you forgive someone who has betrayed you? Someone who deliberately used you?"

A few seconds followed before the senator answered. "It can be done, Braxter, but you have to want to do it. None of us are perfect. All of us have flaws, and we all make mistakes. We don't know why she did what she did initially. The only thing we do know is that in the end, because of you, she couldn't go through with it. Forgiving someone is never easy. It takes a big person to say I'm sorry, but it takes an even bigger person to say I accept your apology and you're forgiven."

Braxter didn't respond for the longest moment, then nodding his head, he turned and walked out of the office.

The snow was coming down in light flakes, the first for D.C. this winter. It took all of Braxter's concentration to operate the car and not think about Celeste. He had not gotten a lot of work done today for thinking about her.

Suddenly his mind became filled with what the senator had said to him earlier that day... "It takes a big person to say I'm sorry, but it takes an even bigger person to say I accept your apology and you're forgiven."

He took a long, deep breath. For so long he had not allowed himself the time to get interested in anyone. He had been too busy to include a woman in his life, at least not seriously.

Not until he'd met Celeste.

When the car came to a stop at a traffic light, he shifted his weight in the seat and massaged the tightness at the base of his neck. No matter how much he tried, he couldn't stop thinking of her. And no matter how much he tried he couldn't stop loving her.

When the light signaled it was time to go, he found himself heading in the direction of Celeste's apartment.

Celeste answered the knock at her door and was surprised to find Braxter's tall figure filling the doorway.

"May I come in?"

Numb, she simply nodded and stepped aside.

For the longest time Braxter didn't say anything to her, he just stood looking at her.

"Braxter, why are you here?"

He shook his head as if to clear it. "I asked myself a similar question while driving over here. I wasn't completely sure until you opened the door. Now I know."

He took her hand in his and led her over to the sofa where they sat down. "There's a lot of things I don't understand, but I want you to talk to me. Let's get things out in the open. I want you to help me to understand your connection with Senator Harris, and why you did what you did."

Celeste met his gaze, not believing he had actually come and was giving her an opportunity to explain things to him. She really couldn't ask for any more than that.

At least it was a start.

Chapter 25

"You're pretty good at flying this thing," Syneda said, watching Clayton at the controls of the Cessna 310. She glanced around the cockpit of the small plane before returning her eyes to him. Although she disliked small planes, she couldn't help admiring his abilities as a pilot. He handled the controls with both ease and competency. They had been in the air fifteen minutes, and she had not experienced even the tiniest bit of queasiness.

"Thanks," Clayton replied, casting her a smile. "And thanks again for taking this trip with me."

"I didn't mind. In fact, I'm looking forward to it." Her lips twitched in amusement. "You evidently made a darn good impression on S. T. Remington when representing Caitlin in that land deal for the two of you to have gotten so chummy. I'm sure not too many people get invited to his ranch for the weekend. Anyone who keeps up with the lives of the rich and famous knows S. T. Remington is a very private person. I understand he's very selective when choosing his friends and associates."

Clayton grinned. "Remington and I aren't chummy. I told you, you're the reason for the invitation. He wanted to meet you."

Syneda rolled her eyes upward. "Yeah, right."

He smiled. He knew Syneda didn't believe him. She thought he was getting together with Syntel Remington on business and had merely invited her along.

Syntel had contacted him yesterday to make sure they were still coming. He had also advised Clayton that after making a few phone calls, he'd been able to track down the investigator who had handled his search for Janeda years ago. Now retired, the man had remembered the assignment well, and what he'd told Syntel was no longer hard for him to believe. He had been paid a hefty sum by Syntel's father to omit certain information in his report. Specifically, any information regarding Janeda's child.

"Tighten up. It's time to take this baby down," Clayton said to Syneda moments later.

Clayton smoothly landed the small aircraft. "Syntel has sent someone to get us," he told Syneda as he motioned to the vehicle parked near the runway. "We'll be on our way to the ranch as soon as I check in."

Not long afterward, they were on their way to the home of one of Texas's richest oilmen. Syneda was not disappointed when the vehicle came to a stop in front of the big sprawling Spanish-style ranch house moments later. She had always thought the ranch house at Whispering Pines was huge but this one took the icing off the cake. It was surrounded by numerous flowering trees, plants and shrubs. "It's beautiful," she whispered to Clayton. "I can't believe he lives here alone."

Clayton took her hand in his. "He doesn't live alone. He has an entire house staff and this is an operating ranch. In addition to being in the oil business, Syntel raises Arabian horses. There's a slew of ranch hands living around here."

"What I meant is that I can't believe he isn't married. He's one of Texas's wealthiest bachelors, and from the pictures I've seen of him, he's extremely good-looking. I'm surprised no one has snatched him up by now."

"I understand he fell in love rather young…in his twenties. The woman died and he never wanted anyone else after that," Clayton replied as the door to the vehicle was opened for them. "He loved her very much."

"How sad."

"Yes, it was, but they did have a daughter together."

Syneda accepted Clayton's words without any further comments or questions. Her attention was immediately drawn to the tall, broad-shouldered, handsome, older man who had come out of the house to greet them. Clayton introduced Syneda to Syntel.

"Welcome to Viscaya." Syntel captured Syneda's hand in his. A lump formed in his throat as he tried suppressing any outward emotions he felt in knowing this young woman was *his* child, his and Janeda's. She had been created in their love.

Syneda smiled up into eyes that she failed to notice were the exact color of her own. "Thanks for the invitation."

Syntel beamed down at her. "Clayton told me how beautiful you were, but I didn't believe him. Now I see he really didn't exaggerate."

"Thank you. You're very kind, Mr. Remington," Syneda replied. For some reason, she had taken an immediate liking to the man. He seemed full of warmth and friendliness and was nothing like the private, closed person the media had painted him to be. "You have a beautiful home."

"I'm glad you like it. And please call me Syntel. Come on inside," he said, leading them through the huge front door made of dark wood. "Emilie is my housekeeper, and she'll show you to your rooms. Later today, after the two of you have unpacked and relaxed a bit, I'll show you around."

Once inside, Syneda couldn't help but view with approval the decor of the house. A few minutes later she and Clayton were led down a long hall where the guest rooms were. The rooms they were given were next to each other. Her room was beautifully decorated and contained a fireplace. A huge window overlooked an interior courtyard filled with lush plants and a small man-made pond. There was also a swimming pool within her sight.

Syneda smiled as she began unpacking her belongings, anticipating what she deemed to be a weekend of fun spent on a ranch deep in the heart of Texas.

True to his word, Syntel took Syneda and Clayton on a personal tour of his ranch. More than once Syneda looked up to find his intense gaze upon her. It wasn't the look of male interest, but a look of something she couldn't quite figure out.

That night she retired to bed early to give Clayton and Syntel a chance to talk privately. After taking a bath in the huge bathtub, she walked out of the bathroom dressed in a silky mauve-colored slip-style nightgown to find Clayton stretched out on her bed.

Her heart began beating rapidly from the sight of him on the bed. He looked so big, powerful and strong. The jeans he wore hugged his muscular thighs, and the shirt he wore greatly emphasized his broad shoulders.

Before she had a chance to realize what he was up to, he reached out and grabbed her wrist, pulling her down to him on the huge bed.

"Clayton, what do you think you're doing?" she asked, laughing.

"I think it's obvious," he said huskily, closing his arms around her like steel bands.

"What will Syntel think if he finds out you're in my room?" Syneda asked moments before her breath caught in her throat. Clayton's hands had begun roaming underneath her gown.

Clayton had thought of that. Syntel had given them separate rooms. Evidently he didn't think it was too late to be a protective father to his daughter. However, as far as Clayton was concerned, it would take more than separate rooms to keep him away from the woman he loved.

"Don't worry about Syntel. He knows we're engaged to be

married. Besides, his bedroom is on the other side of the house. There's no one in this wing but the two of us."

"Are you sure?"

Clayton swiftly and expertly removed the gown from Syneda's body. "I'm positive," he answered moments before savoring the taste of her mouth. And at the same time he let his hands move leisurely over her, finding pleasure in her soft nakedness.

"I want you, baby." He whispered the words against her lips before claiming them again, pressing her back against the pillow.

Syneda was completely aware of Clayton's tenderness as he went about pleasing her. She automatically surrendered to the passion he was stirring inside of her. He teased her by keeping his mouth on hers lightly, toying with her tongue and nipping at the corners of her mouth.

He lifted his mouth from hers and met her gaze. Deep desire flared in his eyes. "I want to love you tonight in the full sense of the word, Syneda. I don't want anything separating us. Not anything. I want to give you all of me. But doing so will put you at risk of getting pregnant, and I don't want to do that. I want you to have my baby but only after we've gotten married and feel the time is right."

Clayton's words echoed in Syneda's head. A rush of emotions surged through her. Clayton Madaris, a man who thrived on being careful and in control, wanted to be careless and out of control with her. What he had held back from numerous other women, he now wanted to give to her. He wanted to be a part of her in the most elemental way, in the most special way. But he thought doing so would put her at risk of getting pregnant.

She looked up at him. Love swelled in her heart. "And I don't want anything separating us, either. I want all of you." Syneda's voice was a mere notch above a whisper when she spoke.

"And don't worry about placing me in any kind of risk. I'm on birth control."

Clayton's surprised gaze held hers for a moment before asking, "You're on the pill?"

Syneda shook her head. "No. I didn't think I'd remember to

take one of those things every day. They're only as reliable as the person who takes them. I had an injection."

His look was thoughtful when he asked, "When?"

"Right after our trip to New Orleans."

"Why didn't you tell me?" he asked, threading his fingers through the softness of her hair.

"I started to tell you a number of times, then changed my mind. Using a condom always seemed to be the most comfortable and safest method to you." She smiled slightly. "Not too many men can boast of having a case of them in their closet. The reason I didn't tell you was because I didn't want you to feel you had to change your way of doing things just for me." She lowered her eyes from his.

"Look at me, Syneda."

When she raised her eyes to his, he brushed his lips across her lips before saying, "I've always believed in safe sex. More men should take responsibility for their actions in the bedroom. But there was never a time when I made love to you that I didn't think about how it would feel to be skin to skin with you, without having some type of covering, no matter how thin, separating us."

He pulled her closer into his embrace. "You don't know how often I wondered how it would feel to make love to you, knowing the very essence of me would become a part of you. I've never made love to a woman without using a condom, but that's all I've ever thought of with you."

Anticipation combined with heated desire flowed through Syneda's body with his words. "Then do it, Clayton. I'm not at risk. I want the full Clayton Madaris experience."

Clayton's heart raced. There was no mistaking the love and trust he read in her eyes. Excitement and desire tore through him. She was a very special woman. His woman. Then he kissed her in a way that left her shivering and murmuring his name. He touched her in a way that made her tremble, taking his time to build their passion until Syneda almost shattered in his arms.

Reveling in his touch, Syneda clung to him. His scent exuded a virility that was a combination of man and heat. His body was warm and hard. She loved the feel of him on her and was ready for the feel of him inside her. She kissed the tender skin underneath his ear and whispered. "Love me, Clayton. Now!"

He did, both mentally and physically.

As he slipped into her body, he gazed down into the depths of her sea-green eyes that were dark with passion. He felt himself losing control. He was powerless in her arms.

They began moving together in rapturous rhythm, the heat of his passion inciting her to move under him and cling to him tighter as he filled her completely.

"I love you." Clayton whispered the words in Syneda's ear just moments before their passion soared to greater heights. All sense of time and place escaped them as their bodies convulsed and their passion crested.

Syneda flexed her inner muscles to hold him tighter within her. She heard herself make a low sexy sound as her senses began slipping. She soon heard Clayton's groan mingle with that sound and felt his body trembling as they simultaneously reached the peak of total fulfillment together. She strained against him when she felt him emptying himself into her.

"Clayton!"

The force of what was taking place made Syneda's entire body grow still as a tidal wave of sensuous pleasure flooded over her. It was a violent culmination for both of them as together they reached the pinnacle of sexual pleasure.

A long time afterward, Clayton lay holding Syneda as she slept in his arms. Her head rested on his shoulder, her soft body tucked into the curve of his.

He leaned down and brushed his lips across hers. Sometime tomorrow her eighteen-year wait for her father would end. He hoped and prayed she would not resent him for interfering, but she needed to deal with her past before the two of them could have a future.

* * *

"Did you get a good night's sleep, Syneda?"

A blush crept in Syneda's cheek. She quickly took a huge swallow of orange juice before answering Syntel's question. "Yes, thanks for asking."

Out of the corner of her eye she saw Clayton's thin smile. Of all the things she had gotten last night, a good night's sleep wasn't one of them. The memories of her lovemaking with Clayton made her body ache with both desire and soreness. She cast a quick glance at him and the delicious tension within her intensified when she watched his lips form a silent message: *I love you.*

"I have a little celebration planned for tonight," Syntel said, unknowingly interrupting the soundless byplay between Clayton and Syneda.

Syneda shifted in her chair. "Oh? What's the occasion?"

"My daughter," he replied smoothly. "She's coming for a visit."

Syneda smiled up at him. "That's really nice."

Syntel took a sip of his coffee. Then he tilted his head and a proud smile touched his lips. "Yes, and I'm looking forward to it."

Syneda sat next to Clayton on the sofa. She glanced at her watch before turning toward him. "What if Syntel's daughter doesn't show up? It's almost seven o'clock," she whispered softly. "He's been acting rather anxious since he mentioned she was coming."

Clayton pulled Syneda closer to his side and pressed a kiss at her temple. "She'll be here."

Syneda lifted a brow, wondering how Clayton was so sure of that, and was about to ask him when she noticed Syntel and Senator Lansing returning to the room. The senator had arrived over an hour ago, and Syneda had finally gotten to meet him.

"I hope you're right. I'd hate for him to be disappointed. He's such a kind person," she said softly before the two men approached.

Clayton smiled. His dark eyes slid lazily over the woman at his side. "So are you. And a rather beautiful one I might add. You look sensational tonight."

Syneda basked in Clayton's compliment. She was wearing an elegant eggshell-colored silk dress that was cut in modest, classic lines. "I wanted to wear something nice for the special occasion."

Syntel and Nedwyn joined them and sat in chairs across from them.

"Tell me about your daughter, Syntel," Syneda asked politely in an attempt to keep conversation flowing.

Unnoticed by Syneda, the three men looked at each other fleetingly before Syntel cleared his throat. "There isn't much I can tell you about her, Syneda. The two of us will be meeting as father and daughter for the first time tonight. I only discovered I have a daughter a few days ago," he replied quietly.

Syneda's eyes widened in surprise. "I don't understand. How could you not know you had a daughter?"

Sadness shone in Syntel's eyes. "It's a rather long and sad story."

Clayton intertwined his fingers with Syneda's. "We would love hearing it anyway, Syntel. That is, if it's not too personal."

Taking a deep breath the older man began. "Almost thirty years ago while attending college, I met and fell in love with the most beautiful woman to walk the face of this earth. I've never met or seen a more exquisite individual. But she wasn't just beautiful on the outside, she was beautiful on the inside, as well. I lost my heart the first time I saw her."

Syntel took a deep breath before continuing. "She'd been in one of Ned's classes and, thanks to him, we were introduced."

He paused thoughtfully before going on to say, "I asked her out and she turned me down." He smiled at the memory. "In fact, she turned me down several times, but I refused to give up. Finally, she gave in on the condition that no one was to know we were seeing each other."

"Why didn't she want anyone to know the two of you were dating?" Syneda asked.

"Because I'm white and she was black. During that time inter-racial dating was not acceptable."

Syneda nodded. She knew that even in this day and time, some people were pretty close minded when it came to interracial relationships. She couldn't even imagine how such a relationship would have survived over thirty years ago. Some people refused to accept the fact that true love was color-blind.

Syntel stood, continuing. "She found out she was pregnant before we graduated but didn't tell me. I had to report to the Air Force Academy the day after graduation. She used that time to disappear, telling no one where she was going. I nearly went out of my mind worrying, but in my heart I believed she would get in touch with me. But she didn't. I never saw her again."

"If you never saw her again, how did you find out about your daughter?" Syneda asked, totally intrigued with the story being told.

"A few days ago her fiancé showed up at my office and told me. He had hired a private investigator to find me with the sole intention of ripping me to shreds for hurting the woman he loved."

A lump formed in his throat. "You see, Syneda, eighteen years ago, the woman I loved died leaving my daughter all alone. All alone but with a promise that I would come for her."

Syneda startled and her fingers turned to ice as they clutched Clayton's. She gazed deeply into Syntel's eyes as he continued speaking. "I'm told her mother had a telephone call placed to me. It was a phone call I never received. That's the only reason I didn't come. There's no way that had I gotten that phone call, I would not have come for my daughter."

He held back an emotional choke. "I loved *your* mother deeply and I believe she loved me. You're living proof of just how much she loved me, and the sacrifices she made. It was her choice not to continue our relationship because of the problems she felt we would have endured as an interracial couple, but it wasn't my choice not to know about you."

He took a deep breath. "There's no way I can turn back the hands of time and undo everything you've endured because of your mother and me. All I can ask is that you find it in your heart to give me a chance, and to allow me to become a part of your life. A life I've already missed twenty-eight years of sharing."

Syneda was transfixed in place, unable to move as her shocked mind absorbed Syntel's words. Tears clouded her eyes.

Clayton's gaze intercepted Senator Lansing's nod. Neither he nor the senator was noticed as they slipped from the room, leaving father and daughter alone.

"I still can't believe S. T. Remington is actually my father." Syneda lay in bed with her head cradled on Clayton's shoulder, staring at the roaring fire in the fireplace. She had returned from talking with Syntel for over two and a half hours to find Clayton pacing the floor waiting for her. She had walked across the room and gone into his arms without hesitation. Then she had cried while he had comforted her.

Clayton leaned on one elbow, smiling down at her. "You may as well get used to the idea. As soon as the media finds out, everyone and their mama will know it."

Syneda nodded. "Syntel and I talked about that, too, and wondered what would be the best way to handle it." She smiled. "One thing is for sure, he doesn't want to keep me a secret."

She snuggled closer to Clayton. "For so long I wanted to hate the man who fathered me, the man I thought let me and my mother down. And now I find it was all lies. Just listening to him talk let me know he loved my mother very much."

Clayton wound his hand in Syneda's silky hair. "Yes, he did. It's just sad your mother allowed what society thought dictate her happiness. Who knows, they could have married and lived happily ever after."

Syneda's smile faded. "Somehow I doubt it. Just look at what Syntel's father did. I don't believe his family would have accepted a marriage between him and my mother."

Clayton raised a brow. "Why are you calling him Syntel's father? He was your grandfather."

"But I can't think of him that way. He didn't think of me as his grandchild, did he?"

"No, he didn't." Clayton had to agree with her on that. "But he's dead now so what he thinks really doesn't matter anymore, does it?"

"No, but it hurts to know he didn't want me as his grandchild."

"And how do you feel about having Syntel for a father?"

Syneda looked up at him. "Scared, overwhelmed. I've had eighteen years of bitterness to fester inside of me. It will take time for all of it to completely go away. It won't dissolve overnight and he understands that. We've decided to take things one day at a time and get to know each other. There's so much we have to catch up on, so much I want to share with him and so little time. I have to begin making plans for our wedding soon. With Christmas right around the corner, June will be here before you know it."

Clayton slipped out of bed to put another log on the fire. When he returned to bed, Syneda couldn't help noticing the serious expression he wore. He pulled her back into his arms.

"Do you want to postpone our wedding for a while?" he asked.

Syneda raised a confused brow and looked at him. "No, why do you ask? Do you want to postpone our wedding?"

"No. I just didn't want you to feel rushed about anything."

She threw her arms around him. "Oh, Clayton, the day I marry you will be the happiest day of my life. Syntel and I will have plenty of time to get to know each other, both before and after our wedding."

Clayton smiled, feeling relieved. "So the wedding is still on?"

"Absolutely."

They kissed with all the deep longing and all the love they had for each other in their hearts. Both of them had waited years to find true, everlasting and eternal love.

"Clayton?"

"Umm?" he asked, brushing small kisses against the base of her throat.

"Have you thought about where we can go on our honeymoon?"

He paused thoughtfully before placing another heated kiss on her lips. He was beginning to ache for her all over again. "No, sweetheart, I haven't thought about it. Any suggestions?"

"Yes." The palm of her hand gently caressed his chin. "I heard St. Thomas is a beautiful place that time of the year, and I've always wanted to go there."

Clayton was grinning. "St. Thomas? Will I get the chance to preapprove the clothes you bring along?"

Syneda smiled. "Do you think you need to?"

"Yes."

Suddenly they were laughing together.

"If you think for one minute, Clayton Madaris, that you're going to start dictating what I can or cannot wear once we're married, you're out of your mind. We need to get a few things straight. No man is going to—"

Clayton kissed her to shut her up. When he lifted his head, his eyes gleamed with amusement. "One thing is for sure, sweetheart, with you I'll never be bored. I can't wait for June to get here."

"Neither can I," Syneda said, pulling his head down for another kiss. "Neither can I."

Chapter 26

A beautiful day in June

Clayton Madaris glared at the seven men standing on the other side of the room. Three of them, Alexander Maxwell, Trevor Grant and Trask Maxwell, were his closest friends. Two others were his brothers-in-law, Daniel Green and Raymond Barnes. But his full glare, the darkest it had been in months, was directed at his two brothers, Justin and Dex, who stood nonchalantly by the window.

"What do you mean Uncle Jake's not coming?" he finally shouted after taking in the announcement Justin had just made. "He has to come! He's in the wedding!"

Jonathan Madaris, dressed elegantly in a white tuxedo, stood leaning against the mantel as he watched his youngest son begin pacing the length of the room in angry strides. He could feel the tension growing in the room. Clayton was a nervous wreck as it was, and at the moment the last thing he needed was his brothers playing devil's advocates. He made a quick decision to intervene before he had a murder on his hands instead of a wedding.

"All right, settle down, Clayton. Jake will be here. He called and said he's running a little late but he'll make it in time for the wedding. Justin and Dex were just teasing you."

Jonathan then turned his serious attention to his other two sons. "Justin Stuart and Dexter Jordan, behave yourselves. Your brother is nervous enough as it is. Don't make matters worse. And I might add that at least he thought enough of me and his mother to let us share in his wedding day. Something neither of you did."

Justin grinned at his father's observation. "I would have loved having you and Mom at my wedding, but if you'll recall, I didn't know about the wedding myself until an hour before the ceremony was scheduled to take place. You have Clayton to thank for that. He schemed with Lorren to pull that one off. So he won't be getting much pity from me today."

Dex Madaris, whose charcoal-gray eyes were warm with amusement, chuckled throatily before coming to his own defense. "I would have loved inviting you and Mom to my wedding, but unfortunately I had to move fast and marry Caitlin. From all appearances, Clayton was trying to make a move on her. I didn't know at the time that he was doing it just to make me jealous."

Clayton had stopped his pacing to listen to what his brothers were saying. He couldn't stop the slow smile that spread across his lips. "The way I see it, both of you owe me a lot of gratitude for Lorren and Caitlin. Without my intervention neither of you would be happily married men."

Dex and Justin looked at each other before smiles of agreement covered their faces. It was a known fact that they loved their wives dearly. "You do have a point there, li'l bro," Justin said, grinning.

"However, your situation hasn't changed. Although we were teasing you about Uncle Jake, you still have to deal with your other problem. There's no way Gramma Madaris is going to let you see Syneda before the wedding," Justin continued. "It's a tradition that the groom sees the bride for the first time on their wedding day when she walks down the aisle. So the way I figure it, you have a couple of hours to go."

Clayton began his pacing again. "This entire thing is totally ridiculous. Gramma has deliberately kept Syneda from me all day."

Jonathan Madaris shook his head. "You know how your grandmother is, Clayton. She's not doing this to torture you. At your sisters' weddings, Raymond and Dan couldn't see them, either. And if I remember correctly, at the time you thought the entire thing was downright funny."

"Well, today is my wedding day, and I don't find anything funny about not being able to see Syneda. And I'm not going to stand for it a minute longer."

Justin chuckled. "What are you going to do? Force your way inside that room where Syneda and all the ladies are being held hostage by Gramma?"

A devilish gleam appeared in Clayton's eyes. "That's not a bad idea."

Jonathan Madaris straightened his stance, recognizing immediately the look of defiance in his youngest son's eyes. He could just see Clayton going head to head with his mother. "All right, Clayton, don't do anything foolish. Your grandmother—"

"Means well, Dad, but this time I can't abide by her wishes."

Before anyone could say anything further, Clayton stalked out of the room and headed down the church's long hall, which was adjacent to the corridor where Syneda was. Without knocking, he walked right into the room.

Ignoring the gasps and surprised expressions of the numerous women in the room, his gaze collided with Lorren's. "Where is she?"

"Clayton! You know you can't come in here. Your grandmother will have a fit if she finds you here."

"Where is Syneda, Lorren?" His patience was beginning to wear thin.

Lorren glared at him. "Clayton Madaris, you just march right back out that door—"

"Where is she, Lorren?" he asked again.

Seeing the determined expression etched on his face, Lorren pointed to another room. "She's in there with your mother getting dressed."

Clayton turned to the other women in the room who were staring at him like he'd gone crazy. "Please make yourselves scarce for a few minutes."

Felicia was the only one brave enough to speak up. "You can't run us out of here, Clayton. This is where we belong. You're the one out of place."

"Out!" Clayton shouted like a madman to the women staring at him. "Out! Now!"

The room quickly emptied.

"What on earth is going on out here?"

Clayton turned when his mother came into the room. A frown covered her face when she saw him. Leave it to her youngest son to be difficult on his wedding day. "Clayton, what are you doing here?"

"I want to see Syneda, Mom."

"That's impossible, Clayton. You know how your grandmother likes traditions. She will have your hide when she returns, and she'll be back any minute. She and Mama Nora left to give last-minute instructions to the florist."

Clayton looked deeply into his mother's eyes, pleading understanding. "I don't mean to cause problems, Mom. Really I don't. But I need to see her. These past few months have been hell. I've barely spent any time with her at all. First it was Syntel demanding most of her time, and then it was you, Mama Nora, and Gramma spending all that time with her planning this wedding. And let's not forget all those bridal showers she had to attend. I feel like an outcast."

Marilyn Madaris was startled by her son's admission. Insecurity was something he rarely had to deal with. Even as a child growing up, he'd always been totally sure of himself. Too sure of himself at times.

She took a deep breath. "All right, Clayton. I'll give you five minutes. Syneda is in there."

Clayton gazed at the closed door. "Does she know I'm out here?"

Marilyn Madaris grinned. "With all that racket you were making, how could she not know." A firm expression covered her face. "Five minutes, Clayton, that's all you got. Besides," she said, chuckling. "I have a feeling someone has alerted your grandmother to your behavior and she's on her way to toss you out on your rear end." She turned and left the room, closing the door behind her.

Clayton walked over to the other door and opened it. His breath caught in his throat.

Standing in the middle of the room wearing her bath-robe was his soon-to-be wife. The essence of her radiant beauty almost brought tears to his eyes. Her hair was arranged on top of her head in a bevy of soft curls. It was a very exquisite-looking style.

Clayton thought his heart had stopped beating when she smiled at him. "Causing problems, Madaris?"

He returned her smile. "Don't I always where you're concerned?" He locked the door before walking over to her. "I had to see you, Syneda."

"You weren't supposed to see me until the wedding."

Clayton raised his hands to cup her face. "I know, and I'm sorry if I've ruined this day for you by not sticking to tradition, but I had to see you. It doesn't matter when I see you, Syneda. Your beauty will always have me spellbound."

Syneda's heart burst with happiness. She thought he looked so handsome dressed in his white tuxedo with tails, and didn't hesitate to tell him so. "You look so good in a tux."

"Thanks. I have something to tell you," he said quietly, taking her hand in his.

"What?" Syneda asked. A nervous tremor touched her.

"I just wanted to tell you how much I love you. So much has happened since you agreed to marry me. We really haven't had a chance to spend a lot of time together lately." He placed her hand over his heart. "Every beat you feel under your palm is for your heart only. I love you very much and will spend the rest of my life showing you just how much. From this day forward, I am eternally yours."

Tears glistened in Syneda's eyes. "And from this day forward, I am eternally yours." She repeated the words he had just spoken. "I love you so very much, Clayton."

Slowly Clayton pulled her into his arms. He couldn't help looking at her lips, full and sensuous. A shock of overwhelming heat spread through him. He suddenly felt hot and hungry for the woman he was about to marry.

"Clayton Jerome Madaris! Open this door!"

The sound of his grandmother's demand from the other side of the locked door echoed loudly in the room.

"I think I'm in trouble," he said to Syneda as his mouth hovered closely over hers. "I may as well make it worth my while, don't you think?"

Syneda nodded, smiling. "Definitely. There's no trouble like big trouble," she replied seconds before placing her arms around his neck to bring her body more fully against his.

Clayton's mouth moved hungrily over hers as Syneda's lips parted for him. She made a small, soft sound when his tongue entered her mouth and rubbed against hers. The byplay was deliciously erotic and promised things to come later.

The heady taste of Clayton made a glowing heat blossom deep within Syneda's belly. The masculine scent of him was embedded in her nostrils, and the desire for him was an ache deep within the core of her.

"Clayton Madaris, if you don't unlock this door, I'll have your father and brothers break it down!"

Abruptly Clayton ended the kiss and looked down into Syneda's passion-filled face. He enfolded her tightly in his arms. "I'd better do as she said, or she *will* have them break the door down." He leaned down and kissed her again. "Remember how much I love you when you walk down that aisle to me."

Syneda nodded. Love was shining in the depths of her sea-green eyes. "I'll remember."

Clayton smiled as he unlocked the door to discover not only his grandmother, but his parents, the minister, Mama Nora, Syntel and the entire wedding party crowded around the door. His grandmother had an annoyed and a disgusted expression on her face.

Before she could say anything he leaned over and kissed her on the cheek. "She's all yours now, Gramma, but in just a little while, she'll be all mine."

Whistling the tune of the bridal march, a much happier Clayton Madaris walked past the crowd of stunned onlookers.

Reverend Moss checked his watch. He then smiled at the faces of the men lined across the room all dressed in white tuxedos. Everyone was accounted for. He frowned when his gaze came to rest on Clayton. He shook his head. Even after the ruckus he'd caused a few hours earlier, Clayton Madaris didn't have the decency to look guilty or ashamed.

"Well, then, gentlemen, it's about that time," he said, adjusting his glasses and smoothing his white robe. "If you'll just follow me, we can get things started. We don't want to keep the bride waiting."

Before turning to leave, he gave Clayton a stern look. "And no more shenanigans out of you, young man. I've had enough excitement for one day."

Beautiful white candles lined the aisles and the altar of the church. The sultry sound of Whitney Houston floated through the building as she enchanted and dazzled the wedding guests by singing a song. Senator Lansing, who was a close friend of the Houston family, had made the arrangements for Whitney's special appearance.

When Whitney's song ended, Syneda watched her six brides-maids drift down the aisle dressed in tea-length peach gowns. Lorren and Caitlin were her matrons of honor. Lorren handed her her floral bouquet while Caitlin was busy straightening her train.

Caitlin had given birth to another girl, Ashley Reneé, and Lorren had presented Justin with another son, Christopher Stuart.

Lorren gave her best friend's hand a little squeeze. "I'm so happy. I've always wanted this for you. You deserve to be happy."

Syneda smiled as tears misted her eyes. "Thanks for always being there for me."

Lorren returned her smile. "And thanks for always being there for me. I have something for you. It's something borrowed." She placed on Syneda's wrist a beautiful pearl bracelet.

"Oh, Lorren. It's your mom's bracelet." She hugged her friend. "Thanks."

When the wedding coordinator took the two flower girls off to the side to give them last-minute instructions, Syneda found herself alone with her father.

The past five months had been somewhat stressful for both of them. After her initial shock had worn off, Syneda went through a few weeks of resentment at Syntel Remington's appearance in her life. As if she had told him in the beginning, she had had eighteen years of hurt and anger to deal with. But through it all, he had been understanding and refused to let her put distance between them or deny him a place in her life as her father. He had braved, tolerated and survived her overwrought and, at times, pushed-to-the-limit emotions. Now she was grateful he had not taken her behavior personally.

Once she had gotten beyond the frenzy of the media's headlines labeling her Syntel Remington's love child, and their constant encampment on her doorstep and place of employment in their search for the entire story, she had discovered something. She and Syntel shared more than just physical resemblance. They were alike in quite a number of ways. They were both outspoken, neither believed in sugar-coating anything and they both didn't mind standing up for what they believed in.

Somehow they had gotten close over the past few months, regretting but accepting Syntel's father's and Clara Boyd's deceit. In the end, father and daughter had forged a strong bond between the two of them. Last month, as he'd done every year for the past fifteen years, Syntel had gone to visit her mother's grave. But this time she had gone with him. Somehow she believed her mother was now truly resting in peace knowing father and daughter were finally united as she had wanted.

After the graveside visit, they had returned to the ranch and had been joined by Senator Lansing and Clayton. With the three of them there, Syntel had not indulged in his two-day drinking spree to drown out his pain. Instead, over iced tea, Syneda and Clayton had sat and listened to the two college friends share fond memories of the time they had spent with her mother, and how difficult it had been trying to keep Syntel and Janeda's relationship a secret. Syntel even shared photographs with her that he and Janeda had taken together. Tears had formed in Syneda's eyes when she had looked at the photos and had seen her parents, young and very much in love. She was thankful to Syntel for sharing that part of his and her mother's past with her.

She had had something to share with him, too: a photo album her mother had kept during Syneda's growing years. The very first picture in the album had been her newborn baby picture that had been taken in the hospital nursery. Following that picture had been others that Syneda had taken each year for the first ten years. Some of them had been pictures she had taken alone. Others were those that she and her mother had taken together. The rest of the pictures in the album had been those she had taken during her junior and senior high school years while living with Mama Nora and Papa Paul. All the pictures had provided Syntel with a pictorial journal of her life; a life he'd been unable to share with her. Their sharing of the photographs had been a special time for them, and had somehow strengthened the bond between them.

"Nervous?"

Syntel's question brought Syneda's thoughts back to the present. She looked up at him, nodding her head. "A little. What about you?"

He smiled. "I'm nervous a little, too." He released a deep sigh before saying, "It seems so unfair."

Syneda raised an arched brow. "What does?"

Syntel took her hand in his, to take his place at her side. "I just found my daughter. It's a pity that already I have to give her away," he said in an oddly hoarse voice.

Syneda looked at him and saw the sadness openly displayed in his eyes. "Be happy for me, Daddy," she said, surprising him by calling him that for the very first time. Up to now she had always referred to him as Syntel.

"I'm marrying a good man. I think he's the best. And don't ever worry about you and me. Now that you're in my life, you're here to stay. Count on it."

She leaned up and kissed his cheek. "Thanks for loving my mother. I know she was only able to make it through all those years without you because she knew she had found true love once in her life. And I know each and every time she looked at me, she must have seen you. That's why she often called me her most precious gift. I was a gift of life she'd received from the man she loved."

Syntel's eyes were misty when he hugged his daughter. "Thank you for telling me that and for believing it. I loved your mother deeply, and I love you. I'm honored to be your father."

"I love you, too, and I'm honored to be your daughter."

Clayton stood next to his father, who was his best man, and watched Jordan, who looked so beautiful dressed in a peach floor-length gown, walk carefully down the aisle, tossing rose petals on the red carpet.

Next came two-year-old Justina. She began tossing rose petals from her basket just like the nice lady had told her to do. She was doing a pretty good job at it until she saw her daddy standing at the altar.

"Daddy!" She tossed the basket down as if saying, "later for this," and ran happily down the aisle to her father.

Justin scooped his daughter up in his arms, shaking his head. He looked over at Lorren who was grinning from ear to ear.

Next came the ring bearer, the four-year-old son of their cousin Felicia. He was followed by Vincent, Justin and Lorren's eight-year-old son, who entered and gave a loud blast from a golden horn. He then proclaimed in a loud voice, "The bride is coming! The bride is coming!"

The sanctuary got quiet. And then the organ began playing the bridal march. In awe, the wedding guests stood on their feet and watched Syneda and her father begin their walk down the long aisle.

A knot caught in Clayton's throat. He had never seen a more beautiful bride. She looked absolutely radiant. Her bridal gown was a soft white satin with a crystal pleated portrait neckline. That neckline gently curved around her shoulders to a cluster of dropped authentic pearls and sequin trim. A lace-trimmed train with embroidered appliques added the finishing touch to the gown. A romantic floral hat that was lavished with fabric flowers, authentic pearls, net pouf and a fingertip-length veil adorned her head.

Both pride and love burst within Clayton. The woman coming to him was everything he could possibly ever want in a woman. They were still both strongly opinionated and at times argumentative, but now they would have a different way of settling their disputes— he smiled—namely in the bedroom.

As he continued to watch her, the sermon Reverend Moss had preached on his grandmother's birthday suddenly came back to him. *"When a man loves a woman he places her above all else, and she becomes the most important person in his life. She becomes his queen..."*

"She's my queen," Clayton whispered in his heart.

The crowd watched as Syntel walked Syneda three-fourths of the way down the aisle. As planned, Clayton was coming the rest of the way for her.

The guests looked on, most of them with misty eyes and breathless anticipation, when Syneda turned and hugged her father. Then they watched as Clayton strode down the aisle toward them.

Upon reaching them he shook hands with Syntel and said, "I promise to take care of her, sir."

Nodding, Syntel then relinquished his place at his daughter's side.

Clayton stood before the woman who had consented to become his wife. She was the woman he loved. He took her hands in his, smiling. Unable to help himself, he leaned down and placed a tender kiss on her lips.

"Lordy, the boy wasn't supposed to do that until after the ceremony."

Clayton smiled when his grandmother's words reached his ears. He then led Syneda to the altar, winking at his grandmother when he passed her sitting on the front pew. He could tell by her deep frown that she was not too happy with what he had done.

Upon reaching the others, he drew Syneda forward as they knelt in front of the altar. After Reverend Moss's brief prayer, they once again stood on their feet. The minister began.

Syneda's hand was held securely in Clayton's. When Reverend Moss asked her to repeat her vows, she looked into Clayton's eyes. "I, Syneda Tremain Walters, take this man, Clayton Jerome Madaris, to be my lawfully wedded husband."

She felt the heat of Clayton's gaze on her as she continued, "…to love and to cherish, from this day forward, for better or for worse…"

Clayton was stunned by the intensity of the emotions he felt, hearing Syneda's words. With iron-clad control he forced himself not to take her into his arms.

"Clayton," Reverend Moss was saying to him. "Please repeat after me. I, Clayton Jerome Madaris, take this woman, Syneda Tremain Walters, to be my lawfully wedded wife."

Finally, after all the vows were said, and wedding rings exchanged, Clayton and Syneda turned to face each other and held hands while Whitney Houston came forward to sing the song Syneda had requested, "I Believe In You and Me."

Syneda looked deeply into Clayton's eyes while the words to the song floated around them, encompassing them in a mist of their love. Tears misted her eyes as she looked at him, remembering how his love had brought her through a difficult time, how he had refused to give up on her until she had sent him away, and how in the end she'd come to her senses and reclaimed his love. She knew the love she felt for him was unhidden and clearly visible for him to see.

Clayton held Syneda's hand in his as the words of Whitney's song touched him. For so long he had not believed in love. He had thought love was not for him. But the woman whose hands he now held in his had changed that. Now he believed in miracles.

After Whitney's song ended, Reverend Moss said, "By the powers invested in me by this great state of Texas, I now pronounce you man and wife." He smiled broadly. "You may kiss your bride, Clayton."

Clayton was more than ready for this part. Lifting Syneda's veil, he whispered, "I love you, Mrs. Madaris." He then took Syneda in his arms and kissed her.

When the kiss seemed endless, Reverend Moss tapped Clayton on the back. "That's enough, son."

Clayton kept right on kissing Syneda.

Reverend Moss frowned. He again tapped Clayton on the back, a little more forceful this time. "You can finish that later, young man."

Clayton released Syneda's mouth. He smiled at the minister. "I kind of got carried away."

Minister Moss frowned at him. "Apparently you did."

Clayton grinned and then to everyone's surprise and to his grandmother's horror, he swung Syneda up in his arms, and after tossing her long, winding train across his shoulder, he carried her out of the church leaving a stunned wedding party behind to follow.

* * *

The grand ballroom of the Hilton Hotel was a spectacular sight. Syntel had gone beyond himself in hosting his daughter's wedding reception.

After the traditional first dance of the bride and groom, Syneda danced first with her father, then with Senator Lansing, who had declared himself her godfather.

Clayton had approached his mother but she strongly suggested that he dance with his grandmother first. "She's pretty upset with you, Clayton. If you ever want to taste her bread pudding again, I suggest you do something to rectify that situation."

Being the smart man that he was, Clayton had immediately taken his mother's suggestion. By the end of their dance his grandmother was all smiles again. But that was only after she had sweetly raked him over the coals.

Trevor Grant stood leaning a shoulder against the wall, holding a half-filled champagne glass in his hand. He smiled, happy for his friend.

His gaze swept over the ballroom. When it rested upon a particular young woman, it stopped. Corinthians Avery, who was head geologist for Remington Oil, was a beautiful woman. She was everything male fantasies were made of. He of all people should know. There wasn't a single night he went to sleep without her invading his dreams.

As if sensing his gaze upon her, Corinthians's head lifted, her gaze met his. She frowned and narrowed her eyes at him.

Trevor gave her his most charming smile then lifted the champagne glass in a silent toast to her. He knew she could tell that his gaze was moving down the full length of her, remembering a night when he'd seen her, wearing nearly nothing at all. It was a night he would never forget.

He smiled when she continued to meet his gaze head-on. He had to hand it to her, the woman was something else. He took a sip of champagne, and still her leveled gaze never flickered from his. He knew she was trying to look straight through him and deny his existence. But he was not about to let her do that. He blamed her for many of his sleepless nights, and one day soon, very soon, she would pay for it.

"How soon can we leave and go upstairs?" Clayton asked his wife as they moved slowly around on the dance floor.

Syneda lifted her head from his shoulder. "It won't be too much longer. You wouldn't leave before most of your guests, would you?"

"Watch me. Besides, they've been well fed, plied with good wine and champagne, entertained with good music and, thanks to your father, most of them have been given plush rooms to spend the night. What more could they ask for?"

Syneda smiled. "I'm so glad all of your friends made it. It was nice getting the chance to meet Alex's brother, Trask Maxwell. He's really nice."

Clayton grinned. "But all of my friends are single. I hope each of them finds a woman to love and who'll make them happy. Like you've done for me." He leaned down and brushed a light kiss across her mouth.

"All right, you two," the wedding coordinator said from behind Clayton. "It's time for more pictures. Then, Syneda, you need to toss your bouquet and, Clayton, you need to take your wife's garter off and toss it to one of those single, unattached, handsome friends of yours."

He smiled. "It will be my pleasure."

Moments later, Syneda was ready to toss her bouquet. All the single women were asked to go to one side of the room. Everyone laughed when Gramma Madaris marched over and pulled Felicia out of the group. Evidently she thought with two failed marriages to her credit, her wild and reckless granddaughter did not need a third.

Syneda had all intention of aiming her bouquet straight toward Christy in hopes of shaking the three overprotective Madaris brothers up a bit over the thought of their nineteen-year-old baby sister being next in line for marriage. Unfortunately, Syneda's aim was off, and her bouquet landed right smack in Corinthians Avery's hands.

Jonathan Madaris came over to join his youngest brother, who was standing against a wall. Both of their tall forms looked elegant in their white tuxedoes.

"I thought I'd better warn you that Clayton is about ready to do the garter toss, and Mama is herding together all the single men to participate," Jonathan said, his eyes twinkling with humor.

Jake raised a dark brow. "Why would you want to warn me about something like that?"

Jonathan smiled. "Because I know for a fact she wants you included in on it. With Clayton out of the way, she wants you to be next. She thinks it's time for you to remarry."

Jake took a sip of his champagne. He then met his brother's gaze. "I have remarried."

Jonathan smiled. "But she doesn't know that, and unless you're ready to share your secret with the family, I suggest you make yourself scarce for a few minutes."

Jake took another sip of his champagne. Only a few people knew about his marriage to Diamond Swain, and Jonathan was one of them. He loved all of his brothers, but Jonathan was the one he was closest to.

"By the way," Jonathan said a few moments later. "How's Diamond? I guess it was hard coming here and leaving her at Whispering Pines."

Jake lifted an inquiring eyebrow. "How did you know she was at the ranch, Jon?"

Jonathan chuckled. "That was pretty easy to figure out. You couldn't leave the rehearsal dinner quick enough last night. You seemed somewhat relieved when Syntel offered to put up the wedding guests at this hotel, which eliminated you from having to put them up at Whispering Pines, and you barely made it to the church on time today. You almost gave Clayton heart failure."

He shook his head, smiling. "Even now you're biting at the bit to get out of here."

Jake laughed a rich throaty laugh. "Am I that obvious?"

"Only to me and Marilyn. And she picked up on it right away. She says you always have a better disposition whenever Diamond is around. She thinks your wife is good for you."

"Oh? And does she still think Diamond and I are making a mistake by keeping our marriage a secret for now?"

"I think she's decided differently after seeing how the media hounded Syneda when word got out that Syntel Remington was her father. Marilyn knows they'll do the same thing to you and Diamond."

Jake nodded. "I want Whispering Pines to always be a place Diamond can come to when she wants to escape the lights and glamour and stress of California for a while."

"And how long will her infrequent visits be enough for you? I can't help but remember why your marriage to Jessie didn't work out."

Jake rubbed the top of his head, struggling to ignore the resentment and old feelings of anger whenever his first wife was mentioned. "I swore after Jessie I would never get involved with another city woman. But when Diamond came along, I couldn't help myself. For as long as Diamond is comfortable with our arrangements, this is the way we'll do things."

Jonathan studied his brother. "And what about you? Are you comfortable with the arrangements?"

Jake's dark eyes met Jonathan's. There was no way he could lie to him. "Not really, but I don't have a choice. I knew what the deal was when I fell in love with her." His gaze sharpened when he saw his mother headed in their direction.

"Look, Jon, here comes Mama so I'm out of here. Tell the newlyweds that I'll see them after they get back from their honeymoon."

He turned and quickly made his exit.

* * *

Clayton looked at the fifteen or so single men gathered around him. None of them looked overly anxious to participate in this part of the wedding ceremony. At least three of them he knew for a fact did not relish the thought of possibly being next in line for marriage.

His gaze sought out those three, Alex Maxwell, Trevor Grant and Trask Maxwell. They were deliberately standing as far away in the back as they could. He smiled when he noticed Trask walking toward him.

"Why do we have to do this?" Trask Maxwell asked when he had reached Clayton.

"Because Gramma Madaris said so. She's all wrapped up in traditions today." Then he used the same tactic on Trask that his mother had used on him earlier. "And if you want to risk making her mad and never eating any of her bread pudding again, then go right ahead and don't participate."

Trask shook his head, smiling. "Do I look like a fool? Now, toss the darn thing. Let's get this over with. Just make sure you throw it to one of those guys in the front." He turned and walked off, returning to his spot in the back.

A few minutes later, Clayton sent Syneda's blue garter sailing through the air and over the heads of most of the men in the front before it finally landed right in Trevor Grant's hands.

"I thought I was never going to get you alone," Clayton said to his wife an hour or so later. Pulling that garter from around her thigh while hundreds of people looked on had been difficult. The feel of his hand on her skin had almost made him lose control. He had wanted to begin making love to her right then and there.

They would spend the night here in the hotel and, bright and early tomorrow morning, they would catch a flight to St. Thomas. He was more than ready for his honeymoon to begin.

He pulled Syneda closer into his arms. "And how do you like my present?"

Syneda laughed softly and tipped her head up to meet Clayton's gaze. "I like it."

When she had entered their hotel room, the honeymoon suite on the twenty-eighth floor, a beautiful gift-wrapped box was in the center of the bed. The card attached to it had indicated it was from Clayton. Like a child on Christmas morning, she had eagerly opened it up to find five brand-new men's dress shirts with designer labels.

"Although you always look sexy as hell in those things, I prefer you not start wearing them until we get back from our honeymoon."

She lifted a brow. "Why can't I take them with me?"

"Because I don't want you to wear anything at all in St. Thomas. I plan to keep you under lock and key those two weeks."

Syneda smiled and placed her arms around his neck. "I think I'm going to like that."

"I'm going to make sure you do," Clayton said, cradling her body even closer to his. "I love you, Syneda."

"And I love you. We aren't going to argue about anything in St. Thomas, are we?"

Clayton smiled down at her. "We'll make love, not war." Clayton kissed the side of her neck. "Besides, I have a new way of dealing with you whenever you get too opinionated and sassy, Mrs. Madaris."

"Oh? And what way is that?"

Clayton grinned as he picked her up in his arms. He began walking toward the bedroom. "You're about to find out."

Hours later, in their darkened hotel room, Clayton and Syneda lay wrapped in each other's arms. Both were very satisfied with how their special day had turned out.

It had been a day filled with love, joy and tears. They had been blessed with the presence of a multitude of family and friends. But most important, it had been a day filled with anticipation, confidence and trust. It was a day they had committed themselves to each other.

"Happy?"

Syneda smiled up at Clayton, mesmerized by the handsome face staring down at her. His features held all the love, tenderness and passion she had come to adore. "Tremendously happy. What about you?"

"Extremely happy." Clayton slipped an arm around her shoulder and leaned down to take her lips in a long kiss.

Syneda wrapped her arms around him, lost in the cravings and desires he could stir within her so easily again. Then in a surprise move, she shifted around until her body was on top of his. She looked down into his dark eyes.

"Now, Mr. Madaris, it's my time to show you how I plan to deal with you when you get too opinionated and arrogant for your own good."

Clayton smiled. "Is that a fact?"

"No, Madaris, that's a promise."

Syneda's scent drifted all around him, and Clayton's passion began flaring anew under the onslaught of her warm lips when she began placing kisses all over his face, neck and shoulders.

His hand came up and cupped her face. He looked up into her eyes, at the love, peace and contentment he saw there. He silently thanked God for bringing this special woman into his life, and for opening his eyes to her beauty, both inside and out. She was the half that made him whole. She was his sunshine after a storm. She would never bore him. With her his life would be filled with never-ending excitement.

She was eternally his and he was eternally hers. Forever.

* * * * *